Sunday Night and Monday Morning

Edited by
James Urquhart

Five Leaves Publications

www.fiveleaves.co.uk

Sunday Night and Monday Morning

Published in 2005 by Five Leaves Publications,
PO Box 81, Nottingham NG5 4ER
info@fiveleaves.co.uk, www.fiveleaves.co.uk

ISBN: 0 907123 52 X

Five Leaves gratefully acknowledges financial assistance
from Arts Council England

'William Marshal' is taken from Elizabeth Chadwick's new book *The Greatest Knight: The Story of William Marshal*, (Little, Brown) published in November 2005.

'Rick Argues' first appeared in Tom Cox's novel *Educating Peter*, published by Bantam Press/Black Swan. Reprinted by permission of The Random House Group Ltd.

'The Drips and the Drops and the Wedding' by Matt Haig is taken from his novel *The Dead Fathers Club* which Jonathan Cape will publish in 2006.

'PMQ' by Robert Harris has previously appeared in *Speaking With the Angel*, edited by Nick Hornby and published by Penguin.

'Home' by John Harvey appears courtesy of *Ellery Queen's Mystery Magazine*, which will run the story in its December 2005 issue.

'The First Punch' by Jon McGregor was first published in *Granta*.

'Electra' comes from Eve Makis's second novel, *The Mother-in-Law*, which will be published in 2006 by Black Swan.

'Mrs Pike' by Julie Myerson has previously appeared in the *Guardian*.

Cover illustration: Sky Mirror, photograph
©Martine Hamilton Knight, www.builtvision.co.uk

Typesetting and design by Four Sheets Design and Print
Printed in Great Britain by Russell Press

Contents

Introduction

A few streets away from me lives Stanley Middleton, who has been publishing a novel pretty much every year since 1960. He was in his forties when the first appeared in print and his thirteenth novel, *Holiday,* shared the prestigious Booker Prize in 1974 with Nadine Gordimer's *The Conservationist.* Now in his eighties, Stanley has just published his forty-second novel. If you include his poetry and other works, Alan Sillitoe is even more prolific than Stanley, but he is still probably most renowned for his début novel, *Saturday Night and Sunday Morning.* His Nottingham working lads possessed a galvanising energy which shook up what was otherwise a fairly staid, London-based literary culture back in 1959. The first review that I wrote for *New Statesman* was of Alan's 1997 collection of short stories, *Alligator Playground.* After nearly four decades, those humble Nottingham terraces were still yielding Alan some powerful stories.

Nottinghamshire enjoys a vibrant literary life beyond the substantial output of Stanley and Alan. It is home to many contemporary writers and a few small publishing houses. Five Leaves Press is marking its tenth anniversary of publishing in Nottingham by putting out two celebratory companion volumes: *Poetry — The Nottingham Collection,* which presents fifty locally-connected poets; and this book, offering an array of short fiction by Nottinghamshire writers. *Sunday Night and Monday Morning* is a playful *hommage* to Alan's famous title, but also a statement of intent. High quality fiction has sprung up from all corners of Nottinghamshire and been published to widespread acclaim since Alan and Stanley rose to prominence. This collection gathers excellent work by fifteen of the county's strongest authors who have established themselves in the last couple of decades, or more recently, or who are currently finding new audiences.

All the contributors to *Sunday Night and Monday Morning* meet two criteria for inclusion: they live in Nottinghamshire (or have previously lived in the county for a significant period), and they have at least one novel currently on the books of a national publishing house. Some of these writers already enjoy substantial international success. Robert Harris and Julie Myerson have been translated into many languages, as has John Harvey, whose 'Resnick' crime series vividly identifies the landscape of Nottingham. His offering here is a new "Resnick" story. Elizabeth Chadwick's reputation for her historical novels is high, and rising with her much anticipated new novel, *The Greatest Knight*, whose opening chapters are included here. Begun whilst he was still at university, Jon McGregor's début novel was called in by the Booker Prize judges in 2002, which helped to bring a wider audience to appreciate his unusual and beautiful reflective prose.

Most exciting is the emergence of a younger generation of excellent writers working in Nottinghamshire, whose fresh claims vie for our attention beside the solid reputations of their more established colleagues. Nine of our fifteen authors are under forty, some of whom are just beginning to forge their writing careers. Three have graduated from Nottingham Trent University's MA in Creative Writing, which also fuels the county's burgeoning literary scene.

Sunday Night and Monday Morning includes three extracts from new or forthcoming novels, and eight new stories that have been commissioned for this collection. The breadth of subject, from twelfth century knights to a future maverick geneticist, from a sinister abattoir worker to Prime Minister's Questions, reflects a diversity of subject and style amongst Nottinghamshire's writers. The short story is an exacting format, demanding precision and clarity from its practitioners. The writers collected here have delivered fifteen very different stories that will all, I hope, entertain you with their exuberance, poignancy, suspense and humour.

James Urquhart

8

Shorty Long and the Long-Long Family Reunion

Kat Pomfret

Before the TV show, we were the Longs: Mom, Dad, Sissy, Kate and me. Now we are the Bridgetown Longs. You might know us from the Family Show. You might have seen our faces on screen in duotone with our names in cartoon letters beneath and the Pointer Sisters singing in back. Anyway, if you do, Crystal Long is my Mom and Joe Long is my father. Sissy Long and Katherine Cooktown-Long are my sisters and I am Shorty Long of the Bridgetown Longs from the *All New Family Show*. And if you're interested, which most people ain't, Shorty's not even my name.

The house is calm like a fed hog for once without the cameras pointing into everything. It's meddling hot; not an hour past breakfast and I'm sweating butter, laying back on the bed and praying for a raincloud while the dogs chase each other, yelping sun-silly in the yard and the hens cluck-crazy roasting in their feather jackets. Mom is standing on the sleeve of my signed Ricky Martin CD and admiring the fit of her new shirt in my mirror.

"Well?" she says. "What do you think?" Her boobies say *Crystal*, her belly says *Long-Long Family Reunion August 2003*.

I shrug. "It ain't no reunion, Mom." We are the Bridgetown Longs so people can tell us from the Washington Longs. That's how the Family Show works, since season one, so there's no point fretting over it any.

"Sure it's a reunion. Family's family," Mom says. That's the twist. Every season there's a twist and this year's is that about a million years ago the Washington Longs were Bridgetown Longs too; only they got out. They, or their great-greats got out and away and now we're running so fast after them we're breathless, crazier than a mutt in a bees nest, but so long as my mother has a plan she will follow it like the yellow brick road, and the rest of us will tapdance behind.

The Washington Longs have sent us their details. It's horribly worse than I thought: the dad's not just a doctor, he's a heart surgeon. Alisha and the crew watch us as we take this in and I don't know who to hate more: Alisha for acting like the fact we poor black trash is any news to us ever, or my family for thinking all we need is our small screen big moment to be Washington Longs, for thinking for thirty seconds that America might even vote for us over them.

Mom hums to herself as she folds up the shirts, and I know she's thinking once we get out of here Katherine will forget about Jackson Junior, and Sissy will meet a nice Washington boy and Shorty, cause that's what she calls me, they all do, Shorty might lose fifty pounds in the Washington air with no fried chicken to be had and if Shorty loses fifty pounds then the sky might change from blue to golden pink and angels will sing Diana Ross songs in three-part harmonies and pee French Champagne on our heads.

"Put it on," Mom throws a shirt at me.

I hold it up. "My name ain't Shorty," I say.

Mom looks at me, but she knows it's true. I lay back on the bed, my sweat-spangled arms sticky on my nappy hair, dust dancing in the room like it couldn't wait for us to be gone, and the sun beating so hard I can hear it. When they got me back from the hospital they put me straight in with Sissy, then when Sissy hollered enough they put me in with Katherine, but that girl's too nasty to like sharing much and in the end they put up a board at the bottom of Mom and Dad's bed and called the space between it and the bathroom wall a room. There's no window and I have to shut the door careful else the board falls out, but I can stick what I like on the walls and when I look at the ceiling the movie star-singer Jennifer Lopez smiles back at me.

"Washington, Shorty, just think."

"What do I care about Washington?"

Mom thinks in Washington the dogs shit chocolate mousse. "Have you packed?" she says.

"I told you, I ain't coming."

"Have you packed?"

"Yes," I say.

Later, Sissy and me pretty up for the camera. Washington men, Sissy says, are rich and sophisticate. Not like boys round here (she means Johnny) throw bottletops at you and call it courting. But it ain't them she's thinking of when she eats tuna for two weeks and stands gazing sideways in the mirror at the little hump of her belly and smelling like bait. Brad Pitt watches the Family Show, and in Sissy's head there ain't a reason in the world why he mightn't phone up and order her take out like she was sweet chilli noodles. Already she's shimmery in the summer sudden sunset, something half-real; I ought to reach out and hold on to stop her dissolving in the lights, camera, action of her best daydream.

Sissy takes off her eye make up and starts to put it on again. I ask Sissy if she's gonna wear her shirt. She rolls her eyes. Sissy is smart but she don't let on. The teachers want her to go to College but Sissy's got too much life in her she says to want to waste it on books. She sure is wild, breathless like a steed wants breaking in only there's nobody round here to do it. Sissy fixes me a look in the mirror.

"What?" I say.

Sissy frowns; she's so pretty it makes me feel almost sick looking at her. "Let me do your eyebrows," she says.

Since I was five years old Sissy's been using me like a doll to make pretty with. She's always after curling something that's meant to lie straight, pulling something that just wants to be left alone. And Sissy hate anything brown. Sissy's own hair is blonde like Britney. That girl can't see a sunset without thinking she can improve on it. "Just a couple hairs," she says.

I scowl, but now she's coming at me with the tweezers. "Get off," I say.

"Just two," she says, "from right here," she puts a finger just on my eye.

Sissy can't stand to be around ugly, acts like she thinks it contagious.

I exhale sharp but I let her pull. "I don't want to go to Washington."

Sissy pouts and frowns like a kitten being vexed, "Sure you do."

"I don't. I told y'all I don't."

"Well it's too bad, Shorty."

"Ain't you frightened?"

"What's to be frightened of?" Sissy looks at me then. She smiles a little. "People will like you. Is that what you skittish for? You think people won't like you?"

"No," I say. I am the only one who can see the horror of it: our faces there, large on the screen and every pimple showing, every pore, the folks at home with their pretzels and beer, watching us like a movie. Sissy thinks a camera is a thing can be fooled with a lick of mascara or a tight panty girdle, but TV ain't no dumber or more blind than God, it gets everywhere, takes a thing and spreads it round like the sweetest gossip. I seen it last season, the Family Show, how the TV can make the smallest lies huge, show you the swell of a tear that don't fall, the breath of a love that don't speak, and I'm frightened of this, more frightened than anything and I don't see why I can't stay here and have this summer just like last: holding Johnny's beer can while he picks guitar on the porch, watching stars and June bugs dance, with the sky big and empty and stretched so thin you can almost see through it. Bridgetown ain't so bad, you know.

"People gonna see us for what we is, Shorty, you know. On the TV. We never did belong here."

Sissy's right, we like a splinter in the palm of the place and squeezed every day. But a splinter ain't a splinter without a palm, is it?

Sissy's down on the floor with me on sudden and holding my hands and squeezing, breathy and her eyes like stars, bright and too far away for me to reach them, "You want to get out, don't you Shorty? Get further than Texas?"

"Not so far as Washington, though," I say, and try and loose my fingers, but her hold's too tight.

"You want to be seen, really be seen, don't you, and be someone and have — " she put her hand on her stomach, "something, glittering, spangling, hope."

"Don't talk at me," I say, for Sissy was always one for picking up fine words and throwing them down like firecrackers when she thought they'd do good.

"Don't you want to be someone, though?" And she's standing again and near dancing round the room as she picks her things together, stepping over her case and her toilet bag, her shoes. Sissy is glorious mess and more marvellous to me than anything.

No. I want to be Shorty, staring in my room at Jennifer Lopez with Sissy next door in her room doing her make-up, laying on shadow

12

and taking it off, laying it on and blending, a picture being painted that the world ain't ready yet to see. I want for everything to be just like always and if Mom and Sissy could only leave this wishing be we'd be happy, I know it.

"Here," says Sissy, and flings me a rag. It's her Pretty Betty's Perfect Poodle Parlour Tee-shirt. "You can keep it."

I hold it up. It won't fit me: Supersize Shorty, they call me, big as all hell and half Texas, but I like the feel of the cotton, brushed soft, when I hold it next to my cheek, and the Sissy-sweet smell of my sister that's on it, and the cute little look on the dog makes me laugh.

"You giving me it?" I say.

"I ain't coming back, Shorty," Sissy says then.

"You got to," I say, cause Sissy fuller of gas than a three-day-dead toad.

"Whatever," she says "I ain't coming back."

"What about Johnny Man?" I say.

But Sissy is holding her new dress against her and swaying in the mirror.

I sit out on the porch then and wait for the TV people and hope that Johnny will walk by. He walks by about a million times a day on account of Sissy, so slow he's just about standing still and the world turning about him. Plenty girls like Johnny, but he don't care for the soft sweet things that hang about the soccer fields. He thinks Sissie's different from all that. She carries his love like henhouse eggs, heedless and hurrying, knowing for all the mess and yolky thick-stickiness she's heading for, there is more to be had. And Johnny knows all this and cares for her still. But he ain't been by, not in the last two weeks since Sissy told him we was going, and when I walk past his place the shutters are all drawn and the music turned loud and after a half hour I give up on him coming out at all. I only know that I'd rather spend my summer waiting for him to come by than anything else and I hate the Washington Longs.

***

We sit in the den, the five of us squashed like peaches on the sofa facing the cameras and Alisha tapping her ring against her Diet Coke can. The whole house smells chicken and not in a good way.

"Forget about the camera," Alisha says. But I have vowed not to.

"So, Mom," she calls my mom Mom, and really she ain't much older than Katherine, "tell us about the Bridgetown Longs."

"We're a happy family," Mom says. Nobody else says anything, there is only Sissy playing with the tie on her blouse and Katherine thinking so loud of Jackson Junior my head hurts. Alisha makes the hand sign that means keep going; the way she does it reminds me of puke tumbling from a mouth.

Mom shuts up tight as a bad clam. Then, "Happy," Mom says.

"Happy how?" says Alisha.

Mom means she and my dad still sleep in one bed and the five of us ain't hungry, but she says, "Happy everyway."

"And what do you think the Washington Longs will be like?"

"Rich," my father says.

"Smart," says my Mom

They will be terrible people, I know it. I know also and don't think I don't that they are asking them the exact same questions and I bet they are saying poor, and dumb, and mean and ugly. My parents know how the show works, the Longs will be everything the opposite of us.

Alisha and the man with the camera frown, like we SeaWorld dolphins who don't jump hoops. "OK," says Alisha, "Shorty,"

"What?" I say.

We been over and over this. I say, "We like to travel," like I was Miss Black America, "and meet different types of people." Around me I feel my family cooling like sugar syrup into brittle shapes.

Katherine turns to look at me then and gives me the look, like someone disguised a turd in a chocolate éclair and she swallowed before she knew.

"We jus wanna spend some time as a family," says Mom, "a big family, whole family, you know?" Her voice is tighter than ever.

The camera goes to Dad. We wait for him to say something. Alisha looks at him and smiles but Dad don't even see her. He looks at the camera, stares right down the lens and don't blink. Dad goes on looking til I think he's gonna pour himself into it and disappear. He could stop it all now with a word, less than that, he could take my mother's hand in his own and squeeze on it and my mother would send these people away, melt into him like Buffy and Spike, but he looks and he

14

stares and sees nothing and says less and I hope that the people at home see whose fault this all is.

***

My father sure can drive slow, and steady, not losing his head when people cut close in front, else ride up right in his tail, flashing, or giving the finger. He just doesn't care. He don't so much as blink and he don't give more gas, he just goes on at the same speed, always. We allowed two hours for the ride to the airport.

Katherine is on her cell phone. "I miss you," she's saying.

I stick fingers down my throat at Sissy and she cackles. She's in a good mood besides since I let her straighten my hair this morning.

"Me too," Katherine says, "I miss you already."

Katherine and Joe are the biggest babies you ever saw. My family thinks he's the best catch; these days Mom is all over him like ugly on an ape. Still, I seen how he looks at Sissy and how Katherine gets quiet about it, too mad to holler; one night I slept over there they was fighting til four in the morning. Plates and all. Katherine tried to be happy, but after Jackson, life got a question too complicated for her to find the answer in plain Joe Cooktown.

Sissy watches Katherine, sly and sad-happy like she knows something too beautiful to share. Mom puts her hand on my father's leg. Today she has spritzed perfume and has taken a gardenia from the yard and fixed it in her hair. She would like my father to tell her she looks beautiful, but it would not be like him to do something so necessary.

My father is a piece of furniture the rest of us manoeuvre round. And not anything so useful as a table or a chair. He is something that we keep a hold of out of habit and because we don't know what to put in its place or how to stand the empty space sitting there always and accusing. All three of us girls know that he is breaking my mother's heart in the slowest way possible, he is holding it still in his fist and squeezing. I wish my father drank. I wish he beat us. Anything other than the silence and worse than the silence, the things Mom says to fill the space. The quieter he is, the louder she talks, the stiller he sits, the more she fidgets and fusses. They've not been near each

15

other in years. Katherine told me. But my mother has bought new underwear and she has had her hair cut. It is plain as summer she's in love with the man, still, and she can't get free no more than a side of ham can suckle piglets.

Sissy is looking at her face in her compact, checking her eyelids and the plump of her lip; full of hope like a ripe mango waiting for someone to bite. Katherine is staring out the window and thinking of Jackson Junior, and worrying at the thought of him like a stain in the carpet she cannot get out.

Their hope makes me sick, the wriggling of it in them, like fish I saw in a bag at the fair, trapped and too big and precious, the squirming something more than I can stand.

***

By morning, there will have been tears and bad language. A punch will be thrown. It always is. They've picked us to fight but until we can figure out what to fight over, we shake hands and smile and laugh at the small things each other say.

In their hallway there are two flights of stairs that curve round like bosoms and meet at the top. Like Scarlett O'Hara in *Gone with the Wind,* they are stairs for dramatics. There are antique vases and a great piano; and it's so clean I can't breathe, a tight kind of clean. But none of this, none of it, is why my eyes are big, why Sissy is laugh-laugh-laughing through her nose, and Mom is struck dumb, my father worrying the rug with the toe of his boot. The reason is that their children, our long-lost Long cousins, unlike their mother and father, are white. They's white. And I don't mean passing, fair nor throwbacks: Alan has blond hair and his eyes are the grey-blue of steel. He comes up to my father and shakes his hand too firmly, like shaking a ketchup bottle for sauce, he goes to kiss my mother and smiles at my sisters, at Sissy most of all, and then sinks his hands in his pockets. Perhaps. I think, no-one has told him. Their Catherine is darker. Her hair is brown, but curls silky about her shoulders like no mixed-race hair ever would and there's a smell about her of Marlboros and patchouli.

16

My mother looks at Celie, who smiles like there wasn't a thing on her conscious, as if birthing white babies came natural to her as passing wind. I could see my mother not knowing what to say; my father looks like someone has pissed in his face.

"What a place," Mom says, "what a place you got here!"

Celie smiles.

"How many bathrooms you got?"

"Oh now," Celie tries modest, like she passed the bathrooms in her own personal stool.

"Seven," says Catherine.

"Seven bathrooms, you hear that Shorty?"

"No," I feel like saying, no, just to see what my mother would do. But I say "yes, seven bathrooms," because I want my mother to know she can rely on me.

Celie smiles again; she is good at it. Already, Sissy feels a love for this woman like my father for processed cheese. She is, not counting singers and movie stars and movie-star singers, the most beautiful woman I have seen. Her hair stands a crown on her head. Her eyes are the light colour of wet sand and they are kind eyes too. I wanted to hate her but I wish my Mom was like Celie, fine-looking as her and smart. The camera catches the way I am standing and staring. I forgot about it, already, like they said.

There's the crackle of plastic as my mother rummages in her bag. Lord, I think, no, but my mother is handing out the Long-Long Family Reunion T-shirts. Celie and Robert look at each other and laugh, then slip their T-shirts on right over their clothes. "Isn't this great?" Alan and Catherine stand there with their shirts limp in their hands like a dog bag full of business.

"Robert," Celie says, "Can you fix our guests a little drink?"

"Sure," says Robert, "what you fancy, folks, a little scotch?"

"Sure," Mom says.

We go through to the sitting room. My father takes the glass from Robert like someone has given him a sick baby to nurse. My mother giggles and chinks the ice in her glass like she ain't ever seen water that's frozen before. Everyone takes a tumbler and Celie makes a little toast and then they look at me.

"Does she —"

"Shorty? No. Oh no, Shorty wouldn't like —"

17

"Yes please, Mrs Long," I say. And everyone laughs, but it would be childish of me to let on it's bad manners. I look at Robert's hands as he squizzes soda in my scotch. I imagine a heart, a beating bloody lump of one, sick of course, fatty maybe, maybe blubbered like a whale. I imagine him holding it there, beating still in his dry hands, right where my glass is. I think about him touching Celie when they are in bed and wonder if she thinks about the hearts ever, the blood and flab oozing out, getting inside her.

"Whatever's the matter with you?" Mom is flapping at me to take the drink, "thank Robert," and the way she gets to call these rich folks by their Christian names I think she might bust with pride.

We sit and drink our scotch. Nobody says anything much. Alisha fetches us one by one to the kitchen. She leaves after that to fetch coffee, swinging her key ring round her finger, so I know that they all squealed louder than hogs. Robert pours more scotch, the camera-man clears his throat, but they don't mind.

At dinner, Celie sits me with Alan. Alisha is back but the camera is up at the other end of the table: we don't need to play nice. His hair isn't blonde after all — more what they call mouse. There are pimples on his neck and he hasn't shaved well. Not enough practice, I think. He is one of those boys that people take for good looking, but his teeth are creamy and the whites of his eyes too, like milk that is yellowing, sat too long in the sun. He's stringy thin but gristly too: beef jerky boy I call him and as soon as I get a name for him it jingle-jangles like dimes, sweet in my pocket.

I'm homesick for fried chicken and chilli, my mother's plain and dumplingy cooking. Even the peas here are things they cannot let be. They have fried them with onion and bacon and cream. The meat is bloody in the mid-part and accusing. The food goes round and around my mouth. Maybe my mother will get her wish: I will be the Amazing Shrinking Girl, win an endorsement deal with Maybelline and we will laugh when we sit hand-holdingly together on Oprah to think I ever loved Texas.

Alan is telling me some dumb ski story; it goes on and his breath smells doggish and I'm so tired of hearing him over my thoughts that I say, "Is Catherine your sister?"

Alan stops talking with his mouth open like a real Texas redneck, which I bet is what his momma is, and her cousin.

"I mean like your actual — I mean, y'all are adopted, right?"

Alan looked at me.

Freaking Mary, I think, I don't see what there's to be pricklish about; I mean it's not as if it ain't plain as the pimple on your neck. And then the camera is there and I don't know since when and Alan cuts his pork chop and pink spreads over his neck like blood in water. I think, like us and Jackson Junior, there are things they talk about and things they don't talk about and all of this crockery and 18 kinds of fork exist on the same principle we do; and this is the point of the Family Show, this is what I am supposed to realise, but it still feels peculiar. Glassy. These games come easy as bleeding to them, but no matter the contract Alisha has had us sign, none of us are sure of the rules any more. Already I know if I need to hurt them, how to do it. And I know we must keep our secrets better hidden and we can, for after all ours are deeper than skin colour, more meaty and breeding, not easily nor cleanly sliced.

***

I wake up thirsty. It's night still and the house is dead. Sissy ain't back yet. Alisha took her and the others to some bar while the parents drank liquor and played cards in the den. I fetch my water from the tap in the kitchen and go back upstairs. As I reach the landing, there's a noise: like a little cat. And before I can think how dumb the idea is I am poking in doorways looking for this lost little thing. A crack of moonlight like a blade cuts through the darkness. I follow the mewing sound to the bathroom.

I push the door open a little and stand looking in. It is quite light enough to see, with the glaze from the moon sparkling on the tiles. Sissy and Alan are screwing against the shower. Alan is standing and Sissy has her legs wrapped round him, clinging on like she was drowning and he was her last hope. He presses and presses her, the screen rattling and him sounding in her like meat slapped raw on the griddle, him pounding away there til Sissy don't look like Sissy no more, with her mouth all open and her head loose on her neck. I let the door stand open and I take my glass of water back to the bedroom and sit there in the dark.

After a minute, something thumps at the door, something massive

19

sounding and I pull the covers up round me but it's Sissy, running in and only a T-shirt on her. Jeesus Jeesus she is saying. Jeesus, and she falls back on the bed, laughing loud like she don't care who hears. I prop up on one arm and look at her. Her eyes are big and shining and I think how beautiful she is. I always thought Kate was the beautiful one and Sissy just pretty, but now I see Sissy got soul and so much of it it's a wonder the girl don't burst with it.

"Sissy you is drunk," I say.

Sissy laughs some more.

"Momma's gonna kill you," I say, "skin you and sell your hide to the Eskimo, girl." I am not jealous of Sissy. I have never been jealous of her; it would be like the moon being jealous of the sun and besides I do not like Alan. But now there is something between us. Sissy's nothing like me, after all; she will leave us like Kate did and then there will only be me, and the ghost of Jackson Junior and our terrible parents, who terrify me. I couldn't stand it. It would rip at me like chicken shredding if Sissy went and I don't know how I could say it to her or what the point would be anyhow since it wouldn't change nothing.

"Does it hurt?" I say.

Sissy sits up on sudden, and moves quick to the little bathroom in our room. I hear her pee fierce, then stumble, then the flush of the john. There's quiet then, but I know Sissy. Sissy is my sister and I've known her longer than anything, like jump rope rhymes I will never forget; she is staring at her face in the mirror and thinking it ugly and I want to tell her that I just saw she was beautiful and that it was nothing to do with him.

Downstairs the dishwasher is gurgle-grinding and the tumble dryer whirring; in the morning everything will be whole still, and clean. The bread machine sings softly to itself. Outside it's quiet. The world stops at the velvet curtains, thick and heavy, I fight my way through and lay my forehead against the glass. Already home seems kind of improbable — my posters, our dogs and their smell and Johnny out on the porch, picking strings and wailing. We will go back, of course, only six more days, but this place will live with us, a speck in our heart it will bleed us slow and cold and the heat, all the heat in Texas, be the hens so hot they lay hard boiled eggs, it couldn't warm us. The silence is heavy about me like clothes that are too big.

"You want me to get Mom?" I say.

Sissy comes out then and throws herself back on the bed, lies looking up at the ceiling, through the ceiling to I don't know what. I curl up on my bed and watch her. She says Jeesus. Jeesus. I wish she'd say something else. Jeesus she says again. There's a click, a quiet one but certain, somewhere in the hallway.

I go to the big bathroom, hunting for Sissy's panties; but Mom has them already, has them hugged to her breast as she sits in the dark on the toilet with the door open, not able to cry and trying to think her way through something that twists shapeless and tight on itself like bad guts. I wonder if she agrees with me that it were better to have been Johnny Mann. Maybe not, cause she just says,

"If we lived in this house, Lord, we'd be happy."

"Happy like the Cosby Show," I say.

"Wouldn't we, Shorty."

My name is Elizabeth, I want to tell her, but it seems mean: needless now. My poor mother: she never did know what was wrong with me, or what happened to Jackson Junior and now she don't know why the Washington Longs are asleep in their beds and she is crying homesick in their bathroom while Sissy bleeds on their Egyptian Cotton sheets down the hall.

I leave her to figure it out and go back to Sissy. "Why d'you let him?" I say. But she's snoring now and there's no reason anyway she could tell me. Just we Bridgetown Longs, always like tumbleweed blowing where it takes us.

Rick Argues

Tom Cox

Matt is sitting on the amplifier, reading from a sheet of A4 paper. I'm leaning against the wall, examining my nails for something non-existent, in that way that people do when they're feeling simultaneously bored and smug. Matt looks up and shakes his head. A smile spreads across his face — a bit like the one you imagine Jagger might have flashed Richards upon receipt of the riff to *Satisfaction*. "This is it," he tells me. "This... This is the greatest thing you've ever written."

It's 1993, and Matt and I are the principle songwriters in Rick Argues, the punk band we have formed at FE college. That is to say: I bring four verses and a chorus of preternaturally banal teen angst to the studio, and Matt constructs a three chord riff around them in the style — we would like to think — of our Californian teen punk heroes, Green Day. Either that, or we just cover a Green Day song. Green Day are still in the hardcore punk ghetto at this point, and have yet to be signed to Warner Music. We look at it this way: liking them makes us very obscure and cool, and if, when we finally get around to playing a gig, someone mistakes one of Green Day's songs for one of ours, we won't go out of our way to correct them.

Matt listens exclusively to three chord punk music. I listen exclusively to three chord punk music and The Smiths. I think The Smiths are brilliant. Matt thinks they are "puff music, for puffs", even though Matt — who, incidentally, won't be homophobic forever — has never properly heard The Smiths. Matt and I argue about The Smiths constantly, but try to meet somewhere in the middle (i.e. I am banned from mentioning The Smiths, Morrissey, ambiguous sexuality, or our college friend, Robin Smith). Today, after three months of hard work, Matt is looking at me affectionately, concluding we have made a major breakthrough. This, I can tell he is thinking from the far off look in his eyes, is the first step on the way to a support tour with our peers, Throaty Toad, a local band with the distinction of "once going out for a drink with the Buzzcocks."

What is the inspiration behind Rick Argues? I don't think either of us can quite put our finger on it. I would ask John and Joe, the other two members of our band, what they thought, but it would probably be a waste of time. John, who drums, and Joe, who plays bass, are never quick to take advantage of Rick Argues's democratic forum for free expression.

"I was thinking of moving the second line of verse one into the third line of verse two. What do you think, John?" I sometimes ask John.

"Okay," John replies.

"What do you think of this riff?" Matt sometimes asks John.

"S'alright," John says.

In an attempt to get John more involved, I write *John's Hair*, a song, built around the central refrain "Once it was long/Now it is short", detailing the journey of his lustrous locks from pony tail to crewcut. "What do you think, John?" I ask.

"S'alright," says John.

Joe, our bassist, isn't quite so loquacious. One of life's great smilers, Joe has such a repertoire of attentive grins, it's possible to have a half hour conversation with him without realising he hasn't spoken. When Matt and I fight over The Smiths, Joe grins. When Matt tells me that what I've written is soppy shite, Joe grins. When I gently suggest to Matt that he might want to add a fourth chord to his repertoire, Joe grins. Joe's grins, despite their diversity, all seem to mean the same thing. They seem to mean "S'alright". Do John and Joe enjoy being in Rick Argues? Who knows. Do John and Joe talk about Matt and I behind our backs? Perhaps, but in our presence they communicate with one another on a purely psychic level.

On the days we can't afford a proper rehearsal room, I drive across town to Matt's front room. First of all, though, I pick up John and Joe, who live on the posh side of town, and load their equipment into the boot of my parents' Vauxhall Astra. I drive in the style of a punk rock Alain Prost, but not quite as slowly. I am an idiot. No-one talks, because I've worked out by now that John and Joe are beyond words and, besides, Green Day's *Kerplunk!*, cranked up on the car stereo, makes conversation difficult. You might say that, as seventeen year-olds go, I'm a reckless driver, but I know the etiquette of the highway. When, for instance, I detect the wail of an ambulance's siren behind me, I pull over to the side of the road with my hazard flashers on.

Only, instead of an ambulance, the Astra is surrounded by three police cars, one in front, one at the back, and one at the side.

Joe, John and I are bundled roughly out of the Astra and get a police car each. I see John's policeman accidentally-on-purpose trap John's leg in the door. For once, John doesn't say "S'alright". He says "Owwww!!". The policeman doesn't apologise.

My policeman doesn't say anything for a couple of minutes, while I sit there, thinking how much he looks like a human version of Basil Brush. He asks me for my name and licence, then inquires what I was doing outside Joe's house, five minutes ago. I tell him I was picking Joe up. He asks me where we are going. I tell him our band, Rick Argues, is on our way to rehearse our new song, *T-Shirt*.

Basil asks me a few more questions, about where I live, how old I am. Then he makes a call via his crackly radio. By this point, his two colleagues are standing outside the car, waiting to talk to him. Joe and John are sitting on the grass verge; Joe looks sad and worried, but is still sort of grinning.

It is clear there has been a terrible mistake. We have been reported by one of Joe's neighbours for breaking into Joe's house and stealing Joe's bass guitar and amplifier. Basil returns to the car and explains this to me in the chuntering voice of the six year-old who knows he is wrong for setting fire to the manger in the school nativity play but doesn't want to admit it in the presence of his tough mates.

"If you're going to have to pick Joe up in the future, just be more careful next time you're in his area," Basil tells me.

I wonder what Basil means by this: How can we be more careful to show Joe's neighbours we aren't breaking into his house? Perhaps I should refrain from driving a twelve year old car with a Dead Kennedys logo painted on the side, or, even better, we should all wear fluorescent t-shirts with name tags and "Law Abiding Citizen" emblazoned on them. I am about to put this suggestion to Basil, but think better of it.

"And there's one other thing," he says. "You went through a red light back there."

"It was amber," I correct him.

"It's the same thing."

I really have to put Basil right here, if only for his own good and his future as a successful policeman. "How can they be the same thing, if one's orange and the other one's red?"

"Both signals request the driver to stop. I'm going to let you out the car now, but just remember: you've been very lucky not to be fined. It's a criminal offence to waste police time, you know."

Police time? What about Rick Argues' time?

We arrive at Matt's place in stunned silence. For once, though, I feel I can rely on John and Joe for support: We're all pretty shaken up, right? Those pigs are such bastards, aren't they? We're innocent punk rock heroes, railing against the system! I recount the experience to Matt, being careful to double the number of police cars and the level of physical violence.

"So then this bastard copper slams John's head against the car bonnet and starts reading him his rights!" I tell Matt.

"Fucker told me I sped through a red light at ninety miles an hour. I told him where to stick it!" I tell Matt.

I look to John and Joe for support.

"S'right," says John.

"..." says Joe, grinning.

Rick Argues' signature song is called "T-Shirt". I genuinely feel it's my masterpiece. Here is the first verse:

Over there you are
Walking in the dark
I don't know your name
But I know your name

The bridge builds the tempo slightly:

I'd like to thank you
For your T-shirt
Congra-tu-lations
On your T-shirt

The chorus goes like this:

T-shirt, T-shirt, I remember
T-shirt, T-shirt, last December

26

T-shirt, T-shirt, look but don't touch
T-shirt, T-shirt, I've seen too much

I like the coda best, though:

Don't throw it away!
Don't throw it away!
Don't throw it away!

T-Shirt is intended to be a meaningful commentary on the eternal search for identity via band logos amongst indie youth at Nottingham's premier alternative venue, Rock City. Through its more profound lyrics — *I don't know your name/But I know your name* — I am trying to convey the sensation of not knowing someone, but feeling like you know someone. Ultimately, though, the song is a love letter to the girl in the Suede T-Shirt who I see at Rock City every week, and who, on the one occasion that I tried to speak to her, told me to "piss off" before I'd even managed to say hello. One day, I hope, she will sit in the front row at a Rick Argues gig, and I will be able to sing our signature song to her. As I said, I am an idiot.

Rick Argues are called Rick Argues because we have a friend, Rick, who argues. We invite Rick along to our rehearsals as our mascot, one time, but he just disrupts the creative process by arguing.

"Why did you call yourselves Rick Argues?" asks Rick.

"Because you argue a lot," Matt and I tell him.

"No, I don't," argues Rick.

Rick argues about everything, but doesn't seem to realise it. I've noticed that when I abruptly change my mind and agree with him on a topic on which I previously disagreed with him, he'll change his original argument and borrow my original argument, just because he likes arguing so much. I don't think Rick has ever agreed with anyone in their presence. Matt and I don't only have a band called Rick Argues; we have a song called *Rick Argues*, too. It doesn't have a chorus, and the verses simply consist of me shouting out random topics which I've argued about (apart from The Smiths, of course, who are banned). For example:

Argued about my mum
Argued about my leg

27

Argued about John Major
Argued about hedgeclippers
Argued about third division footballers
It makes me happy!

We don't think of it as one of our classics.

The microphones in the rehearsal rooms where Rick Argues practice smell of regurgitated parmesan. The crusty who owns the studios, Chiz, usually sits in the room adjacent to the room where Rick Argues rehearse, reading the *Daily Star*, smoking weed, and feeding Kentucky Fried chicken to his dog, KFC. "Here, KFC, want some KFC?" inquires Chiz.

"Wuff!" replies KFC.

Our plan has been to spend six months honing our style, before cutting a demo or playing a gig. However, we feel, with our polished version of *T-Shirt* and a new song, *Bike Mother (I Want Your Omelette)*, we are ready to book time in the Big Room, where people record things.

"Chiz, we want to cut a demo," Matt and I inform Chiz.

"Are you sure?" asks Chiz.

We eventually convince Chiz that we're ready lay down some tracks, and we're booked in for the following Monday. When we arrive, though, Chiz claims he has double-booked us. The week after that, Chiz tell us his mixing desk is playing up. He sends us back to the rehearsal room with a small, early nineteen-eighties tape recorder and a C90 cassette. Matt and I see the rehearsal through in a dolorous mood, both of us thinking the same thing, but not wanting to say it.

"Matt, do you think we're actually any good?" I ask Matt the next day at college, in the refectory.

"Of course we are," Matt replies.

"But, y'know, I mean proper good. Like on-tour-with-Green-Day good."

"Easily. I've told you, *T-Shirt* could quite easily be off *Kerplunk!*"

"So when I sing it back to back with a Green Day song, it sounds just the same?"

"Yeah."

"And that's all we want, really, isn't it?"

"Yeah."

I've never wanted to be a rock star — I just want to meet the girl with the Suede T-shirt (I am an idiot). Matt doesn't want to be a rock star, either, but he has different reasons, chief of them being that rock stars are corporate scum. I think if Matt could bring himself to admit it to his subsconscious, he would *really* like to be a rock star. I would like to be in a band, definitely, but I don't think I'm particularly musical. I've thought about the band I want to be in, and I think it should have horns and mandolins and lyrics about nothing in particular and everything in the world, all at once. It should be gentle and poetic, or epic and surreal, not laconic and primitive. Matt would kill me if he knew.

Matt calls me up one night. "Up for a rehearsal this weekend?"

"Yeah, deffo," I say. I'm panicking, because droning away in the background in my bedroom as I speak, is *Bona Drag*, a solo album by Morrissey, from The Smiths.

When I come to college in a t-shirt which doesn't say 'Too Drunk Too Fuck', 'Never Mind The Bollocks' or 'I Am Not What I Own', Matt tells me off. "What the fuck you wearing that for?" he asks me, when I turn up in the bootleg Teenage Fanclub shirt I bought from outside Rock City the night before. I'm growing my hair out slightly, and hoping he hasn't noticed. At lunchtime, in the college refectory, I often think I'd quite like to sit next to Nick and Steve from my design class, but they have long hair, and Matt says all people with long hair are "townies" or "hippies". Matt also says you can't trust a song which doesn't include swearing. The few lyrics Matt writes for Rick argues invariably contain the words "coagulate", "enema" and "pigfuck".

I think I'm in the process of re-evaluating my artistic relationship with Matt.

"... This is the greatest thing you've ever written," Matt is repeating, still shaking his head at the piece of A4. "I mean it. This is it, Tom. This is what I knew you had in you."

John fiddles with his drum sticks. Joe grins. I slouch against the wall, shrug, and smile internally. I'm wasting more of Rick Argues' time, but I have to admit I'm quite enjoying this. Maybe I'll let Matt construct a few chords around my lyrics. Then, at some point, I'll gently explain to him that the words on the piece of paper are not mine, that I copied them this morning from the sleeve of The Smiths' 1983 album, *Hatful Of Hollow*. But not yet. Not just yet.

Damocles

Clare Littleford

Anyone who knows me will tell you that I'm not an impulsive man. I like to think things through, look at the potential outcomes, make informed choices. That's Angela's main complaint, that I'm not spontaneous enough, and maybe that's why I decide to move in with Carmel — I deliberately don't think about it. If I'm honest, I suppose I want Angela to hear about it, and maybe it will change her opinion. Not that I want her to come begging, telling me she's made a mistake, asking me to move back home — no, that isn't it at all.

I can't really tell you what Carmel's like, and that probably sounds like a strange thing to say when I'm moving in with her, but you'd understand if you met her. She isn't like anyone else I've ever known. She's an actress and singer, or she wants to be; I have no doubt that she'll get there, she's got that certain something, star quality or whatever. But she isn't like the stars you get these days. You won't ever see her on reality TV, or baring all for the lads' magazines, or spread across the gossip-mags. There won't be any paparazzi-shots of her sunbathing topless on the deck of a yacht, or draped over a bad-boy popstar in a West End nightclub, or giggling up a red carpet in Leicester Square. Flashguns popping and crowds pressing against the railings calling out her name — that isn't her scene at all.

Not that she lacks confidence, or is prudish, or anything like that; she knows she's beautiful, you can see that in the way she carries herself, but she's got integrity. She knows she's worth more. She's like an old-fashioned star; Audrey Hepburn, or Grace Kelly. Think black-and-white photos, a half-smile like the camera is sharing a secret, eyes so liquid you could swim in them. Think of slow-dancing on a hotel terrace, under the moon and a sky strung with stars. Think of a convertible with the roof down on a summer's day, the sky so blue it looks painted, and Carmel, headscarved and sunglassed, in the driver's seat. Think of dinner-dances with Big Band musicians in black-tie and little round tables with white tablecloths and waiters who bend to light Carmel's cigarettes as if the pleasure is all theirs.

Think of all of that, and you're still only part way to knowing what I mean when I say her name.

Carmel. The name drips off your tongue.

It's Lawsy who introduces us. Dougie Law, broad and red-cheeked, gold cufflinks and Rolex always on show, soft pink hands constantly running to pockets full of cigars and business cards, and if he'd known what was going to happen he never would have introduced us.

This is when I move into the flat in Mapperley, out towards Carlton Hill. Top of the city, with views all the way to smudged green countryside. The block was built in the eighties; even the architecture encapsulates the spirit of that age — four small flats stacked like a cube, two-across, two-up, with an uncompromising layout, a Thatcherite meanness to the room proportions, no allowances made for the human eye's need for detail. Each flat has its own front door onto the parking area, with private staircases to the upstairs flats — technically, that makes them maisonettes, but nobody ever calls them that — and Carmel has the flat directly above mine.

I hear Carmel many times before I meet her — hear her hard heels on the stairs, and her phone ringing, ringing, ringing late at night, and her muffled laughter when she answers the calls. I hear her singing — she's Doris Day at the piano, she's Ursula Andress emerging from the ocean, she's an old Blues record on a wind-up gramophone. And I hear her dog, Pepsi, yap yap yapping like it thinks it can sing along.

Lawsy owns the whole block, of course. That's just his style. When things go wrong with Angela he jumps straight in and offers me a place, all credit for that, but he has to make a point of it, he can't let it lie. I'm working from home, writing analysis software on short-term contracts — long hours at the computer on coffee and Pro-Plus, heart pounding, brain singing with exhaustion but too wired to sleep — and that's when Lawsy starts dropping in.

"I was just passing," he'll say, leaning against the doorframe, jingling his keys in his trouser pockets. "Thought I'd see how you're settling in," or, "Had ten minutes before my next appointment, thought you might have a brew on the go?" or, when I've made up my mind that this time I'll say I'm busy, he comes with an iron that he's noticed I haven't bought myself yet, and he says, "I know it's hard, you and Angela were together so long, it must be hard." Looking at my crumpled shirt, and I haven't shaved for a few days, and what can I say?

This is only four and a half weeks after Angela asked me to move out, so all of that is still raw and I'm jumpy-nervous about it, torn between wanting to engage in furious, bitter discussions of all her faults, all the things she said that aren't true, and that sickening, tiring paranoia that maybe people think they are true, I am that bad, I did bring it on myself. I'm desperate for news, opinions, anything, and I'm too scared to ask and I hope he'll tell me anyway. So I invite Lawsy in, and he looks around at the boxes I haven't unpacked yet, and I make tea, and we sit and drink, and I try to think of something to say.

He says, "I saw Angela last night. Julia and I saw her at Cassidy's. All the old gang was there."

Cassidy's is where I met Angela. Lawsy's wife Julia brought Angela along. This is before Lawsy and Julia had kids, back when we were still young. The gang hasn't been round to the flat yet. I say, "How is she?"

"She seems fine. You know, considering." A neutral tone, like he's trying to stop me reading into it. Typical Lawsy — he'll give you so much and then he'll shut up, and there's nothing you can do to draw him out.

For years, we never even liked each other — or at least, I didn't like him. School years, all those awkward years; our parents were friends but we never even acknowledged each other. He was too much about the money, even then — like he was in such a hurry to get into the world and get rich that he didn't have time for anyone who couldn't help him on his way. He was the kind of kid who talked loudly about what he got for Christmas; he was the kid who got the supervisor's stars on his name-badge at his weekend job. But it's one of those strange things — we were indifferent to each other all through school, but as soon as we started working it was like we couldn't get away from each other, we were always in the same place at the same time. After a while we couldn't keep up the indifference any more. Does that count as friendship? I don't know. He's helped me out, he found me my flat, and that has to count for something.

He sips his tea, picks a book out of the top of a box and drops it back in without reading the cover. I start formulating a question.

Carmel turns on her stereo upstairs and we hear the opening bars to some old tune, Ella Fitzgerald or someone like that, and when Carmel starts to sing Lawsy cocks his head and listens, face lit up with expectation. "Ah!" he says. "Just listen to that! Have you met Carmel yet?" I shake my head. "I'll introduce you."

We go to Carmel's door and he rings the bell. I can still hear the stereo, but she stops singing. Lawsy rings again, and I hear her at the top of her stairs. "All right, all right," she's calling. I see her approach through the patterned glass in the front door, and then she says, sweet but firm, "Dougie, I told you I couldn't see you today, I've got to prepare for my audition."

Lawsy flushes and glances at me, but I pretend not to understand. I know Julia, after all; she's friends with Angela. Lawsy says, "I only wanted to introduce you to Nick. Your downstairs neighbour. Open the door, won't you?"

There's a pause, then she lets out an extravagant sigh and says, "Okay, okay." I can see her outline through the patterned glass; a distortion of white cotton dressing gown and a towel like a turban on her head. "Oh, where did I put that key? Hold on."

She runs back up the stairs. Lawsy says, "We, uh, had a little thing, you know? But there's no need — Julia, I mean."

"Don't worry," I say. I want to add that I'm unlikely to see Julia anyway, or any of the old gang the way it's looking, but Carmel is back and unlocking the door.

"Come in," she says, standing aside for us to pass. She's taken the towel off her head and wet black curls fall to her shoulders. She has dark eyes, and a honey glow to her skin that makes me think of olive groves and cicadas and bleached skies.

I follow Lawsy upstairs. Where my flat is all cardboard boxes and bare magnolia walls, hers is effortlessly clean, tidy, with pale furniture and modern art prints on the walls. There's a folding music stand arranged with sheet music by the window. The dog, Pepsi, is curled up on the sofa, a little ratty brown thing with big eyes that give it a permanently surprised expression, like someone's given it a facelift and pulled the skin too tight.

"The flats are all pretty similar," Lawsy says to me, as if Carmel isn't there. "I'm thinking about extending these top-floor flats, there's access into the loft space. Put another bedroom up there no problem." He's walking over to the hallway that runs into the back of the flat, signalling the access panel in the ceiling. Then he smiles at Carmel. "That'd be all right, wouldn't it, love?"

She shrugs, eyes on him as he glances down the hallway towards her bedroom. He turns back, sees both of us watching him, smiles a magnanimous landlord smile.

"I can't offer you anything," Carmel says, moving over to the music stand. "I have to get ready."

"I only wanted you to meet Nick," Lawsy says, but he's settling on the sofa. The dog rearranges itself and looks at me, so I sit too.

Carmel says, "Well, now we've met." There's fury in her expression, but she looks away when I meet her eyes.

"Nick's an old friend," Lawsy goes on, a relaxed tone. "We go way-back. He needed a place, and downstairs was vacant, so I'm helping him out." He pauses, but she says nothing. "He's just separated from his wife."

She looks at me with sympathy then, and I feel a rush of anger for Lawsy. I say, "We should let you get on, Carmel," and I stand up. "It was nice meeting you."

"You too," she says, but there's a faraway look in her eyes. Lawsy gets to his feet reluctantly. She turns away from him, holds out her hand to me. It's an oddly formal gesture. "I'll see you around, I'm sure."

I shake her hand. Thin, brittle fingers and a light grip. Lawsy engulfs her in his arms, gives her an extravagant kiss on the cheek; she pulls away and laughs and he laughs too, a great dirty laugh that seems too big for the room. The dog joins in, yap-yap-yap from its place on the sofa; as we go down the stairs I look back and see her pick it up, cradling it to her chest.

I'm still feeling that unaccountable anger towards Lawsy when we get back to my flat. He must see it in my expression; his face twists and he says, "What?"

"Nothing," I say.

"It isn't nothing," he says. "I know what you're thinking, I always do." And he sinks down onto my sofa, throws his hands over his face, stays like that, silent, for a full minute. I sit next to him, and he says, "You don't understand."

I don't say anything. He's right, I don't understand. I'm not sure what he's talking about.

He rubs his fingers across his eyes — for a moment I think he's rubbing away tears, but when he looks up he's angry. "I can do what I like," he says. "You don't think Julia does whatever she likes?"

"I don't know," I say. "What about the kids?"

He turns his face away for a moment. "Look," he says. "You seem to think I've had it easy, but it isn't like that. I've worked for everything I've got, but people always criticise me. People look for any chance to knock me down. I set out to make money, and I've made some. I don't think I should suffer because of that, do you?"

"No, no, no," I say. "I wasn't –"

"You have to be dedicated if you want to get anywhere. Be prepared to sacrifice. That's what I've done, I've sacrificed. I've taken risks. Your trouble," and here he leans in towards me, like he's imparting a secret. "Your trouble, Nick, is that you haven't ever taken any risks. You don't let that adrenaline flow. That's what life's all about — the adrenaline, the excitement. That's how you get anywhere in this life."

He sits back, waiting. I'm not sure what he wants — me to leap up and say that he's right, I've just never seen it that way before? That he's wrong and I can tell him why? My life isn't so great; my life isn't something to emulate. But he is right about one thing — he isn't afraid to go after the things he wants. And I can learn from that.

He says, "The thing with Carmel, it's nothing. You know? Nothing to do with Julia or the kids or any of that."

He stands up, goes to the window, looks out. I don't know what to say — there's something like anger, I still want to be angry but I don't know why. Maybe that transmits to him, because he turns back from the window, looks around like he can't find anything for his eyes to settle on, and then says in a falsely jovial tone, "Well, I should leave you to it."

I don't say anything. He's waiting for me to protest. He stands there, jingling his keys in his pocket. Finally, he cracks a smile and says, "She's really something, though, isn't she? Carmel? A real free spirit."

I say yes, she seems very nice, and he laughs that same dirty laugh, all innuendo. Then he says, "I'll drop in again another day."

"Sure," I say, because I can't say no.

As he's leaving, Carmel begins to sing again upstairs. He throws a delighted smile up at the ceiling, then nods at me and goes out to his car.

When he's gone, I look around at the mess of my flat, and I think about Carmel's flat, so beautiful. I sit on the carpet and look into the nearest box, but I can't find the energy to unpack anything. I don't want any of the stuff. I want to phone Angela again, tell her I miss her, but she hasn't returned my other calls. I want to phone her friends — Julia — but I just sit there instead, listening to Carmel sing.

Later, I'm lying on the bed when my doorbell rings. The boxes are still on the living room floor. I have a headache. But I think maybe it's Angela, so I heave myself off the bed and answer the door.

It's Carmel, carrying a bottle of wine. She's wearing sunglasses even though it's almost dark. She says, "I didn't welcome you properly earlier. Can I come in?"

I let her in. She hesitates on the threshold, seeing the state of the place, then gives me a smile. "Have you got a corkscrew?" she asks, holding out the wine.

I take it from her, go into the kitchen and pour out two large glasses. When I return she's standing by the stereo, looking through the stack of CDs.

"Put something on," I say, and she smiles back at me and continues to look. "How did your audition go?" I ask.

She puts a CD on — one of those late-night jazz compilations, it came free with a newspaper, I've barely listened to it — then takes the glass of wine I'm offering and sits next to me on the sofa. "They'll call me, they say," and she rolls her eyes. "I'm sorry about earlier, just I had to prepare."

"That's okay," I say.

"It wasn't you," she goes on. "It's Dougie, he can be so demanding."

I want to ask her if she knows he's married, has kids, but I can't think how to phrase it so it isn't an accusation. The silence is filled by the rising sound of a sax. We sit listening to the CD, and the weariness rises up through me again.

"Dougie talks about you all the time," Carmel says suddenly. "He really admires you."

37

"Admires me? Why?"

She sips her wine, thinking about something, the music, I don't know; for a long time I don't think she's going to answer me. Then she says, "He thinks you've done something with your life. Got skills, you know. He's very big on people having skills. Having something to fall back on." She screws her nose up, thinking about that. "He's very practical."

There's something behind her words. "He knows what he wants," I say, watching her. "If he sees it, he just goes and gets it."

"He's very forceful," she says. Her expression is fixed, but she's turning the wine glass between her fingers, swirling the remains, the wine washing up the sides of the glass.

I say, "I'll get the rest of the bottle," and I go into the kitchen. When I return, she's drained the glass and holds it out. I fill it almost to the top and she takes a gulp and wipes some from her chin. I put the bottle down. "How did you get together?" I ask, but that isn't what I want to know, and she smiles as if she realises that.

The CD has finished, and she gets up and hits play again. She has her back to me. "I don't know that I'd say we are together," she says. Then the music starts and she turns with a smile. "I love this sound." She repeats that, changes the emphasis: "I love this *sound*." She lets out a long sigh. "It's like — it's like New York, it's how I imagine New York by night. Harlem, back in the day — Louis Armstrong and Billie Holiday and all the others, and crowded little basement jazz clubs that keep going all night, and everyone just tuned in to this *sound*."

I don't say anything.

"I've always wanted to go there," she says. "Dougie has no idea. He doesn't have any sensitivity. He doesn't have any *soul*." She gives a little laugh, steps towards me so I have to put my head back to see her face. Her eyes seem very bright. "You know what I mean, don't you? You've got soul, I can tell."

I'm not sure if she's teasing me; I have a feeling she might be.

She sits down next to me again and closes her eyes, swaying slightly as if she's picturing herself in one of those jazz clubs. I listen to the music, trying to hear what she can hear. The music is soporific; I can feel my eyelids growing heavy. "I'd love to sing in one of those clubs," she says. "That's a dream of mine."

Her voice is soft as the music. I lean back, aware of her weight pressing into the sofa beside me, and she tells me about being on stage, about the feeling when she sings. She tells me that she feels alive.

With my eyes half-closed and her so close to me and that music coming through her words, I feel like I've been transported to some other place.

"But it's just a silly dream, I know that," she says. Then, "Do you think dreams can come true?"

"I don't know," I say.

"I think they can," she says, as if I've disagreed. "I'm a big believer in following your heart. You can't go too wrong if you follow your heart, that's what I think."

"You could be right," I say.

"Dougie says that, but I think he's just humouring me. He's got a businessman's heart." Then she says, "You're not humouring me, are you?"

"God, no," I say. "I've heard you sing, you're amazing." And it seems like I've blurted the words out, too quickly, too suddenly. "I mean, if he can't see that — you deserve — you shouldn't –"

She looks at me for a moment, coolly, and then she laughs. But there's nothing malicious in that laugh. "You're very sweet," she says. "Really, I mean it." And then she gets up, and says, "Poor thing, look at you, you're worn out. It's late, I should let you rest. I shouldn't have burst in like this."

"No, no," I say quickly; I don't want her to go. But she's insisting I don't get up, and when she reaches the door she turns and smiles, and I think she's going to blow me a kiss but she doesn't, she doesn't.

I lie there on the sofa for a long time, long after the CD has finished. I'm not thinking about anything, not even about Angela. When I finally go to bed, I dream about the music, about New York. I dream that I'm trying to find Carmel in New York, but everywhere I turn there's crowds of people and none of them are her.

I see her a few times in the next few days, coming and going from her flat. She waves at me. Angela doesn't phone. I don't see Lawsy for another week; I think he's avoiding me. I think maybe he's embarrassed, but I don't mind.

I work on another programming contract, test strings of code, but I can't get very far with it. I think about unpacking the boxes, but every time I open one I'm overwhelmed by this sense that I don't want any of the stuff inside, none of it connects to me any more.

I listen to Carmel singing. I lie on the sofa with my eyes closed and listen to her voice coming at me through the darkness. It's like she's in the room with me, it's like she's singing just for me. When she stops, I put on the CD she selected and play it over and over, trying to hear what she heard, trying to find that place she transported me to.

And then, finally, she comes round.

When I open the door she pushes past me into the living room. "Who's Julia?" she demands. "It's his wife, isn't it? Isn't it? He's fucking married, and now she's writing me letters — she's sent me photos of his kids, for god's sake. Who does he think he is? You knew, didn't you, all along?"

"I thought –" I start to say weakly.

"You knew and you didn't warn me! I'll kill him, I swear to god!"

She pushes past me again, shoulder in my chest. At the door she looks back, and I open my mouth to tell her I'm sorry, and she says, spits, "Forget it," and marches away. Slams my door on her way out; slams her own door on her way in; stamps up the stairs like she wants to come through them.

I lie back on the sofa, put my arms over my face. I think about Angela telling me to move out. I want to cry.

I hear Carmel upstairs, walking around. The creak of floorboards and I can follow her around her flat. The dog barks but she doesn't put any music on, she doesn't sing.

Later — it's night time, it's dark outside and I haven't switched on any lights — later I hear a car brake suddenly in the parking area, and a door slam. I don't move. And then there's someone banging on my door.

"Nick!" Lawsy calls. "Come out here, Nick, I want to talk to you."

He thumps the door again. He's drunk, I can hear it in his voice. I heave myself back from the edge of sleep. He's kicking the door and it's rattling in its frame, each pane of glass rattling.

"Open the fucking door," he's saying as I open it.

He's very drunk, stupid drunk, blind drunk. He has to hold himself up against the doorframe. I think he's going to fall when I open the door and I grab his shoulders to stop him, but he staggers away from me.

"Nick, you bastard," he says. "You fucking told her."

"She already knew," I say. "She asked me."

He pulls himself upright, heaves his shoulders back to steady himself. "You just can't stand people having things you don't have," he says. And then, before I realise what he's doing, he swings his fist, and makes contact with my jaw, and I go down hard, smack against the doorstep. He's on top of me; his hands grapple mine; I can smell the booze on his breath, the rancid stink of it. His fingers mesh with my hair and he slams my head down. I can hear a roaring sound, and I don't know if it's him or me or the blood rushing through my ears.

I hear the dog, Pepsi; I hear its high bark, and Carmel shouting. I push Lawsy away and he staggers back. The dog is around his ankles, Carmel is pulling his arm. He shakes free of her, stands over me, gasping for breath. His face is red. The dog yaps again, running at his feet, and he gives a great roar and aims a kick and there's a terrible sound of pain as he sends the dog flying.

"Pepsi!" Carmel cries, and rushes for the dog. It cowers, whimpering. "Oh Pepsi," she says, scooping it up in her arms, and turns to face Lawsy, furious.

"Leave it," he says, before she can speak. "Just leave it." And then he's stumbling away across the car park — I think he's going to try to drive, but he staggers past his car towards the street.

"Come back here!" Carmel calls. "You come back here! Dougie!"

She's helping me to my feet. I tell her I'm okay, hand to my head, feeling soft tissue and blood and what must be bruises forming. Then she says, "I'm sorry, I've got to — here, will you?" and she thrusts Pepsi into my arms and starts after Lawsy. "Go up to my flat," she calls back at me. "Go up, I'll be back soon."

I can't think clearly. I can't think at all, blood is pulsing through my brain, my ears are aching, but I snick the lock on the front door so that Carmel can get back in, and I carry Pepsi up Carmel's stairs. The dog is whimpering. I can hear each of its breaths. There's a little blood at the corner of its mouth, but I can't worry about the dog, it's all I can do to get myself up those stairs and onto her sofa. I lie down, and the dog wriggles free and runs under a table and watches me, eyes wider than ever.

I close my eyes. Everything spins. I remember how hard I hit my head, Lawsy's fingers in my hair as he smashed my head down. I remember that people with head injuries shouldn't sleep, and I force myself to stand. Every muscle in my body burns. My breath hurts in my chest.

After a few minutes, I switch all the lights on and lie on the sofa again. The brightness hurts my eyes but I'm determined not to sleep. I look up at the ceiling, focus on it not spinning, on not feeling sick. The dog whimpers once and shuts up.

I don't know how long it is before Carmel comes back. I wake briefly when she puts a duvet over me; I know she speaks to me, hand brushing my forehead, and I reply. When morning comes, she's sitting on the floor beneath the window, arms wrapped around her knees. I have the feeling she's been watching me.

And everything seems very clear. It's like I've been asleep for my whole life, it's like everything before now has just been shadows. She asks how I am, and makes tea and toast, and all the time I'm marvelling at how much sharper everything seems. I sit up, look at the pale blue sky beyond the window. I don't want to be here any more. It's like, all this time I've been occupying the wrong space. My life doesn't fit this space.

"I've been thinking about going away," I tell Carmel. "I've been thinking about what you said, about following your heart, and you're right. I need to find my space. I'm going to do it, right now, today." I'm seized by sudden euphoria; I grab her hands, overwhelmed by the feeling. "Come with me," I say.

She pulls free, laughing, and says, "What are you talking about?"

"Getting out of here," I say. "Don't you want to see New York? Isn't that what you said?"

I can see the city — streets like canyons, the roar of traffic and crowds and sirens; summer heat and exhaust fumes, the music steaming from jazz bars, those old black guys blowing their saxes and trumpets and they're calling to us. "Imagine it," I say, and the feeling's so strong, I can see it so clearly, she must feel it too. "Come with me. It's like you said, you have to follow your heart, make your dreams come true."

"Go with you?" That silly smile. "But Nick, I can't do that. My life's here," she says, and there's something like pain in her eyes. "I

42

can't leave, not now — I have commitments, I have a show, it could be my break — can't you see?"

She sounds so sorry, so regretful. The timing — "It's all about timing," Lawsy told me once. Drunk, talking into his glass. "See your opportunity, and grab it when the timing's just right." He knows, he always has known, and ever since school I've been running behind him, wondering how he does it.

"Come on," I say to Carmel. "Follow your heart, that's what you said. Seize the moment, take a chance." And then I'm babbling, trying to get her to see, but my words are tumbling out, muddled by the excitement until I'm not sure what I'm saying. I tell her to grab opportunities; I tell her that life is about adrenaline, about taking risks, making sacrifices. I tell her we have to risk everything if we want our dreams to come true.

But her smile has died. She's looking at me like she hasn't ever seen me before. I want to take the words back, start again, show her that I mean all of this, but I can't do that, I can't. Desperation fills me — I'm losing her and I won't be able to get her back.

She goes into her bedroom and closes the door. I stand at the other end of the hallway. I think about Lawsy standing here, his plans for the flats, and the anger rises up again. He makes everything seem so easy.

When she comes out of the bedroom, she's dressed. "I have to take Pepsi to the vet," she says.

I follow her down the stairs. She has the dog in her arms; it looks back at me over her shoulder, a contemptuous, proprietorial look.

"Forget the dog," I say, and it blinks and rubs its nose against her shoulder. "Just forget it," I say, and the anger's there again, and it's all I can do not to grab her and force her to stop. And then I see. "You're going to look for him, aren't you?"

We've reached the parking area. She turns, as if she's going to say something, then changes her mind and says instead, "Close the door."

I slam it behind me, and she walks away.

I watch her until she's out of sight. All I can think is that she's going after him, and he wins again, and it's just like with Angela — people blaming me when things go wrong, and I can't control this, I can't control anything.

I turn to go to my flat, but her door's slightly open. It must have bounced when I slammed it — the snick on the lock must still be down from last night.

I push the door open, look at those stairs leading up. My mouth is dry.

Upstairs, I stand in her living room looking down the hall towards the bedroom. Stand where Lawsy stood, see what he saw.

I don't need to see the world — I have the world right here, with her. She's the whole world, she's everything that's in it. She's what I've been missing; she can help me find my way back. If I stay with her she will rescue me.

That's when I decide to move in with her.

With the tips of my fingers, I can reach the hatch into the loft space. The cover is only thin chipboard — I can slide it across easily, and it only takes a little jump to hook my hands into the space, and a couple of attempts to pull myself up.

Sheets of chipboard have been laid across the joists in the centre of the loft. Lawsy's right, there's plenty of space for another room. The air is warm and stale. It's dark, but with bright streaks of light between the roof tiles.

I go down to my flat and collect the things I'll need. My laptop, a torch, a sleeping bag. Water and clothing. A screwdriver, a kitchen knife. It's like building a nest, a cocoon.

I go back to her flat, climb into the loft, close the hatch behind me. I lie down on the chipboard. Light is shining up through a small hole in the plasterboard. I take the screwdriver and make the hole a little bigger, and with my eye to the hole I get a partial view of the living room; a corner of the sofa, a patch of carpet.

I check from below, and it's nothing but a dark spot, barely more than a pin-prick. She'll never know. So I crawl along the chipboard on my knees, estimate the distance to her bedroom, and then I make another small hole.

This is what I need to do. It's like Lawsy said, it's like Carmel said; you have to follow your heart, you have to take risks.

I don't know how long I'll stay here. A week, a month, a year — it doesn't really matter. People will forget about me — Angela, Lawsy, Carmel, they'll all forget I was ever here. I'll be in my nest and nobody will disturb me and I have everything I need.

That's how I came to be here now, with Carmel, lying on my belly in the hot roofspace. Looking down into Carmel's bedroom. Lawsy is there, standing talking. I can see his arm, the cufflinks and the Rolex but he's taken his jacket off. Carmel is there, sitting on the bed looking up at him. He's explaining something. I hear him tell her he's sorry; I hear her say he treated her badly.

"It's all this pressure," he says. "I can't stand this pressure."

She says again that she won't put up with it, and he tells her again that he's sorry.

My breath is warm and damp around the eyehole. I'm thinking about him telling me about adrenaline, and how you have to seize your chances when the timing's right. I'm thinking about her saying that you have to follow your heart, that she believes dreams can come true.

I'm thinking about things said in the heat of passion, and how she's going back to him, back on all of it.

I'm thinking about lying here in the heat for a long time, the sweat crawling down my back. I'm thinking about Angela and Julia and how they deserve better. And I'm thinking about the difference between having dreams and acting on them, about what it means to really do something. Act, act, that's what I'm thinking. Time to do something.

Stun to Stick

Stephen Booth

The last one of the day is dying badly. You wouldn't think she had the strength left by now, would you? But look at her, kicking and screaming as the skin splits and the blood flies. It could get really bad in here. Sometimes, they thrash around so much they come off the shackles and fall into the blood pit. *That* makes a mess, all right.

In a way, I admire the ones like this. The refusal to give in is something I can relate to. And some of them fight death to the end — all the way to the last twitch of a muscle, the slightest spasm of a nerve in a leg. As if they could run from the knife when their blood is already pooling on the floor.

As always, the worst thing is the mess, though. It's all over the tiles and halfway up the wall, backing up the drain until it overflows the gutter. Someone's going to have to clean that up later. Me, probably. And right at the end of a shift, too, when I'm ready to wash off the blood and go home.

Some folk would panic at this point, when they see the kicking and screaming. Anyone less experienced, that is. But not me, not Marty Cook. I know to stay calm and follow the training. I always go by the rules, you see. Everything by the book for Marty. All within the law and according to regulations.

So that's what I do — I stay calm and watch the blood for a bit. It runs across the floor and slides into the gutters, nice and slow. It swirls and picks up scraps of flesh. Then it's just a trickle, and the drain catches up and swallows the lot. Naturally, I keep out of the way until it's all over, and she's properly dead at last. No point in getting more of the stuff on my boots than there is already.

I spend this time thinking about Brenda. Because your mind has to be thinking about something, no matter what. You can't have a big gap where your thoughts ought to be. If I didn't have thoughts, I wouldn't be human, I'd be an animal. Most likely it'd be me hanging there with my throat cut.

47

So I have this little thought slipping into my mind, and when I picture the shock on Brenda's face it makes me smile for a second. Only a second, but it'll do for now. A little bit of pleasure to finish off the day.

But, oh shit, wouldn't you know it? Here's Big Barry coming down the aisle, wanting to know what the hell's going on at this end of the room. So I tell him there wasn't enough current in the stunner, but I can see straightaway he doesn't believe me. He just stares at me and says: "There must be something wrong with the failsafe then, Martin." And he uses that tone of voice he has — real sarcastic, like. Sneering, that's what you'd call it.

I never have been able to stand this way he has of saying my name. He makes it sound as if the fact I'm called Martin explains all my faults somehow, as though all the things I've ever done wrong in my entire life can be boiled down into two syllables. The way Barry says it, you'd think my name is enough to mark me out as thick as pig shit, useless at my job, crap with women, short, ugly, going bald, a loser who'll spend the rest of his days up to the knees in animal guts until he chucks in his apron and hangs up his knife belt, and spends the rest of his sad life in front of the telly in a council home, smelling of wee. Bastard. But somehow he gets it all into that tone he uses, like one long sneer. "There must be something wrong with the failsafe then, *Ma-artin.*"

Well actually, Barry, I just didn't use the tongs right, as you damn well know. Probably I put the electrodes in the wrong place, and they didn't span the brain properly. Sloppy work, eh? So sack me then, Barry. I couldn't care less. So sack me, *Bar-ry.*

But I don't say anything like that, obviously. The last thing I want is for Big Barry to sack me right now. That wouldn't fit in with what I've got planned for Brenda. In fact, that'd put paid to my plans in one fell stroke.

So instead I saw off the pig's head and clean up the mess. I've got to keep up the standards, got to stick by the rules. Lucky I know them so well. If Marty forgot the rules, where would we all be?

Extract from Quality Meat processing standards
Paragraph 3.3: Slaughter

Animals must be restrained immediately before slaughter and stunned by one of the following methods:

(a)   a mechanically operated instrument which penetrates the brain;

(b)   a mechanically operated instrument which administers a blow to the brain;

(c)   electro-narcosis with cardiac arrest.

**THE MAXIMUM STUN TO STICK INTERVAL
MUST NOT EXCEED 60 SECONDS**

I never did like being called Brenda. It doesn't even shorten to anything. It just goes to show how much imagination my mum had. But sometimes she's right.

"Brenda," she says to me. "Brenda, that's his trouble — he has too much time to think. It's okay for us women, but it doesn't do for men. You ought to keep him occupied more. What about a family, for a start? What about me seeing some grandchildren?"

Well, that's a laugh. As if I didn't do everything I could to get pregnant those first few years. But after a while, you have to give up. There's no point in fighting it any more.

The first time I met him was at the club. I was working behind the bar then, making myself a bit of money, saving up to buy a car. I had my eye on a Fiat with a sunroof and not too many miles on the clock. That had to go, along with everything else. I wonder what happened to it. Scrap, I expect.

Well, he came up to the bar and I pulled him a beer. He didn't move away, so I knew he was on his own. You can tell the usual types when you're behind a bar, believe me. But I talked to him for a bit, and we got on all right. I thought he had a nice smile. Of course, he didn't let on then where he worked. As it happened, he was done up in his best suit because it was a Saturday, and he'd been to his cousin's wedding. I thought he must always look like that. What an idiot I was.

49

I was too busy that first time to find out much about him. But he said he understood that. "The job comes first when you're at work," he said. "Pleasure has to be separated into a different part of your life." He talks like that sometimes. I don't know where he gets it from. But that's where it all started. That's when my life changed.

He was always such a good-looking bloke, you know. But look at him now. He thinks he's clever. He thinks he's funny, with his smart little remarks. Funny? I reckon I'm as tough as most, but sometimes his words can cut like a knife.

That's a joke, by the way — *one fell stroke*. Look it up, if you don't believe me. Fell is what they call an animal's hide with the hair still on it. I used to work at a fellmonger's near Derby, before they closed it down. They shut it because the neighbours complained about the smell. Can you believe that? What do they expect when they live near a fellmonger's? The scent of roses? Fresh pine with a hint of lemon bloody balm? Well, you can't hide the stink of death. The flies can smell it miles away.

I'm not smiling any more. After Barry's said his piece and sneered a bit longer, he wanders off again, his boots slapping in the water where the floor is being hosed off down the aisle. When he's gone, I finish up and check the clock. Time to knock off at last.

We don't have a high throughput here, not like some of the massive outfits. But we don't cut corners either. I'm quite proud of that, funny as it may seem. Take an example. Everybody knows a captive bolt pistol isn't the best thing for stunning pigs. A pig's brain is really deep down inside the head, and it's hard to reach it with the bolt. But some slaughtermen still use it — and that's sheer laziness, in my opinion. We don't do it here, you see. That's what the tongs are for. You put the electrodes either side of the head, then you flick the switch and down goes the pig. If you've done it properly, the animal lies good and still, with its legs all folded up, easy for shackling to the killing rail. A nice job done.

But only if you've done the stunning right. I have to admit, it's a bit too easy to get the tongs in the wrong position, around the cheeks or on the snout. Then the animal only gets half stunned, and it wakes up while it's shackled and bleeding. Sometimes they're still alive when they go into the scalding tank. I've seen it happen.

But that's inexperience again, or not enough training. Some blokes don't have the dedication to the job like I do. They never bother to learn the rules. But me, I like to do things right every time. And if I lose concentration now and then — well, I know I've done wrong and I don't need the likes of Big Barry to tell me. At the end of the day, I'm a professional like any other.

If the worst thing about working at the fellmonger's was the smell, the best thing was learning how to use a knife. I know how to make a clean cut with the fewest strokes of the blade, and without injuring myself in the process. Not everybody has the knack of that, but I picked it up fast. A very handy skill it is, too. You ask Brenda.

No, don't ask her now. Ask her later. She won't get the point just yet...

The trouble is, I've been dwelling too much on other things lately. It's put me right off my job. I mean, when I'm killing, I ought to concentrate on killing, and that's that. If I don't, I'm bound to make the odd mistake. I'm only human, like I said.

But Barry wouldn't understand, even if I tried to tell him. Just because I spend all day wading in blood and guts, watching creatures die, cutting through warm meat like so much wet putty, he thinks I shouldn't have any feelings. But as far as that goes, he's wrong. Hey, you're wrong, *Bar-ry*. Wrong, wrong, wrong. I just go by the rules, that's all.

At last I'm stripping off the apron and gloves, dumping the cap and the boots. On the way out, I pass the head bin. For a second, I look them over to see if I can make out the one I missed stunning properly. Piggy, piggy, are you there? But they all look the same — open mouths, glazed eyes, bloodied necks. Like a lot of weird fish laid out on a slab. But then, they don't know me, either. Old Marty Cook is just the grim reaper in a green apron to this lot. The rats will get some of them later, I bet.

They say pigs are as close to humans as you can get, in some ways. Their skin is a lot like ours, and gets sunburned. The meat tastes much the same, if you're a cannibal. Yes, you could cook a bit of human and pass it off as pork. Long pig, they call it. And a decomposing pig smells so like a dead person that they use it for training police dogs to find bodies.

51

The stuff you can learn is amazing. It's not part of the job exactly, but it helps. I think of myself as a student. Maybe a scholar, or a philosopher.

In the locker room, I change into clean clothes. The only thing that goes out with me tonight is the knife belt. Personal to a man, that is.

Even here, the rules are up on the wall. Before I go home, I like to read them again, though I know them all by heart. This is my Bible, you see. My Ten Commandments. Moses and Mount Sinai, I love all that stuff. *For I am a jealous God.*

Welfare of Animals (Slaughter or Killing) Regulations. Schedule 6

3. (1)   Subject to sub-paragraph (3), any person engaged in the bleeding of any animal that has been stunned shall ensure that

  (a)   the bleeding is rapid, profuse and complete;

  (b)   the bleeding is completed before the animal regains consciousness; and

  (c)   the bleeding is carried out by severing at least one of the carotid arteries, or the vessels from which they arise.

4. (1)   Where one person is responsible for the stunning, shackling, hoisting and bleeding of animals, such operations must be carried out by him consecutively in respect of one animal before being so carried out by him in respect of another animal.

**THE MAXIMUM STUN TO STICK INTERVAL
MUST NOT EXCEED 60 SECONDS.**

Of course, that's the other thing about him — he's what you'd call a creature of habit. And most of them are dirty habits, my Mum would say. "I don't know why you married him, Brenda. He's not fit to be in a decent person's home. I'd rather have one of those pigs of his in the house, and let him get hung up from a hook instead."

I never thought she was right, not at first. But now, it's different. I've got into such a state that I depend on his habits to make my life tolerable. He leaves the house at seven every morning, and it's like the sun coming out.

I wish I could move away from this town. I can't walk past that place, can't go within a mile of it, or even think about it. It seems as though I can smell it all the time, and hear the screams of dying animals. I feel as though the flies are in the house at night, buzzing in the corners, looking for something to feed on.

Sometimes it's like a black shadow hanging over me, a pressure inside my head, as if I'm about to get a really bad migraine. Yesterday, I walked home half-blind, ignoring someone who spoke to me in the street. They must have thought I was mad, or sick.

I know he's watching me. He's a jealous sod, suspicious all the time. Now and then, he gets these crazy fantasies. So I know it's him that's watching the house at night when he's supposed to be at the pub. I know it's him phoning but not speaking, just to make sure I'm at home. I know it's him that follows me from the club, whispering my name from the alley to scare me.

He thinks I should be afraid of him, but I'm not. I know he's all talk. A prick with a mouth, Mum called him. And not so much of the first, either. Otherwise, we'd have had children, and things might have been different. I just need to stand up to him, or get in first. Maybe that would be best.

Well, God, we've been together for a long time now. Too long by half. If I don't do something soon, it's going to kill me.

Sixty seconds, that stun to stick interval. A whole minute. And a minute can be a long time, believe me. Try counting up to sixty, and you'll see what I mean. It's more than long enough for whatever you need to do. Long enough for this business, anyway. Provided you're quick and accurate with the knife, of course. Quick, like I am.

And this is what you have to remember. An animal shouldn't regain consciousness during bleeding-out. That's the worst possible thing that can happen. It's a real crime in our business. So that's why they have this stun to stick interval. Sixty seconds, right? Longer than that, and they start coming round again while their throats are being opened up by the knife and the blood is draining out. Messy, messy.

53

There are inspectors here all the time, making sure the animals are healthy enough to be killed. Now, *that's* a joke, isn't it? They have to be healthy enough to die, fit for the knife like a rabbit is fit for the bullet. No, I can see you're not laughing. But, believe me, it's a joke.

God, there was such a fuss when we had Foot and Mouth a few years ago. All those townies getting in a lather about animals being killed in the fields. What a farce. The only reason they cared was because they could actually see the carcasses on the TV and in their newspapers every morning. Talk about out of sight, out of mind.

What do they think happens to those animals normally? Do they imagine there's some bloody great retirement home for cows somewhere, with herds of 'em playing bingo and watching *Countdown*?

The difference is, the folk who eat the meat don't usually see the killing. They ought to appreciate people like me, because Marty Cook keeps all the killing nicely out of sight for them. They don't see my handiwork until it turns up in a supermarket cabinet, wrapped and labelled. When they're popping a juicy rump steak into the trolley, they don't stop to wonder 'How come there are no bones or blood vessels attached to these dead cow's muscles that I'm planning to eat?' They don't ask themselves who took the skin off, whose hand sliced it away from the warm body, lifted the hide and the layer of fat underneath, separated the muscles from tendon and bone. Or who used the tongs to stun the beast before it died, and who sluiced the blood into the gutter.

It was me, Marty Cook. Me and my knife, that's who. My knife brings death, and it gives life. *In the midst of blood, we are surrounded by meat...*

Barry doesn't like me, because I think too much. That's what he says. And he's right on this one. You don't find many abattoir workers who think as much as I do.

We slaughter nine hundred million animals a year in this country, just for food. That's hard to imagine — even when you see a fair number of them queuing up to get the chop when you arrive at work every morning. So I reckoned it up. Nearly two-and-a-half million a day, a hundred thousand an hour, seventeen hundred a minute, twenty-eight every second. Okay, so one or two of them don't quite get done according to the book? Get a life, that's what I say.

Mind you, most of these nine hundred million are chickens, which don't really count. I never saw a chicken yet that had a brain. Then there's turkeys — twenty-eight million of them being fattened up right now. One turkey between every two of us, veggie or not. So don't blame the likes of me for what I do, just because you're all fat, greedy pigs who can't resist stuffing your faces at Christmas. I kill it, you eat it. We need each other.

When I go out of the door, some of the blokes are hanging around in the car park, having a fag and scraping their boots in the gravel. They smirk, but don't say much. One of the younger lads calls out my name, taking the piss as usual. He doesn't get the sound of it the way Barry does, but Barry's had plenty of practice.

These lads don't last long here. They're soon off to easier jobs, for a bit more money. Not an ounce of dedication in any of them, you see. Chicken killing, that's all they're good for. So I ignore them and get in the van to go home to Eastwood. A bit of something to eat, and then I'll be ready for whatever comes. Marty doesn't bother with chicken killers.

Personally, I've never done poultry, but I reckon you must hardly notice them going by. They'd just be a never-ending blur of feathers and claws. And this is where things go wrong mostly — in the poultry slaughterhouses, not the red meat houses like ours. If you were in one of those places, you'd see the turkeys coming in with their eyeballs pecked out and their beaks hacked off with a hot blade. That last bit is to stop them killing each other. They turn into cannibals in those fattening sheds, unless they're kept in the dark.

Darkness is a good thing, sometimes. Darkness means you don't have to see what's coming.

And I don't like the way they stun birds. What happens is, a bunch of them have their heads dipped in an electrical water bath. Those that don't get stunned are supposed to be decapitated by the back-up killer. Well, the poor sod who gets the killing job is coping with a line speed of about nine thousand birds an hour, and any that he misses just carry on to the neck-cutter with the rest.

It's not like my job, you see. I'm a bit particular, which is why I work here. Red meat, low throughput. It suits Marty fine.

Report by Compassion in World Farming Trust:

After stunning, there follows what is called sticking or knifing. The animal's throat is cut or, in the case of pigs and cattle, the blood vessels in the chest. Sticking may be performed while the animal is still prone. Alternatively, the animal may be shackled by a rear leg after stunning and hoisted up on to a rail, where it is then stuck.

That's why we don't have any children. Even before I started to realise I couldn't bear him to touch me. We've been sleeping in separate rooms for a while now, ever since I complained that he smelled of blood when he came to bed at night. I told him the stink was giving me nightmares, and I was always thinking about what he'd been doing with his hands all day. He just said you can put that kind of thing out of your mind. Separate work from home, that's all you need to do. Some chance.

And then he goes and sees some bloke he says has been hanging around near the house. So he puts two and two together and he gets ninety-five, as usual. Common sense was never his strongpoint, but these days I think the smell of blood has gone to his head.

"You're seeing someone else," he says. "You've got a fancy man." A fancy man? Where does he get this stuff? He sounds like my mum sometimes.

"You mean a lover," I say, just to wind him up, like. And he goes ballistic, right through the roof, raving like a lunatic. But he knows better than to a lay a finger on me, because I'd have him in court before he could blink.

"If you're going to thump me, you'd better make a good job of it," I tell him. "Because you'll never get another chance."

He used to be such a good-looking bloke, At least, I thought so. Tall, with big shoulders on him, a real man. I thought the other girls would envy me.

On the other hand, there's Barry Simmons. He doesn't give a damn, Big Barry. He likes to be the one to use the electric goad on a beast to get it into the stunning pen. I think he'd use it on me if he thought I was slacking.

It makes you think, being in this business. I get some funny ideas now and then. I imagine a big conveyor belt running non-stop, all day long. There's life at one end, and death at the other. Well, we're all on a conveyor belt like those chickens, I reckon. Ours might run a bit slower, maybe — but we're all going to reach the end of it, just the same. We're all going to meet the neck-cutter, aren't we? I wonder if one of those chickens knows when it's next in line to feel the blade.

The fact is, Barry thinks I'm stupid. He ought to know better, because he's got my CV in his filing cabinet with all that other stuff he keeps. Personnel files. Well, if he ever read my file, he'd know I've got GCSEs. That's more than any of the other blokes who work here. So I'm brighter than average, as you can probably tell.

I bet *she* thinks I'm stupid, too. Amazing, isn't it? Of course, she doesn't really know me, even after all this time. Stupid or not, it didn't take me long to work out what she was up to. For weeks now, she's had that look on her face like a cow that's just been served by the bull. Smug, self-satisfied, hugging a little secret inside.

She has no right to treat me the way she does, like some piece of shit to scrape off her shoes or ignore when she feels like it, with that look of disgust on her face. As if she didn't know what was going on, as though she could pretend there was nothing between us and I'm just a stranger she met in the street, some short, bald loser who'll never amount to anything but a bad smell and skin so cracked that I'll never get the blood out... Bitch.

And that look on her face. I can't forget that look.

So this is the deal. Tonight, I'm going out with some mates I bought a few drinks for at the Stag's Head. Two of them have terriers, and we're going rabbiting at the back of Hanging Wood. At least, that's what my mates will tell the coppers, if they ask. *"He was with us all night rabbiting, officer. No, we didn't catch any rabbits — just giving the dogs a bit of exercise, really."*

The lads are really off badger digging, which is a crime. So they're not likely to be telling the coppers the truth anyway, are they? In that case, they might as well lie about me being there. I thought that was pretty clever myself. Neat, somehow.

Actually, I don't agree with badger digging. Those badgers turn nasty when they're cornered, and a dog can get ripped up bad. I wouldn't risk my dog with a badger — if I still had one, that is.

My old Labrador got smashed up by a car. Some pillock joy riding, it was — fifteen years old, and more acne than sense. He came round the corner of our street like an arse on two wheels, making as much noise as he could, so someone would call the cops. Well, the old dog couldn't get out of the way quick enough, and she was badly messed up. Obviously, I had to put her out of her misery myself — a vet would have cost a fortune. But I did a proper job. The captive bolt goes right through the brain on something the size of a dog. In through the top of the skull and out through the throat. Instant stunning. And if you bleed an animal properly, it takes only seconds for the brain to stop. I'm an expert with a knife, like I say. Quick and accurate. The old bitch never knew a thing.

No one understands what a skill there is to this business. *She* turns up her nose the moment she sees me.

Still, it makes no difference now. There's one more old bitch that won't know a thing. First comes the stun, the nasty little surprise when Marty greets you with his electrodes at the end of the passage. And then comes the stick.

FOR SALE — Abattoir equipment

1. Freund Sticking Knife:
   For the collection of blood, and hygienic transfer of blood away from the bleed area. Suitable for all species.
2. SIG Dehiding Knife:
   Quick and easy sharpening, lightweight to use.
   Practically no hide laceration.

The thing is, slaughter's a two-stage process, and it has to be done properly. Everything in the right order and according to the rules. This isn't some no-brain labouring job that any plonker off the dole queue can do without any training. It's skilled work. I mean, you wouldn't want some sweaty-arsed navvy turning up in the operating theatre to take your appendix out with a chisel, would you? You'd want someone who knew what they were doing with a knife.

So there are entire laws written to tell people like me how we should do our jobs. The rules are up there on the wall in the locker room, covered in plastic so we don't get bloody fingermarks on them trying to spell the words (only joking — we wash our hands all the time, that's another rule).

You don't get that in your soft office jobs, do you? Nobody writes a law telling you how to shuffle bits of paper from one tray to another, or what sort of pen you should use, or how long you can leave between tea break and lunch. Because it doesn't matter, see. Your job isn't important; it isn't life and death.

But my job definitely matters. Without me and my knife, you'd all starve to death on beans and cabbage, farting your way to the end of life's conveyor belt like a lot of jet-propelled chickens. You'd never do the killing yourself. It takes a special sort of person to kill.

So when it's dark, I nip back into town and park my old van in a side street near the house. It's an old British Telecom Bedford that I got sprayed white by a bloke I know with a workshop just off the M1. He does any little jobs you want and no questions asked. Another pro, you see. Okay, maybe the van is a bit clapped out, like me, but it only cost me five hundred quid and it has these really neat shelves fitted in the back, so you can keep all your tools tidy and in the right place.

No one pays any attention to me as I walk up the alley behind the house and slip through the gate into the back garden. I'm not the sort of person anyone notices much. As long as I get the job done, they'd rather not notice me at all. This has its advantages.

I'm standing near the old brick privy that she uses for some kind of potting shed, with soil trailing across the path and bits of broken plant pot getting under my feet. The gate still creaks a bit, the same as when I was here last. And that wheelie bin stinks. Doesn't she ever look after her stuff properly? If you ask me, she deserves what's coming.

Here's the back door at last. Not locked, of course, but what do you expect? Give me five minutes, and then ask me who's the stupid one. Now it's time to see how well she dies. Time to do the job and clean up the mess.

I touch my belt, and there's the handle of the sticking knife. Smooth from use, worn to the shape of my hand. Bringing death, giving life. In the midst of blood...

Piggy, piggy? Are you there?

And I smile as I open the door. Smile, before the whole world falls in on my head.

My God, there's so much blood. He's lying on my kitchen floor, twitching and gasping, and his blood is spreading across the tiles like a tide. It's a red tide, coming in to cut me off and drown me. I've never seen so much blood in life.

And I don't know who he is. I mean, I really don't know him — I've never seen him before. He's some funny little skinny bloke with bad teeth and no hair, but he's wearing one of those knife belts like they have at the abattoir. One of Barry's mates? Does my husband know this man? Did he send this person to hurt me? You bastard, Barry.

I can tell that he's dying. I ought to do something, but I don't know what. The black shadow is closing in, the pressure on my head. I can smell the blood now. It's everywhere. My kitchen is full of it.

I didn't see him coming, but I saw the knife. Get in first, I thought. And all I did was pick what came to hand. I don't even know what I hit him with. But there's so much blood. What have I done? Barry? Help me, Barry...

A kitchen knife? I mean, a kitchen knife? A cheap plastic-handled thing from the pound shop in the High Street. That is just not the right tool for the job. It's got a serrated edge, for a start, which means it's for sawing, not sticking. Doesn't everybody know that? I've never seen one that was kept sharp. How can you expect to do a proper job with badly maintained tools?

So they did for me between them, Barry and Brenda. They must have had it all worked out, to trick me. I'm not stupid, but I'm too trusting. That was always my problem.

But Barry should have told her there's an art to killing. There's a technique. You have to be trained, and follow the rules. Has she ever read the Slaughter Regulations? I don't think so.

Which is how she wouldn't have known that if you don't stun an animal properly first, it stays conscious right through the sticking and bleeding. That's why you get all this screaming and kicking, and the mess. I can see it now. I can feel it, my life pooling on the floor. Stuck and bled. Rapid, profuse and complete, just like it says in the book.

But there's one thing the rules never mention. They don't tell you about the pain. They don't describe the agony of the hot blade sliding into your body, or the sick, bursting terror as your skin rips apart. No one explains the screaming hell as your tendons snap and your muscles slice through to the bone. Oh, God help me. Butchered like so much long pig. They could pass me off as pork...

Report of Home Office pathologist Professor J.M. Frazer

At the request of the Coroner, I conducted a postmortem examination on the body of a well-nourished Caucasian male aged thirty to thirty-five, five feet eight inches in height, weighing a hundred and forty pounds.

I concluded that death had been caused by severe internal trauma and loss of blood resulting from multiple stab wounds. The wounds were consistent with a single-sided blade six inches in length, with a serrated edge. One had penetrated the aorta, and a second the carotid artery. Upon opening the chest cavity, I found the body to be almost completely exsanguinated.

In my opinion, the injuries would have caused immediate loss of consciousness, with cessation of brain function and subsequent death within a short period, possibly as little as sixty seconds.

Despite the severity of the injuries, I am convinced the deceased would have suffered no pain.

William Marshal

Elizabeth Chadwick

Fortress of Drincourt, Normandy, Summer 1167
1

In the dark hour before dawn, all the shutters in the great hall were closed against the evil vapours of the night. Under the heavy iron curfew, the fire was a quenched dragon's eye. The forms of slumbering knights and retainers lined the walls and the air sighed with the sound of their breathing and resonated with the occasional glottal snore.

At the far end of the hall, occupying one of the less favoured places near the draughts and away from the residual gleam of the fire, a young man twitched in his sleep, his brow pleating as the vivid images of his dream took him from the restless darkness of a vast Norman castle to a smaller, intimate chamber in his family's Berkshire keep at Hamstead.

He was five years old, wearing his best blue tunic, and his mother was clutching him to her bosom as she exhorted him in a cracking voice to be a good boy. 'Remember that I love you, William.' She squeezed him so tightly that he could hardly breathe. When she released him they both gasped, he for air, she fighting tears. 'Kiss me and go with your father,' she said.

Setting his lips to her soft cheek, he inhaled her scent, sweet like new mown hay. Suddenly he didn't want to go and his chin began to wobble.

'Stop weeping, woman, you're unsettling him.'

William felt his father's hand come down on his shoulder, hard, firm, turning him away from the sun-flooded chamber and the gathered domestic household, which included his three older brothers, Walter, Gilbert and John, all watching him with solemn eyes. John's lip was quivering too.

'Are you ready son?'

He looked up. Lead from a burning church roof had destroyed his father's right eye and melted a raw trail from temple to jaw, leaving him with an angel's visage one side, and the gargoyle mask of a devil on the other. Never having known him without the scars, William accepted them without demur.

'Yes, sir,' he said and was rewarded by a kindling gleam of approval from John Marshal's one eye.

'Brave lad.'

In the courtyard the grooms were waiting with the horses. Setting his foot in the stirrup, John Marshal swung astride and leaned down to scoop William into the saddle before him. 'Remember that you are the son of the King's Marshal and the nephew of the Earl of Salisbury,' his father said as he nudged his stallion's flanks and he and his troop clattered out of the keep. William was intensely aware of his father's broad, battle-scarred hands on the reins and the bright embroidery decorating the wrists of the tunic.

'Will I be gone a long time?' he asked in a high treble.

'That depends on how long King Stephen wants to keep you.'

'Why does he want to keep me?'

'Because I made him a promise to do something and he wants you beside him until I have kept that promise.' His father's voice was as harsh as a sword blade across a whetstone. 'You are a hostage for my word of honour.'

'What sort of promise?'

William felt his father's chest spasm and heard a grunt that was almost laughter. 'The sort of promise that only a fool would ask of a madman.'

It was a strange answer and the child William twisted round to crane up at his father's ruined face even as the grown William turned within the binding of his blanket, his frown deepening and his eyes moving rapidly beneath his closed lids. Through the mists of the dreamscape, his father's voice faded, to be replaced by those of a man and a woman, arguing in a tent.

'The bastard's gone back on his word, bolstered the keep, stuffed it to the rafters with men and supplies, shored up the breaches.' The man's voice was raw with contempt. 'He never intended to surrender.'

'What of his son?' The woman asked in an appalled whisper.

64

'The boy's life is forfeit. The father says that he cares not — he still has the anvils and hammers to make more and better sons than the one he loses...'

'He does not mean it...'

The man spat. 'He's John Marshal and he's a mad dog. 'Who knows what he would do. The king wants the boy.'

'But you're not going to... you can't!' The woman's voice rose in horror.

'No, I'm not. That's on the conscience of the King and the boy's accursed father. The stew's burning, woman; attend to your duties.'

William was seized by the arm and dragged roughly across the vast sprawl of a battle camp. He could smell the blue smoke of the fires, see the soldiers sharpening their weapons and a team of mercenaries assembling what he now knew was a stone throwing machine.

'Where are we going?' he asked.

'To the King.' The man's face was one of hard, square bones thrusting against leather-brown skin. His name was Henk and he was a Flemish mercenary in the pay of King Stephen.

'Why?'

Without answering, Henk turned sharply to the right. Between the siege machine and an elaborate tent striped in blue and gold, a group of men were talking amongst themselves. A pair of guards stepped forward, spears at the ready, then relaxed and waved Henk and William through. Henk took two strides and knelt, pulling William down beside him. 'Sire.'

William darted an upward glance through his fringe, uncertain which of the men Henk was addressing, for none of them wore a crown or resembled his notion of what a king should look like. One lord was holding a fine spear though, with a silk banner rippling from the haft.

'So this is the boy whose only value to his father has been the buying of time,' said the man standing beside the spear-bearer. He had greying fair hair and lined care-worn features. 'Rise, child. What's your name?'

'William sir.' His dream self stood up. 'Are you the King?'

The man blinked and looked taken aback. Then his faded blue eyes narrowed and his lips compressed. 'Indeed I am, although your father seems not to think so.' One of his companions leaned to mutter in his ear. The King listened and vigorously shook his head. 'No,' he said.

A breeze lifted the silk banner on the lance and it fluttered outwards, making the embroidered red lion at its centre appear to stretch and prowl. The sight diverted William. 'Can I hold it?' he asked eagerly.

The lord frowned at him. 'You're a trifle young to be a standard bearer, hmm?' he said, but there was a reluctant twinkle in his eye and after a moment he handed the spear to William. 'Careful now.'

The haft was warm from the lord's hand as William closed his own small fist around it. Wafting the banner, he watched the lion snarl in the wind and laughed with delight.

The King had drawn away from his advisor and was making denying motions with the palm of his hand.

'Sire, if you relent, you will court naught but John Marshal's contempt...' the courtier insisted.

'Christ on the Cross, I will court the torture of my soul if I hang an innocent for the crimes of his sire. Look at him... look!' The King jabbed a forefinger in William's direction. 'Not for all the gold in Christendom will I see a little lad like that dance on a gibbet. His hellspawn father, yes, but not him.'

Oblivious to the danger in which he stood, aware only of being the centre of attention, William twirled the spear.

'Come child.' The King beckoned to him. 'You will stay in my tent until I decide what is to be done with you.'

William was only a little disappointed when he had to return the spear to its owner, who turned out to be the Earl of Arundel. After all, there was a magnificent striped tent to explore and the prospect of yet more weapons to look at and perhaps even touch if he was allowed — royal ones at that. With such a prospect in mind, he skipped along happily at King Stephen's side.

Two knights in full mail guarded the tent and various squires and attendants waited on the King's will. The flaps were hooked back to reveal a floor strewn with freshly scythed meadow and the heady scent of cut grass was intensified by the enclosing canvas. Beside a large bed with embroidered bolsters and covers of silk and fur stood an ornate coffer like the one in his parents' chamber at Hamstead. There was also room for a bench and a table holding a silver flagon and cups. The King's hauberk gleamed on a stand of crossed ash poles, with the helmet secured at the top and his shield and scabbard propped against the foot. William eyed the equipment with longing.

The King smiled at him. 'Do you want to be a knight, William?'

William nodded vigorously, eyes glowing.

'And loyal to your king?'

Again William nodded but this time because instinct told him it was the required response.

'I wonder.' Sighing heavily, the King directed a squire to pour the blood-red wine from flagon to cup. 'Boy,' he said. 'Boy, look at me.'

William raised his head. The intensity of the King's stare frightened him a little.

'I want you to remember this day,' King Stephen said slowly and deliberately. 'I want you to know that whatever your father has done to me, I am giving you the chance to grow up and redress the balance. Know this; a king values loyalty above all else.' He sipped from the cup and then pressed it into William's small hands. 'Drink and promise you will remember.'

William obliged, although the taste stung the back of his throat.

'Promise me,' the King repeated as he repossessed the cup.

'I promise,' William said, and as the wine flamed in his belly, the dream left him and he woke with a gasp to the crowing of roosters and the first stirring of movement amongst the occupants of Drincourt's great hall. For a moment he lay blinking, acclimatising himself to his present surroundings. It was a long time since his dreams had peeled back the years and returned him to the summer he had spent as King Stephen's hostage during the battle for Newbury. He seldom recalled that part of his life with his waking memory, but occasionally, without rhyme or reason, his dreams would return him to that time and the young man just turning twenty would again become a fair-haired little boy of five years old.

His father, despite all his manoeuvring, machinations and willingness to sacrifice his fourth born son, had lost Newbury, and eventually his lordship of Marlborough, but if he had lost the battle, his fortunes had rallied on the turn of the tide. Stephen's bloodline lay in the grave and Empress Matilda's son, Henry, the second of that name had been sitting firmly on the throne for thirteen years.

'And I am a knight,' William murmured, his lips curving with grim humour. The leap in status was recent. A few weeks ago, he had still been a squire, polishing armour, running errands, learning his trade at the hands of Sir Guillaume de Tancarville, chamberlain of Normandy and distant kin to his mother. William's knighting had announced his arrival into manhood and advanced him a single rung upon a very slippery ladder. His position in the Tancarville household was precarious. There were only so many places in Lord Guillaume's retinue for newly belted knights with ambitions far greater than their experience or proven capability.

William had considered seeking house room under his brother's rule at Hamstead, but that was a last resort, nor did he have sufficient funds to pay his passage home across the Narrow Sea. Besides, with the strife between Normandy and France at white heat, there were numerous opportunities to gain the necessary experience.. Even now, somewhere along the border, the French army was preparing to slip into Normandy and wreak havoc. Since Drincourt protected the northern approaches to the city of Rouen, there was a current need for armed defenders.

As the dream images faded, William slipped back into a light doze and the tension left his body. The blond hair of his infancy had steadily darkened through boyhood and was now a deep hazel-brown, but fine summer weather still streaked it with gold. Folk who had known his father said that William was the image of John Marshal in the days before the molten lead from the burning roof of Wherwell Abbey had ruined his comeliness, that they had the same eyes, the irises — deep grey, with the changeable muted tones of a winter river.

'God's bones, I warrant you could sleep through the trumpets of Doomsday, William. Get up you lazy wastrel!' The voice was accompanied by a sharp dig in William's ribs. With a grunt of pain, the young man opened his eyes on Gadefer de Lorys, one of Tancarville's senior knights.

'I'm awake.' Rubbing his side, William sat up. 'Isn't a man allowed to gather his thoughts before he rises?'

'Hah, you'd be gathering them until sunset if you were allowed. I've never known such a slugabed. If you weren't my lord's kin, you'd have been slung out on your arse long since!'

The best way to deal with Gadefer who was always grouchy in the

68

mornings, was to agree with him and get out of his way. William was well aware of the resentment simmering among some of the other knights who viewed him as a threat to their own positions in the mesnie. His kinship to the chamberlain was as much a handicap as it was an advantage. 'You're right,' he replied with a self-deprecating smile. 'I'll throw myself out forthwith and go and exercise my stallion.'

Gadefer stumped off, muttering under his breath. Concealing a grimace, William rolled up his pallet, folded his blanket and wandered outside. The air held the dusty scent of midsummer, although the cool green nip of the dawn clung in the shadows of the walls, evaporating as the stones drank the rising sunlight. He glanced towards the stables, hesitated, then changed his mind and followed his rumbling stomach to the kitchens.

The Drincourt cooks were accustomed to William's visits and he was soon leaning against a trestle devouring wheaten bread still hot from the oven and glistening with melted butter and sweet clover honey. The cook's wife shook her head. 'I don't know where you put it all. By rights you should have a belly on you like a woman about to give birth.'

William grinned and slapped his iron-flat stomach. 'I work hard.'

She raised a brow that said more than words, and returned to chopping vegetables. Still grinning William licked the last drips of buttery honey off the side of his hand and going to the door, braced his arm on the lintel and looked out on the fine morning with pleasure. The peace of the moment was broken by the sound of shouts from the courtyard. Moments later the mail-clad Earl of Essex and several knights and serjeants raced past the open door towards the stables. William hastened out into the ward. 'Hola!' he cried. 'What's happening?'

'The French and Flemings have been sighted in the outskirts!' a knight panted over his shoulder.

The words hit William like a bolt of lightning. 'They've crossed the border?'

'Aye, over the Bresle and down through Eu. Now they're at our walls with Matthew of Boulogne at their head. We'll have the devil of a task to hold them. Get your armour on, Marshal. You've no time for stomach-filling now!'

69

William sprinted for the hall. By the time he arrived his heart was thundering like a drum and he was wishing he hadn't eaten all that bread and honey for he felt sick. A squire was waiting to help him into his padded undertunic and mail. Already dressed in his, the Sire de Tancarville was pacing the hall like a man with a burr in his breeches, issuing terse commands to the knights who were scrambling into their armour.

William pressed his lips together. The urge to retch peaked and then receded. As he donned his mail, his heartbeat steadied, although his palms were slick with cold sweat and he had to wipe them on his surcoat. Now was the moment for which he had trained. Now was his chance to prove that he was good for more than just gluttony and slumber, and that his place in the household was by right of ability and not family favour.

By the time the Sire de Tancarville and his retinue joined the Earl of Essex at the town's West Bridge, the outskirts of Drincourt were swarming with Flemish mercenaries and the terrified inhabitants were fleeing for their lives. The smell of cooking fires had been overlaid by the harsher stench of indiscriminate burning and in the Rue Chausée a host of Boulonnais knights were massing to make an assault on the West Gate and break into the town itself.

Eager, nervous, resolute, William urged his stallion to the fore, jostling past several seasoned knights until he was level with de Tancarville himself. The latter cast him a warning glance and curbed his destrier as it lashed out at William's sweating chestnut. 'Lad, you are too hasty,' he growled with amused irritation. 'Fall back and let the knights do their work.'

Flushed with chagrin, William swallowed the retort that he *was* a knight and reined back. Glowering, he allowed three of the most experienced warriors to overtake him but as a fourth tried to jostle past, William spurred forward again, determined to show his mettle.

Roaring his own name as a battle cry, de Tancarville launched a charge over the bridge and down the Rue Chausée to meet the oncoming Boulonnais knights. William gripped his shield close to his body, levelled his lance and gave the chestnut its head. He fixed his gaze on the crimson device of a knight on a black stallion and held his line as his destrier bore him towards the moment of impact. He noticed how his opponent carried his lance too high and that the red shield was tilted a fraction inwards. Steadying his arm, he kept his eyes open until the last moment. His lance punched into the knight's shield, pierced it and even though the shaft snapped off in William's hand, the blow was sufficient to send the other man reeling. Using the stump as a club, William knocked the knight from the saddle. As the black destrier bolted, reins trailing, William drew his sword.

After the first violent impact, the fighting broke up into individual combats. Nothing in his training had prepared William for the sheer clamour and ferocity of battle but he was undaunted and fed upon the experience avidly and with increasing confidence as he emerged victorious from several sharp tussles with more experienced men. He was both terrified and exhilarated; like a fish released from a calm stewpond into a fast-flowing river.

The Count of Boulogne ordered more troops into the fray and the battle for the bridge became a desperate crush of men and horses. Armed with clubs, staves and slingshots, the townspeople fought beside the castle garrison and the battle swayed back and forth like washing in the wind. It was close and dirty work and William's sword hand grew slippery with sweat and blood.

'Tancarville!' William roared hoarsely as he pivoted to strike at a French knight. His adversary's destrier shied, throwing his rider in the dust where he lay unmoving. William seized the knight's lance and urged the chestnut towards a knot of Flemish mercenaries who were busy looting a house. One man had dragged a coffer into the street and was clubbing at the lock with his sword hilt. At a warning shout from his companions, he spun round, but only to receive William's lance through his chest. Immediately the others closed around William, furiously intent on dragging him from his mount.

William turned and manoeuvred his stallion, beating them off with sword and shield, until one of them seized a gaff resting against the house wall and attempted to hook William from his horse. The gaff lodged in his hauberk at the shoulder, the lower claw tearing into the mail, breaking several riveted links and sinking through gambeson and tunic to spike William's flesh. He felt no pain for his blood was coursing with the heat of battle. As they surrounded him, trying to grab his reins and drag him down off the horse, he pricked the chestnut's loin with his spurs and the stallion lashed out. There was a scream as a shod hind hoof connected with flesh and the man

71

dropped like a stone. William gripped the stallion's breast strap and again used the spur, forward of the girth this time. His mount reared, came down, and shot forward so that the soldiers gripping the reins had to let go and leap aside before they were trampled. The mercenary wielding the hook lost his purchase and William was able to wrench free and turn on him. Almost sobbing his lord's battle cry, he cut downwards with his sword, saw the man fall, and forced the chestnut forwards over his body. Free of the broil of mercenaries, he rejoined the bulk of the Tancarville knights, but his horse had a deep neck wound.

The enemy had forced the Drincourt garrison back to the edge of the bridge. Smoke and fire had turned the suburbs into an antechamber of hell, but the town remained unbreached and the French army was still breaking on the Norman defence like surf upon granite. Bright spots of effort and exhaustion danced before William's eyes as he cut and hacked, no longer any finesse to his blows. It was about surviving the next moment and the next... in holding firm and not giving ground. Every time William thought that he could not go on, he defied himself and found the will to raise and lower his arm one more time.

Horns blared out over the seething press of men and suddenly the tension eased. The French knight who had been pressing William hard, disengaged and pulled back. 'They're sounding the retreat!' panted a Tancarville knight 'God's blood, they're retreating! Tancarville! Tancarville!' He spurred his destrier. The realisation that the enemy was drawing off, revitalised William's flagging limbs. His wounded horse was tottering under him but undaunted, he flung from the saddle and joined the pursuit on foot.

The French fled through the burning suburbs of Drincourt, harried by the burghers and inhabitants, fighting rear guard battles with the knights and soldiers of the garrison. William finally ran out of breath and collapsed against a sheepfold on the outskirts of the town. His throat was on fire with thirst and the blade of his sword was nicked and pitted from the numerous contacts with shields and mail and flesh. Removing his helm, he dunked his head in the stone water trough provided for the sheep and making a scoop of his hands, drank greedily. Once he had slaked his thirst and recovered his breath, he wiped the bloody patina from his sword on a clump of loose wool caught in the wattle fence, sheathed the blade, and trudged back to the bridge, suddenly so weary that his shoes felt as if they were made of lead.

His chestnut was lying on its side in that ungainly way that told him even before he knelt at its head and saw its dull eyes that it was dead. He laid his hand to its warm neck and felt strands of the coarse mane scratch his bloodied knuckles. It had been a gift at his knighting from the Sire de Tancarville, together with his sword, hauberk and cloak, and although he had not had the horse long, it had been a good one — strong, spirited, and biddable. He had expended more pride and affection on it than was wise and suddenly there was a tightening of grief in his throat.

'Won't be the last you'll lose,' said de Lorys gruffly, leaning down from the saddle of his own dappled stallion which had several superficial injuries but was still standing, still whole. 'Fact of war, lad.' He extended a hand that, like William's, was bloody with the day's work. 'Here, mount up behind.'

William did so, although it was an effort to set his foot over Gadefer's in the stirrup and swing himself across the crupper. The cuts and bruises that had gone ignored in the heat of battle now began to strike him like chords on a malevolently plucked harp, especially across his right shoulder.

'Wounded?' Gadefer asked as William caught his breath. 'That's a nasty gash in your mail.'

'It's from a thatch gaff,' William replied. 'It's not that bad.'

De Lorys grunted. 'I won't take back the things I've said about you. You're still a slugabed and a glutton... but the way you fought today — well that makes up for everything else. Perhaps my lord Tancarville has not wasted his time in training you after all.'

That night the Sire de Tancarville held a feast to celebrate a victory that his knights had not so much snatched out of the jaws of defeat, as reached down the throat of annihilation, dragged back out and resuscitated. Badly mauled, the French army had drawn off to lick its wounds and, for the moment at least, Drincourt was safe, even if the neighbouring county of Eu was a stripped and pillaged wasteland.

William sat in a place of honour at the high table with the senior knights who fêted him for his prowess in his first engagement.

Although exhausted, he rallied beneath their camaraderie and praise. The squabs in wine sauce, the fragrant, steaming frumenty and apples seethed in almond milk went some way to reviving his strength, as did the sweet, potent ice-wine with which they plied him. His wounds were mostly superficial. De Tancarville's chirugeon had washed and stitched the deeper one to his shoulder and dressed it with a soft linen bandage. It was sharply sore; he was going to have the memento of a scar, but there was no lasting damage. His hauberk was already in the armoury having the links repaired and his gambeson had gone to the keep women to be patched and refurbished. Men kept telling him how fortunate he was. He supposed that it must be so, for some of the company had left their lives upon the battlefield and he had only lost his horse and the virginity of his inexperience. It didn't feel like luck though when someone inadvertently slapped him heartily on his injured shoulder in commendation.

William de Mandeville, the young Earl of Essex, raised his cup high in toast, his dark eyes sparkling. 'Hola, Marshal, give to me a gift for the sake of our friendship!' he cried so that all those on the high table could hear.

William's head was buzzing with weariness and elation but he knew he wasn't drunk and he had no idea why de Mandeville was grinning so broadly around the trestle. Knowing what was expected of him, however, he played along. The bestowing of gifts among peers was always a part of such feasts.

'Willingly my lord,' he answered with a smile. 'What would you have me give to you?'

'Oh, let me see.' De Mandeville made a show of rubbing his jaw and looking round at the other lords, drawing them deeper into his sport. 'A crupper would do, or a decorated breastband. Or a fine bridle perchance?'

Wide-eyed, William spread his hands. 'I do not have any such items,' he said. 'Everything that I own — even the clothes on my back are mine by the great charity of my lord Tancarville.' He inclined his head to the latter who acknowledged the gesture with a sweep of his goblet and a suppressed belch.

'But I saw you gain them today, before my very eyes,' de Mandeville japed. 'More than a dozen you must have had, yet you refuse me even one.'

William continued to stare in bewilderment while a collective chuckle rumbled along the dais and grew in volume at William's expression.

'What I am saying,' de Mandeville explained, between guffaws, 'is that if you had bothered to claim ransoms from the knights you disabled and downed — even a few of them — you would be a rich man tonight instead of an impoverished one. Now do you understand?'

A fresh wave of belly laughter surged at William's expense, washing him in chagrin, but he was accustomed to being the butt of jests and knew that the worst thing he could do was sulk in a corner or lash out. The ribbing was well meant and behind it, there was warning and good advice. 'You are right, my lord,' he agreed with de Mandeville. The shrug he gave made him wince and brought a softer burst of laughter. 'I didn't think. Next time I will be more heedful. I promise you will receive your harness yet.'

'Hah!' retorted the Earl of Essex. You've to get yourself a new horse first, and they don't come cheaply.'

On retiring to his pallet that night, William lay awake for some time despite his weariness. His mind as well as his body felt bludgeoned. The images of the day returned to him in vivid flashes, some, like his desperate fight with the Flemish foot soldiers repeating over and over again, others no more than a swift dazzle like sharp sun on water, there and gone. And through it all, running like a thread, needle-woven into a tapestry was de Mandeville's jest that wasn't a jest at all, but hard truth. Fight for your lord, fight for his honour, but never forget that you were fighting for yourself too.

2

The cloak that William had received at his knighting was of Flemish weave, felted and thrice-dyed in woad to deepen the blue, and edged with sable. The garment was designed to cover the wearer from throat to ankle in a splendid semi-circular sweep of fabric. Brushing his palm over the expertly napped cloth, William's heart was heavy with reluctance, regret and shame.

'I will give you fifteen shillings for it,' the clothes trader said, rubbing his forefinger under his nose and assessing William with crafty eyes.

'It's worth twice that!' William protested.

'Keep it then, messire,' the trader shrugged. 'I've a wife and five children to feed. I cannot afford to give charity.'

William rubbed the back of his neck. He had no choice but to sell his cloak because he needed the money to buy another horse. The Sire de Tancarville had shown no inclination to replace the chestnut. A lord's largesse towards his retainers only went so far and it was up to the individual knight to account for the rest. William was not at fault for losing a valuable warhorse in battle; his blame lay in his omission to recoup that loss from the men he had defeated. His problem was compounded by the fact that the kings of England and France had made peace and Lord Guillaume no longer needed so many knights in his retinue — especially inexperienced ones lacking funds and equipment.

'Being as it's never been worn, and it's a fine garment, I'll give you eighteen,' the merchant relented.

William's gaze was steel. 'No less than twenty-five.'

'Then find another buyer. Twenty-two, and that's my final offer. I'm robbing myself blind at that.' The trader folded his arms, and William realised that this was the sticking point. For a moment he nearly walked away, but his need was too great and although the taste was bitter, he swallowed his pride and agreed to the terms.

Leaving the stall he hefted the pouch of silver. Twenty-two Angevin shillings was nowhere near enough to buy a warhorse. It might just pay for his passage home across the Narrow Sea with his light palfrey and pack beast, but arriving at his family's door in such a penurious state would be tantamount to holding out a begging bowl. It would have been difficult enough were his father still alive, but now that William's older brother John had inherited the Marshal lands, he would rather starve than receive his grudging charity.

Forced to a grim decision, he used the coin to buy a solid riding horse from a serjeant's widow whose husband had been killed in the fight for Drincourt. It was a decent beast, well schooled and although a trifle long in the tooth, had plenty of riding left in it — but it wasn't a destrier.

Having stabled the beast, he visited the kitchens and availed himself of bread, cheese and a pitcher of cider, hoping that the latter would wash away the sour taste of what he had just been forced to do. The cloak was the thin end of the wedge. Next it would be his silk surcoat and his gilded sword belt. He could see himself trading down and down until he stood in the leather gear of a common footsoldier or became his brother's hearth knight, undertaking petty duties, living out his days in ennui, and growing paunchy and dull-witted.

The cook tossed a handful of chopped herbs into a simmering cauldron, stirred vigorously, and glanced round at William. 'I thought you'd be in the hall,' he remarked.

'Why?' William took a gulp of the strong, apple-scented cider.

'Ah, you haven't heard about the tourney then.' The cook's eyes gleamed with the relish of the informed in the presence of the ignorant.

William's expression sharpened 'What tourney?'

'The one that's being held in two week's time on the field between Sainte Jamme and Valennes. The herald rode in an hour since with the news. Lord Guillaume's been invited to take part.' He pointed his dripping spoon at William. 'It'll be a fine opportunity to build on your prowess.'

A spark of anticipation blazed up and died in William's breast. 'I don't have a destrier,' he said morosely. 'I can't ride into a tourney on a common hack.'

'Ah.' The cook scratched his head. 'That's a pity, but surely my lord Tancarville will give you a warhorse for the occasion at least. He's taking as many knights as he can muster. Why don't you ask him?'

The spark rekindled, making William feel queasy. If he did ask and was refused, he would have no option but to return to England, his tail between his legs. To ask at all was humiliating, but he had little alternative. Besides, his pride had already taken a fall; it couldn't sink much lower. Gulping down the cider, leaving the food, he hurried to the hall.

The news of the tournament had created a festive atmosphere. William stood on its periphery, his emotions finely balanced between hope and despair. Going to his sleeping space, he sat on his pallet and began checking over his equipment — his mended mail shirt, his neatly patched gambeson, his shield and spear and sword. The squires ran hither and yon as if their legs were on fire as they sped on errands for the knights.

Men came up to him, slapped his shoulders and spoke excitedly of the tourney. William laughed, nodded, and worked at concealing his anxiety. Buffing his helmet with a soft cloth, he wondered if he should have spent the coin from the sale of his cloak on a passage home instead of a horse. His mother would be overjoyed to see him, and perhaps his sisters, but he harboured doubts about his brother John. The latter had been furious that William and not he had been chosen to go for training to Normandy. Instead John had remained at Hamstead, his likely fate that of service to their two older brothers Walter and Gilbert from their father's first marriage. As it happened, Walter and Gilbert had both died, leaving John to inherit the Marshal lands, but that did not mean John would forget old jealousies and resentments.

Their younger brother Henry would not be at Hamstead as he was training for the priesthood and like William was expected to have fledged the nest for good. Ancel, the youngest, a wiry, freckled nine-year-old when William had last seen him would be of squiring age now, although his training would probably be at John's hands, God help him.

William polished his helm until it glittered like a woman's hand mirror. He didn't want to return to his kin in an impoverished state, but he very much desired to see them; even John. And he wanted to pay his respects to his father whose funeral mass he had been too far away to attend.

'You look troubled, William.'

He raised his head and found Guillaume de Tancarville standing over him, hands at his hips and amusement crinkling his eye corners. He was sensitive about his receding hairline and concealed it with a brightly coloured cap pulled low at the brow and banded with small gemstones.

William scrambled to his feet. 'No, my lord, just deep in thought.'

'And what does a lad of your age have to think deeply about, hmm?'

William glanced down at his reflection, distorted in the polished steel of his helm. 'I was wondering if I should return to my family in England,' he said.

'A man should always keep his family in his thoughts and prayers,' de Tancarville replied, 'but I expected your mind to be on the tournament. Everyone else's is.' He smiled and gestured around the bustling hall.

'Yes, my lord, but they have the equipment to take part, and I do not.' He forced himself to hold the Chamberlain's gaze.

'Ah.' De Tancarville stroked his chin.

William said nothing. He wasn't going to tell his lord that he had been forced to sell his knighting cloak in order to buy a common rouncy.

De Tancarville allowed the moment to stretch beyond comfort and then released the tension with a sardonic smile. 'You displayed great courage and prowess at the fight for Drincourt, even if you were a rash young fool into the bargain. You'll be a fine asset to my tourney team. I've arranged for a horse coper to bring some destriers to the tourney field on the morrow. You weren't the only knight to lose his mount in the battle. Since you've been taught a lesson, I'll replace your stallion this time. The rest is up to you. If you capture other knights and take ransoms, you'll be able to redeem your finances. If you fail...' de Tancarville shrugged and let the end of the sentence hang. He didn't need to put it into words.

'Thank you my lord!' William's eyes were suddenly as bright as his helm. 'I'll prove myself worthy, I swear I will!'

De Tancarville grinned. 'You're a good boy, William,' he said, slapping him on the shoulder. 'Let us hope that one day you'll make an even finer man.'

William managed not to wince despite the lingering tenderness from his wound. It was a small price to pay; everything was suddenly a small price to pay. He would show de Tancarville that he was a man, not a boy, and capable of standing on his own two feet.

William eyed the stallion that two grooms were holding at the de Tancarville horselines. Its hide was the colour of new milk, its mane and tail a silver cascade. Spanish blood showed in the profile of its head, the neat ears, the strong curved neck, deep chest and powerful rump. It should have been the first to be chosen, not the only one left. William had been busy erecting his pavilion and whether out of spite, oversight or heavy-handed jesting, no one had told him that the horse coper had arrived and that the new destriers were being apportioned to their owners.

'We left you a fine horse, Marshal!' shouted Adam Yqueboeuf, a belligerent, stoutly-set young knight who disliked William and baited him at every opportunity. 'Only the best for our lord's favourite relative!'

Pretending indifference to Yqueboeuf's taunt, William approached the stallion and saw from the sweat caking the line of the saddle cloth and breast band that the others had probably had their turn at it. Like a new whore in a brothel he thought. Used and overused on the first night until of no use at all to the last man in line. In dismay he took in the laid back ears, the tension in the loins; the way the grooms were holding tight to the restraining ropes.

'He's wild, sir,' one of them warned as William approached side on to the horse's head so that it could see him. Its hide shivered and twitched like the surface of a pool in the rain. He reached out to pat the damp, gleaming neck and for a while quietly soothed the stallion, letting it drink his scent and grow accustomed to his presence.

'Wild?' he questioned the groom in a soft voice. 'In what way?'

'He's a puller, sir — bad mouth. No one's been able to manage him.'

'Ah.' William glanced over his shoulder at his jeering audience and continued to stroke the destrier's quivering neck and shoulder. After a time, he set his hand to the saddle bow, placed his foot to the stirrup and swung astride. Immediately the stallion lashed out and sidled crabwise.

'Whoa, softly now, softly,' William crooned and gingerly set his hands to the reins, exerting no pressure. Its ears flickered, and it continued to prink and dance. William applied firm pressure with his heels and the destrier sprang across the ward towards the watching knights. When William drew on the rein to pull him round the stallion fought the bit, plunging, sawing his head and swishing his tail. The audience scattered amid a welter of curses. William had no time to laugh at them for he was too busy trying to stay astride a dervish. Dropping the reins he grabbed the mane instead, gripped with his thighs, and clung like a limpet. As soon as the pressure on its mouth relaxed, the horse quietened and after a moment, William was able to leap down from its back.

'Let's see you win a tourney prize with that!' sneered Yqueboeuf from the corner into which he had leaped. Stone dust and cobwebs streaked the shoulder of his tunic.

William's open smile was belied by the narrowness of his eyes and his swift breathing. 'How much would you wager?'

'You're a pauper, Marshal,' Yquebeouf scoffed, dusting himself down. 'What have you got that I could possibly want?'

'My sword,' William replied. 'I will wager my sword. What will you put up?'

Yqueboeuf laughed nastily. 'If a sword is what you want to lose, then I'll put my own up against it — even though it's worth more.'

William raised his brow but managed not to comment that half a sword's value lay in the fist that wielded it. 'Agreed,' he said curtly and turning back to the horse set about removing the bridle and examining the bit.

The morning of the tourney dawned fine and bright and the Chamberlain's company was up early.

'Where's Marshal?' de Tancarville demanded, for the young knight's tent was empty and his bed roll neatly folded up. The chamberlain had half-expected to find William still sleeping as was his wont.

'Probably breaking his fast at one of the bakers' booths,' said Gadefer de Lorys with a knowing roll of his eyes.

'No my lord,' said a squire. 'He's been working half the night on a new bridle for his horse, and he's gone to try it out.'

De Tancarville quirked a brow at the information. 'Which horse did he take yesterday?' he asked de Lorys.

'The Spanish grey,' said the knight in a neutral tone. 'He was late to the choosing and it was the only one left. 'It has a ruined mouth.'

De Tancarville frowned and hitched his belt in an irritated gesture. 'That's unfortunate,' he said, 'I wanted to give the boy a chance.' Glancing down the rows of striped tents and pavilions, he saw William striding cheerfully towards them and shook his head. Predictably the young knight's right hand was occupied by a large hunk of bread and his jaw was in motion. He was wearing his padded under-tunic so was at least part-dressed for the joust and his expression was one of almost child-like delight. Stopping short when he saw de Tancarville and de Lorys outside his pavilion, he hastily swallowed the mouthful he had been chewing and his gaze grew anxious.

'My lord, is there some trouble? Did you want me?'

'Only to wonder where you were, but I've been told you were tending your horse. I understand you had some difficulty with it yesterday?'

'Nothing that can't be solved,' William replied enthusiastically. 'I have let out the bridle by three finger-widths so that the bit's lower in his mouth and not resting on the part that hurts him.'

'You'll not have the control,' de Lorys warned, folding his arms.

'At least I'll have a rideable mount. I've been out practising, and the change seems to work.'

De Lorys raised a sceptical brow and turned his mouth down at the corners, but held his peace.

'I did not mean for you to receive a bad horse,' de Tancarville said gruffly.

'It isn't a bad horse my lord,' William answered, smiling. 'Indeed, it is probably the best of all those given out.' He hesitated as he was about to duck inside the tent. 'I would ask you not to say anything to Adam Yqueboeuf about that. He has wagered his sword that I won't win a tourney prize on Blancart, and I want to surprise him.'

De Tancarville gave a snort of reluctant amusement. 'William, you surprise us all,' he said. 'I won't say anything; it'll be evident soon enough. Make haste now, or you'll not be ready to form up with the rest of the mesnie.'

'Yes, my lord.' William crammed the last chunk of bread into his mouth, moistened it with a swallow of wine from the pitcher standing on his camp stool and, chewing vigorously, beckoned a squire to help him arm.

Compared to William's baptism in battle at the desperate, bloody fight for Drincourt, the tourney was a jaunt. Death and injury were hazards of the sport, but the intent was to capture and claim ransom, not to kill. His stallion was fiery and unsettled, but William could deal with that. It was a matter of remembering to go lightly on the reins and do more work than usual with the thighs and heels. When he lined up in close formation with the other Tancarville men, his heart swelled with pride. He had chosen a place in the line well away from Adam Yqueboeuf, but each knight was aware of the other's presence. William did not allow himself to think of failure. He would make gains today; his honour and his self-esteem depended on it and he would rather die than yield his sword to a conceited turd like Yqueboeuf.

Their opponents were a medley of French, Flemish and Scots knights, as eager for the sport as the Normans, English and Angevins. De Tancarville stayed at the rear of his mesnie. For him, the tourney was a place to meet friends and peers and to display his largesse and importance through the number and calibre of knights fighting for him. The sport was for the young and reckless whilst he and the other sponsors looked on.

At the trumpet call from a herald, the two opposing lines spurred towards each other. William felt Blancart surge under him, the motion as smooth and powerful as a wave in mid-ocean. He selected his target — a knight wearing a hauberk that glittered silver and gold like the scales of a carp, his warhorse barded in ostentatious saffron and crimson silk. As the two stallions collided like rock and wave, crashing, recoiling, crashing again William wrapped his fist around the knight's bridle and strove to drag him back to the Norman pavilions. 'Yield!' William's voice emerged through his helm in a muffled bellow.

'Never!' The knight drew his sword and attempted to beat William off, but William held on, ducking, avoiding blows, striking back in return, and all the time drawing his intended prize towards his own lines. A second French knight who tried to help his companion was beaten off by Gadefer de Lorys. William saluted in acknowledgement, ducked another assault by his now desperate adversary, and spurred Blancart.

'Yield my lord!' he commanded again, dragging his victim far behind the Norman line.

The knight shook his head, but at William's determination and bravado rather than conveying refusal. 'Yielded,' he snarled. 'I am Philip de Valognes and you have my pledge.' He gave a lofty wave. 'You were fortunate to catch me before I had warmed to the sport.' His tone suggested that William's vigorous assault and grim determination to hold on were not quite chivalrous. 'Release me and have done... and I would know to whom I have yielded the price of my horse.'

'My name is William Marshal, my lord.' William replied, his chest heaving, his fist still tight around the knight's bridle. 'I am kin to

Guillaume de Tancarville, nephew to the Earl of Salisbury and cousin to the Count of Perche.'

'And by the looks of you, one of de Tancarville's young glory hunters without a penny to your patrimony,' growled de Valognes.

'Not until now, my lord,' William said pleasantly.

De Valognes acknowledged the quip with a snort of reluctant humour. 'I will have my attendant bring the price of my horse and armour to the sharing of the booty,' he said.

With a bow, William released the bridle, letting de Valognes spur back into the tourney like a carp reprieved by an angler and returned to river. 'Hah!' cried William and urging Blancart into the fray, went to net more fish.

A muscle working in his cheek, Adam Yqueboeuf unbuckled his swordbelt and handed it across to William. 'You win your wager,' he muttered gracelessly. 'I've never seen anyone with so much luck.'

William had gained the price of four war horses in the tourney and half the price of another which he had shared with Gadefer de Lorys. The amount might be no great sum to the likes of Philip de Valognes and Guillaume de Tancarville, but to William it was a small fortune and proof of his ability to provide for himself. Smiling at Yqueboeuf, he inclined his head. 'Some would say that a man makes his own luck, but what do they know?' He studied the swordbelt and the attached scabbard, but did not draw the weapon. 'A man's blade is made to suit his own hand. I gift it back to you with my goodwill.' Bestowing a courtly bow, he returned Yqueboeuf's sword, his smile becoming a grin.

If Yqueboeuf had been struggling to swallow his mortification before, now it was choking him. Uttering a few strangled words of insincere gratitude, he closed his fist around his scabbard and, turning on his heel, strode away.

'You make enemies as well as friends in life, remember that, lad,' said de Tancarville, drawing William aside for a quiet word before the carousing started. 'You've a rare talent there and lesser men will resent it.'

'Yes, my lord,' William said and looked troubled. 'Yqueboeuf's sword would have been of no use to me. I thought about asking him for its value in coin, but it seemed more courtly to return it to him.'

De Tancarville pursed his lips. 'I cannot fault your reasoning, but high courtesy will not protect you from malice.'

'I know that my lord.' William's eyelids tensed. 'I have endured the years of being called 'Guzzleguts' and 'Slugabed.' Perhaps some of it is deserved, but as much stems from being your impoverished kin as from the truth. At need I can go without food and sleep.'

'I'm sure you can.' The Chamberlain cleared his throat with unnecessary vigour. 'What will you do now?'

The question shook William, for he understood what it presaged. Whatever his skill, de Tancarville was not prepared to continue to furnish his helm. The tourney had been a great success, but it was over and now he had a surplus of young knights. William was being as good as told he was too troublesome to keep.

'I have been thinking about visiting my family,' he said, swallowing his disappointment.

'You have been many years away; they will be glad to see you again.' De Tancarville showed his discomfort by rubbing his forefinger over the jewelled band on his cap.

'Perhaps they won't recognise me,' William said, 'nor I them.' He looked thoughtful. 'Tourneying is not permitted in England, and Gadefer told me that there is another contest three days ride away. I thought I might try my fortune there first — with your permission.'

The last three words gave de Tancarville a way to make a graceful and formal ending to the obligation that had tied him to William for the past five years — and William to him. 'You have it,' he said, 'and my blessing.' He clasped William's shoulders and kissed him soundly on either cheek, then embraced him hard. 'I have nurtured and equipped you. Now go out and prove your knighthood to the world. I expect to hear great deeds of you in the future.'

William returned the embrace, heat prickling his eyes. Guillaume de Tancarville had never been especially paternal towards him, but he had given him the tools with which to make the best of his life and William acknowledged the debt owing. 'I will do my best, my lord,' he said, adding after a hesitation, 'There is one last boon I would ask of you.'

'Name it and it is yours, and let there be no talk of 'last boons' between us,' said de Tancarville, although his mouth quirked as he spoke the words. Within reason said the look in his eyes.

'I ask that you send a messenger to the Earl of Essex with this.' William produced a fine jewelled breast band and crupper off one of the horses he had claimed in the tourney. 'Bid him say that William Marshal pays his debts.'

De Tancarville took the gilded pieces of harness and suddenly he was laughing. 'It's a good thing you were not taken for ransom today,' he chuckled, 'for I doubt you have a price.'

William grinned. 'Does that make me worthless, or worth too much?' he asked.

Flyboats

Nicola Monaghan

Paris, August 1996

Unlike most of the city, which had dabbed a touch of eau de old urine behind its ears, the Cathedral smelt nice. Burning wax and furniture polish. Bekah walked over to the box of votive candles and bought one. Kneeling, she lit it, and the flame cut through the black air of Notre Dame de Paris. She liked the Cathedral. It didn't make her feel uncomfortable, not like York Minster near where she grew up. In the Minster she felt dead people everywhere, tapping her on the shoulder or poking at her, telling her God wasn't there. This didn't happen in Notre Dame, and it felt warmer too. Perhaps this was the heat from candles, everyone's wishes warming up the place.

A hand on Bekah's shoulder made her start. She turned to see Gordon.

'You really are a Catholic girl,' he said. She wondered what he meant by that. Men often used that phrase with less than religious implications. Bekah ignored him and looked back at her candle. She remembered an RE teacher telling her votive meant a wish, but warning the class it was more complicated than that. He said you needed to be careful what you wish for because God doesn't like selfish requests. It's not like rubbing on a lamp and talking to a genie. Bekah thought about nice things she could ask, for other people, then prayed for Gordon, that he would be happy for the rest of the holiday. Too late she realised she'd made this wish for herself after all.

She did love Gordon, even if he was a difficult man. He raised his voice quite a lot, and had screamed in her face once, and reckoned he'd caught hay fever from her, and that he'd never had a temper before they'd started dating and other ridiculous things. But there was that saying about rough and smooth and Bekah knew love couldn't stay all hot and shivery or it'd burn itself out. It needed to settle into something steady. It couldn't be Belgian chocolates and expensive perfume the whole time. It couldn't be one long trip to Paris. But it could be the odd week or so there if you nagged for it long enough and offered to pay more than half.

Gordon had appointed himself tour guide and it was clear to Bekah he loved the job. He'd come armed with three guidebooks, Paris trussed up like a hostage inside them. Yellow post-it notes stuck out from the books where he'd marked important facts, sights, names. Bekah would have preferred to wander round, take the city as it came to her, but you can't be like that. In a relationship you have to compromise. So she let Gordon show her Paris. Potted Paris, ground up meat and bones and offal squeezed into a plastic tub so you can spread it on white bread.

The sun shone through Notre Dame's famous rose windows, making a laser show. Bekah turned away from her candle to see Gordon walking off. As he strode towards the exit, he killed the coloured beams of light that shot from window to floor. Bekah crossed herself and got up, followed him. She pushed the heavy door aside and was blinded by the summer. Walking into the square outside, she found Gordon waiting. He kissed her, but his eyes were focused some way behind her, like he was trying to remember something more important. He turned then, and rushed off, and Bekah had to walk double pace to keep up with him. She wondered if her wishing candle could do any good. They'd seen the Unknown Soldier under the Arc de Triomphe earlier in the week and he had an eternal flame lit for him, but he was just as dead and anonymous as he'd always been. What good could lighting a candle do when it was made of wax and would burn away in a matter of hours?

For the first time since they'd arrived in Paris, Gordon and Bekah were at a loose end. Gordon had a surprise planned but he said it was something they couldn't do until it got dark. In the meantime, they wandered round the Latin Quarter and found a café. Bekah ordered milky coffee and Gordon drank hot chocolate. They sipped the drinks without talking. Bekah wanted to curl up on the chair and fall asleep. Being on holiday was exhausting.

When dusk came down they left the café and took the Métro to the Champs Elysées. Gordon looked at his map outside the Métro, then walked off. Bekah followed him down a road lined with designer shops, classy looking bars, and restaurants she wouldn't have dared to walk into in case they were too expensive. The road was wide as a river and led to the Seine, just by the Liberty flame and the Alma tunnel. Bekah saw lasers ahead of them, spanning round over the river like searchlights. The trees glittered with white sparkles. A huge blue sign said 'Bateaux Mouches' and pointed down to the riverbank. She'd wanted to do the boat trip all week but Gordon kept knocking her back. Now she understood why.

Bekah climbed onto the top deck of the boat and Gordon put his arm around her. 'Do you have a great boyfriend or what?' he said. She didn't answer, and thought about whether she preferred to be surprised this way, or if it would have been nice to be allowed to take part in the planning.

People were flooding onto the boat, filling the seats around them. Then a horn sounded and the boat started to move out into the middle of the Seine, heading towards the Alexandre III Bridge. Lit up in the dark it looked beautiful. So did the Musée D'Orsay and the Louvre, the Grand and Petit Palais. Bekah didn't look beyond them or between them or further than the glow. She sat back and lapped up the lightshow, enjoying not rushing, not being curled up in a tight ball trying to move too fast through people.

The boat passed Notre Dame de Paris, bringing them full circle on the day. The church looked magnificent, sticking out into the river like the hull of a cruise liner. Little stone arches clung to the outside like cobwebs and gargoyles menaced, keeping out the demons and scaring away the dead. The recorded commentary said the boat was about to pass under the Petit Pont, the city's smallest bridge. It said you could make a wish the first time you passed under and it would come true within a year. Bekah screwed up her face and wished hard to move to Paris. Then she kissed Gordon. Just at that moment Bekah loved him so much. How could she not, right outside Notre Dame with the whole of Paris lit like a filmset around them? It was a scene out of a Disney movie, the boat dragging a trail of fairy dust in its wake. Though, of course, this wasn't anything to do with magic at all but fireflies, basking in the lights around the hull. Bekah was deep under the strongest enchantment. But it was all the wrong way around. The kiss is supposed to break the spell.

As Gordon pulled away, Bekah realised she'd not included him in her wish. She wondered if that meant something about the two of them. But it was too late. You only get one first time under the bridge.

Paris, August 1997

'They' say strange things happen 'once in a blue moon' but half the time 'they' don't even know what a blue moon is. 'They' say loads of things, like to be careful what you ask for and not to put eggs in baskets or count them before they've hatched. Not to look gift horses in the mouth but beware if they're borne by Greeks. 'They' are mostly full of shit. But as it happens, there was a blue moon when Bekah went back to Paris. The second full moon of the month.

It had been a bad year for Bekah. She'd lost her grandmother, who'd died of cancer, and though she'd been expecting it, it was still a nasty shock that she wasn't around anymore. She'd hated every minute of the nursing course she was doing at St Mary's. Everything about it. The theory classes and exams, the placements in hospitals where she got to do all the dirtiest jobs. She'd split up with Gordon too and, even though she knew it was the right thing to do, it had wrenched her heart out. He'd not made her life easy either, turning up at her mum's house, following her home from college, making aggressive phone calls and generally doing all he could to bully her into getting back together with him. To make matters worse, her best mate Zoë had met a new man and was so engrossed with him she had no time for Bekah. So Bekah took the money her grandmother had left her and ran. All the way to the nearest Eurostar platform, next stop Gare du Nord.

Gordon had bought Bekah a pull-along bag for her birthday. The lack of romance in this gesture had been the end of things for Bekah. It was as if he didn't know her at all. Still, it came in handy now she was moving country. She dragged it behind her, off the Métro and onto the platform at Bastille. She could see water straight ahead and wondered if it was the Seine, except it didn't seem to be moving like a river. Was it a canal, and if so which one? She made for the stairs and picked up the bag. It was heavy, so she let it bump down the steps.

Bekah surfaced into madness, the quiet of the station blown to pieces by a busker a few yards away, hitting a drum hard. She turned to see a restaurant called Tex-Mex Indiana, its door guarded by a cut-out Chieftain with a feather headdress. She headed towards the taxi rank. There was no one queuing.

'Boulevard Richard Lenoir,' she said, through the window of the first taxi.

'*Où?*' said the taxi driver.

This reminded Bekah of trying to order water with dinner when she'd visited with Gordon. Neither of them had been able pronounce '*de l'eau*'.

'*Où, où, où!*' Gordon had said over and over. The waiter looked suitably confused, his face like a question mark. 'What's the word for jug?'

'*Un carafe*, I think,' she'd said.

'*Une carafe? Ah, vous voulez du vin. Rouge où blanc?*'

'*Blanc,*' Gordon had said. '*Blanc!*' And he'd looked at Bekah and rolled his eyes. 'What's he talking about, red water?'

'*Où?*' said the taxi driver, a year later.

'Boulevard Richard Lenoir,' Bekah said again. She held her handbag between her knees and pulled out a tourist map she'd picked up at the station. She pointed.

'Ah, Boulevard Richard Lenoir,' he said. And Bekah thought: that's what I said. The taxi driver launched into a stream of words she didn't know but she understood he was sending her away. He pointed diagonally across the square, presumably at the Boulevard she was looking for, and threw a few more French words in her direction. She made her way around the Bastille Circus towards where he'd pointed, thinking how the word circus described the crazy place just fine, and headed up Boulevard Richard Lenoir. Along the middle of the road were the hoods of empty market stalls. The road was wide as she'd ever seen and looked so strange. *Etrange* means foreign and strange in French, Bekah thought, wondering how she could know that when she couldn't remember how to ask for sugar in her coffee. Wondering if she was even right. Everything was so different from home. The crossings with low level traffic lights and green and red men as well as lines on the road. The pharmacies marked with huge green crosses and piled high with miracle creams that claimed to smooth wrinkles or melt cellulite. The promised perfect thighs and faces were displayed six feet high in the windows. She could smell unfiltered cigarettes trodden into the pavements. And when she heard people speak it was guttural, the words half swallowed, half spat. Nothing like the soft versions she'd been taught at school by some English lady who'd spent a year in Nice.

Then something familiar made Bekah smile. Les Golden Arches. She walked inside and ordered a Big Mac and fries, Coca-Cola. Hardly haute cuisine but it filled a gap. She'd never felt further away from Paris in her life. It was like the city had turned to jelly as she headed over on the train. When she reached out to touch it her fingers slipped through.

Bekah finished her meal and headed up the boulevard. She found the Résidence Orion and walked through the automatic doors and over to the counter. The receptionist told her *'bienvenue'* but she didn't smile as she handed over the key and a list of rules. The 'key' was a card, in fact, an electronic thing. The lady pointed to the lift.

The elevator was small and grey inside. When she got to the second floor corridor, that was painted grey too, with dark red borders. She followed it to room 205 and pushed the card into the door. Nothing happened. She turned the card over and tried again. She heard a click and a light flashed green, open sesame. It wasn't exactly like a treasure trove inside.

The room had a sofa bed and a kitchenette. Bekah noseyed around, opening up the cupboards, which were full of caravan crockery; small plates, teacups and saucers. She opened the drawers and touched the cutlery, cold against her fingers. In the bathroom was a row of light bulbs, Hollywood dressing room style. There was a hairdryer that switched on when you pulled it from the wall. A hotel hairdryer. The whole apartment had the air of a hotel about it, except without the mini bar or room service. It was hardly the Parisian dream Bekah had wished for under the bridge. But then, she'd just said 'Paris' to the bridge. And the bridge knew Paris much better than she did.

Bekah was wrenched from sleep by a foghorn of an alarm the previous tenant must have left set. It was not a nice way to wake up. Her eyes opened wide but didn't see. Shapes formed around her and she realised quickly that she was not in her usual bedroom. It took a minute or so for the sleep to clear from her head so she could work out where she was.

The heavy red curtains didn't let light through and so it could have been any time of day inside the room. Bekah was hungry and thought about breakfast: *café au lait, pain au chocolat.* She wondered if people would understand her when she said these words. She practised them aloud.

Bekah switched on the radio and listened to babble, punctuated by names and songs she recognised. She was in Paris. She thought about that fact for a while and made a list of the things she would do. She would go to the Louvre. She would walk up the hill to the Sacré-Coeur, go inside and light a candle. She would sit in the Tuileries Gardens and eat ice cream, read a book. She shuffled over to where she'd left her handbag, wrapping the red quilt around her shoulders. She pulled out the tourist map. It covered all of central Paris and had pencil sketches of the landmarks in three dimensions. She saw the address of the Résidence, where she'd scribbled it the night before at the station, in the space between the Grand and Petit Palais. She wished she'd not picked such a dump. She corrected herself. Not a dump, so much as a soulless place.

Bekah made strong coffee and sipped it black as she unpacked. There were several vital items missing from her bags. She was good at forgetting things and not so good at packing or unpacking. Gordon used to joke about her designer luggage, like the plastic carrier bag she brought with her for the overspill from her suitcase when they came to Paris together. He'd said that he would always be able to find her by following the trail of spilt things. She hoped not.

Bekah did not empty her bag but dug for the clothes and toiletries she needed, spilling unwanted items over the side. The apartment around her looked bare, clinical. It smelt of stale sweat and every time Bekah looked at it, really looked at it, her stomach swelled with something heavy and hard. All she had of England was a small bag. She'd left most of her belongings at her mum's house in London and felt like part of her was still there too. Her tummy tied itself in knots as she thought about Gordon. Would he be missing her? Would he come looking?

Bekah walked out of the Résidence Orion and shut its heavy door behind her, listening for the click that confirmed it was closed. She was setting out to find Paris. She was wearing her best clothes in the hope this would help, a new black skirt and a red blouse. The skirt had that cleanness, the freshness things have only the first time you wear them.

The Résidence Orion lay on the corner of a wide-open boulevard and a small lane. Bekah walked down the lane away from the Résidence and found it led to another boulevard, wide as a river. The road and pavements were busy with people rushing from one place to another, tutting and cursing at those who slowed their progress. She felt glad not to be one of them but, at the same time, left out. They knew Paris in a way she couldn't yet, as home, as commonplace, as ordinary, wrapped around them. She looked for a street sign. Rue du Faubourg Saint Antoine, she read. Something to do with Saint Anthony then. The saint she prayed to too often, begging him to bring back or reveal lost watches, jewellery, people. 'The art of losing isn't hard to master,' the poem said and Bekah had found it told the truth. She touched her hands together and asked Saint Antoine to help her find Paris.

Bekah walked all the way along Rue du Faubourg Saint Antoine until she came to the Place de la Bastille. She recognised it as the place she'd arrived at the previous day and realised she'd gone a distance out of her way. There was a bar-cum-restaurant on the corner that was crowned with a huge neon advert for Kanterbrau. It looked like the kind of place where old men would drink and so Bekah passed it by. She tried to read the inscriptions on the wall explaining the area and its history. She could find no English translations and her French was not good enough. Across the road she noticed the busy Tex-Mex restaurant. It looked as good a place as any to acclimatise.

Bekah crossed the road and sat in one of the wicker seats that littered the terrace. The waiter approached her. He was holding something in his hand that resembled a Psion organiser, except a little bigger. Bekah ordered fajitas and a beer and he stared at her blankly. She opened and closed her mouth, making as much difference as a goldfish in a bowl. She pointed at the menu, and he used the handheld device to radio her order to the kitchen.

Sitting outside the Tex-Mex felt more like being in Paris than anything she'd done so far, and Bekah stayed for several hours. She drank frozen Margueritas, letting them melt and slip down her throat as the daytime slipped away. Afternoon turned into evening, getting cooler, noisier, darker. The lights came on around the Bastille Monument and then in the windows of nearby apartments. The street lights came on too, even though it was only dusk. Bekah was reading a cheap thriller about the stock market, the kind of book Gordon used to say she read too much. Around her people arrived and then left, eating different food and speaking different languages. Only Bekah and Liberty were constant, watching the transients come and go. She knew that the statue was of Liberty now, not Cupid. Gordon had put her right when they'd been here last summer. As she thought about that moment, the sharp edge to Gordon's voice, his unjustified irritation with her, the way he always expected her to know things before anyone told her, as she remembered the argument that had followed his comment, a pigeon shat on her skirt.

Bekah went inside the restaurant to try to clean up. She used wet tissues but before long the front of her skirt was smeared with a mixture of pigeon droppings and dissolving tissue. She took it off and put it under a running tap. The yellow-brown mark spread rather than washing away, and her skirt was left covered in a fine layer of the pigeon-shit tissue. The more she rubbed, the further it spread. She tried to dry the skirt under the hand dryer even though it wasn't clean, because she had to wear something to walk back to the Résidence. The smell as she dried it was not good.

Bekah headed back along Boulevard Richard Lenoir wearing the dirty skirt. But she didn't want to go back to the depressing apartment, not even to change. She turned off the main road and trailed through narrow streets choosing each new direction without thinking so that her route was random. She came across a small busy square named after Saint Catherine. The square was cobbled and surrounded by cafés and bistros with patios, and their lighting gave the paving stones a pretty yellow glow. It was packed with people. It was the Paris she'd wished for under the bridge, the Paris she'd prayed for to Saint Anthony. She fell onto a café stool and ordered a milky coffee. The waiter brought it over straight away, and it was strong, brewed to suit the French palate. She drank it slowly. The square was so alive that its life seeped into her, as she sipped, down into her stomach. It made her feel alert and strong, or perhaps that was just the caffeine doing its temporary best. The air was choked with garlic and cooking food smells. Diners sat and chatted with claret-stained lips and dogs yapped as they sat in handbags or on the laps of their owners. And a miracle happened, courtesy of Saint

95

Anthony and Saint Catherine, who made Bekah forget completely about what the pigeon had done to her skirt. She emptied the bottom of her coffee and thought about ordering another one, or perhaps a glass of wine.

A hand on Bekah's shoulder made her start. She turned and saw Gordon. '*Excusez-moi?*' he said, with a strong English accent. But it was a North-Western accent, from Manchester or somewhere near, not Gordon's soft Durham tones. It was not him at all, just a similar looking tall blond man.

'You're English,' she said.

'Yeah. So are you. I was after your salt and pepper if you're not using them,' he said, grinning. Bekah passed them to him. '*Merci beaucoup*,' he said.

She smiled at the lack of effort he made to make his accent sound anything like French. Just like Gordon.

'You been here long?' the man asked her.

'An hour or so,' she told him.

'I mean, in Paris,' he said, grinning again.

Bekah smiled back. 'Not that much longer. I arrived yesterday.'

'I'm Martin,' he said, holding out his hand to her. She shook it and he told her 'enchantey' in such a funny accent she had to work at not laughing. 'I could show you around sometime if you like, take you out to some cool bars. This city can be hard work when you first get here,' he said.

'I wouldn't want to put you to any trouble,' she said.

'It wouldn't be trouble.' And Martin asked the waiter for a pen and scribbled his number on the napkin. Bekah noticed he spoke really good French, despite the strong English accent. She watched him walk away and wondered if he had an agenda. But she was hardly in a position to turn down a night out even if he might. She folded up the napkin and put it in her pocket.

Bekah spent the next few days sightseeing and trying to find places to eat or drink coffee where she didn't feel uncomfortable. Mostly she went to McDonald's. She'd thought she'd felt lonely when she broke up with Gordon, but she'd been wrong. Back in England, she'd had friends around. Sure there was still a cold space next to her in her big double bed and she'd found it hard to sleep. But she hadn't really known what loneliness was. What it was like to have no one to meet up with. No job to go to. No family on the other end of a train journey. She did now.

She'd been determined not to call Martin too soon in case he got the wrong idea and thought she was interested in anything other than a tour of the city's bars. But on Thursday everything changed.

She was on her way to visit the Luxembourg Gardens where she intended to sit in the shade with a novel and perhaps some ice cream. As she slipped her *billet* into the Métro turnstile and pushed, she felt someone right behind her. She'd seen this a few times, people dashing into the Métro right behind other passengers to avoid paying, and assumed that was all the boy was doing. Then she felt his hand reach and grab for her, sneak underneath her skirt. She pulled away and rushed off, down the steps towards the platform. As she reached the bottom of the staircase, she heard someone moving fast behind her. She turned, but not fast enough to get out of the way of the same lad, who was following her. He wasn't on his own; a gang of his mates were following behind. They were laughing as he grabbed for her again.

She walked right along the platform as fast as she could and up to the exit without getting on the train. The boys had destroyed any desire she had to go looking round the city. She rushed back to the Résidence and up to her room, taking the stairs because she felt exposed standing waiting for the lift in reception. She climbed onto the sofa bed, which was still laid down from the night before, and cried until her eyes were red and so swollen they felt rubbery to the touch. Still shivering with tears, she picked up the phone and rang Martin. She would take the risk. Assume he was genuine.

They arranged to go out in the Bastille area, not far from the Résidence, on Saturday night. Martin assured Bekah the area was *sympa*, short for a French word *sympathique*, which he said had no proper English equivalent but meant it was a good place to hang out. Bekah wasn't sure whether she thought he was cool or a prat for speaking Franglais this way. She dressed carefully that night. She didn't want the same kind of trouble she'd had in the Métro station. And she didn't want to give Martin the wrong impression. He was waiting for her outside the Tex Mex, the only place she could think of to suggest meeting. He smiled as she walked up and Bekah relaxed, decided she would have a good time.

They went to a bar that had a low beam over the door, so that they both had to duck as they walked in. Salsa music blared out from only half decent speakers and there was a black and red picture of Che Guavara on the wall, reminding Bekah of University where everyone had had this poster.

'This Brazilian bloke runs this place,' Martin said, 'I met him a couple of times.'

Bekah nodded, and they headed to the bar. They served cocktails so Bekah ordered a mudsling, several measures of spirits with cream and chocolate. It was delicious and didn't taste of alcohol. One of those dangerous drinks. She sipped and smiled at Martin, who insisted on paying.

'What are you doing in Paris then?' she asked him.

'I work for a French bank called UBF. Real boring stuff so I won't go on about it but it pays the bills pretty nicely, ta,' Martin told her. 'You?'

'I split up with my boyfriend and it seemed like a good idea,' she said.

'Yeah, but what are you doing here? Gonna get a job? Write? What?' Martin said.

Bekah shrugged. She realised she didn't know. Didn't have a clue what she was doing there.

Martin laughed. 'That's cute. But it's not such a good idea to be here in Paris without a plan. It's a city that needs a plan.' The drink tasted nice and Bekah didn't know what to say so she took big gulps instead. Martin waved at the barman and ordered some more. 'You're on a mission tonight, looks like,' he said, as the guy shook the drink together and served it with a flourish.

Bekah felt awkward for the first few drinks but as she became infused with alcohol, she relaxed. Martin told Bekah about his experiences of Paris, his friends, his job, his life back home before he moved. Bekah talked a little about Gordon, the breakdown of their relationship. She told Martin about the boy in the Métro station.

'That sort of shit happens all the time here,' he told her. 'I don't have a single female friend, not one, who's been here for six months

98

and hasn't had a man masturbate in front of her on the Métro. They know you're foreign.'

'What can I do?'

'Not a lot. Best to ignore them and look away. Whatever you do, don't try to speak to them. Once they know you don't know the language so well you've had it,' he told her. Bekah took a huge gulp of drink then. She thought, maybe I should start seeing this guy. Maybe it'd be better than putting up with shit like that. Then she almost laughed to herself. She wasn't prepared to cop out that easily.

They moved on to a place called 'The What's Up Bar', though it was more like a club than a bar. It had metal chairs and tables, and sold cheap beer, played house music. A projector shot images onto a white wall behind the dance floor. A bloke offered them pills. Bekah and Martin looked at one another, trying to suss what the other thought about the idea.

'What the hell,' Martin said, and pulled some notes from his pocket.

Bekah laughed. 'Just what I was thinking,' she said. And they both washed them down with beer.

They danced till they came up on the pills, then they danced some more. They had conversations with the people around them, Bekah even attempted some of the French she'd been trying to learn. She giggled when people didn't understand her, and they giggled too, and reverted to English.

When the rush of the pill buzz had worn off, they sat down and grinned at each other. Martin was gurning a bit, his jaw off-centre and grin lopsided, and this made Bekah laugh.

'If I tell you a secret do you promise not to tell?' he said.

'Course,' she said, laughing and leaning towards him.

Martin stuck his tongue out at her. Impaled through the middle of the pink flesh was a big metal stud.

'No way,' said Bekah, touching it and shrieking.

'It's dead useful, if you know what I mean,' he told her, winking. Bekah didn't, but she liked touching it. She didn't even think about what he was trying to say.

'Cool,' she said.

'You wanna come back to mine for a bit?' Martin said. And through a feel-good pill haze Bekah thought, why the hell not?

Martin had a lovely flat with stone floors and a balcony over a flow-ered courtyard. He made coffee and Bekah looked through his bookshelves. There were some novels, but mainly self-help books. He handed her a drink and she sat down. She felt a wave of lightheaded-ness hit her and hoped that she wasn't going to be sick.

'I should go,' she said, putting down the mug.

'Don't,' he said, standing up. 'Please stay.'

Something in his voice moved her, a sadness she recognised.

'I just want someone else in the place. I've got a spare room, I'm not trying it on here,' he said. It was the loneliness of all of Paris welling up in his voice, something Bekah knew intimately. Staying seemed the right thing to do.

'Bless you,' she said, and hugged him. He squeezed her hard, and showed her where she could sleep, gave her a T-shirt to wear in bed.

Bekah slept anxiously and lightly in the spare room. At about four o'clock she was woken by the instinctive feeling of not being alone. She felt hands on her waist and turned to find herself nose to nose with Martin. He tried to kiss her but she could feel his tongue stud and it made her gag. It struck her what he'd been getting at in the club, about how the piercing was 'useful'. She pushed him away but he read the signal badly, trying to demonstrate exactly what he'd meant in a hungry embrace. Bekah pushed him away hard.

'Martin!' she said. She felt prickles of water in her eyes.

'Princess Diana died. Just down the road from here. It was on the radio,' he told her.

Bekah couldn't process what he was saying against what was hap-pening. She couldn't get her head round any of it. She got out of bed and got dressed. She wanted more than anything to run but she had to regain control. So she walked away slowly.

'Bekah!' Martin called after her.

She heard her name echo behind her, following her out of the flat, and the urge to run away from it was strong. Martin, the boys in the Métro, it was like some disease was going around Paris, a desperate, hungry illness that ate at men. Bekah didn't want to be near it. She wondered why he'd been going on about Princess Diana.

She thought about his tongue dipping inside her and shuddered. She tried to work out how it could feel so bad, something that could be delicious with a good measure of attraction and a pinch of love. That recipe was spoilt and she felt poisoned. She threw up in a bin on the side of the street.

As she lifted her head a man walked past, swaying a little from too much to drink.

'Lady Di,' he said. *'Elle est morte.'*

For once the French didn't pass Bekah by. She understood what he was saying and that Martin hadn't been lying about that at least. She understood too that she really didn't know what she was doing in Paris and that Martin was right, it was a city where you needed a plan or you'd get into trouble. She didn't have a good enough reason to stay.

Paris, September 1997

Bekah wanted to say goodbye to Notre Dame and light some candles. She had three franc pieces in her pocket. She pulled one out and looked closely at its surface. Liberté, egalité, fraternité. Freedom, equality and brotherhood were all very well, but what about the girls? She put the coins in the wooden box and took her candles.

Bekah lit a candle for Paris, a city where men were so lonely they were frightening to be around. She lit another candle for Gordon and prayed for him. She could hear his voice, as if he'd left an echo when they'd been in the cathedral together. 'You really are a Catholic girl.' She lit the next candle for herself. She took no notice now of the advice she'd had on being selfish and made a wish; that she might find whatever it was she wanted and know where to look. All she'd learnt so far was she wouldn't find it in Paris.

Bekah had spent the last of her inheritance on a designer dress from one of the shops near the Champs Elysées, and a first class Eurostar ticket. She didn't feel guilty, she knew her grandma would have approved. She was going home. Not back to nursing though, and not back to Gordon either. And she would stand up to anyone who tried to make her. Most of all she would stand up to Gordon. She wasn't going to let anyone push her around again, touch her when she didn't want it, manipulate her into compromising situations. She sat in a big, cushioned seat sipping champagne, on her way home. She raised her glass in a toast to the stronger girl she wanted to be. Then the train entered a magical tunnel under the sea in a rush of

101

air, and that was it, the Paris she'd conjured up under the bridge vanished, blown out by the backdraft. She sipped the standard issue Eurostar champagne. All the bubbles were gone.

She sat back in her seat, thinking how deceptive everything was, especially Paris. It'd looked so beautiful from the boat at night, the City of Light and its damn fireflies. In the daytime, though, it was just a city, they were just flies.

An Autumn Encounter

Stephan Collishaw

How long my fever lasted I don't know. I woke in the hospital under the shadow of the old city wall. Cold winter sunshine lay flat across my sheets, and looking through the window I could see that the trees had lost their leaves. A nurse came into the room and, seeing me awake, smiled.

"Well," she said, "look who has woken up."

I haven't seen him since then. Not once. I have looked, of course: have scoured every corner of the city. But he's nowhere. He is gone.

'When was it that you first met... him?'

Yevgene Petrovich sat back in the leather seat of the coach to Petersburg and eased a cigarette between his lips. He looked at me fleetingly before his gaze turned out to the passing countryside, the endless deep forest broken only for still lakes, deep silken rivers that flowed like veins across the country and small meadows, pock-marked with isolated wooden farm buildings.

I touched the flask in my jacket pocket, but decided against it. Noticing the flutter of my hand Yevgene offered me his cigarette case, a slim, handsome box inlaid with amber. I thanked him and took a *Davidoff's*, lighted it and began enjoying the light, aromatic smoke.

'The city was dark, that first time,' I said, my words emerging rich with tobacco fumes, 'the narrow lanes empty.'

My mind skittered back across the months, beyond the bright new spring, that long dark winter to the autumn of the previous year. Early autumn. September. It had rained in the morning and I had looked up from my piano where I had been practicing and noticed the heavy spots forming dusty trails down the window and realised how lonely I was.

It struck me so crushingly that I was unable to play anymore that morning. I got up and stood by the window and gazed out into the street. I thought of calling Katya and had even lingered a moment over the telephone, but had resisted in the end. I went for a walk and ended up in a café on the far side of the city.

I took another drag on the cigarette and exhaled the smoke slowly, leaning back against the leather headrest. Yevgene was gazing still out of the window but I could tell he was listening.

'My footsteps echoed on the cobblestones as I made my way back to the apartment,' I said. 'Turning into my doorway I fumbled with my keys. I had drunk a bottle of wine at the café, drowning my self-pity, and it took a while to fit the key into the hole. I cursed a little. A chill wind cut through my jacket. The key found its place and the lock turned with a solid clunk.'

Yevgene nodded as if he recognised this detail, as though the locks all turned with solid clunks in that city we had both come from. He flicked the ash from his cigarette and turned to flash me a glance, knowing that I was coming to the strange beginning of my tale.

'The stairwell smelled musty. It was pitch-black when the door closed behind me. I heard footsteps descending the stairs. I grabbed for the door, pushing it open, feeling, at the same time, for the light switch on the wall. The footsteps had grown quite close by the time my fingers reached it. I pressed the switch and turned to the figure squeezing past me. My heart leapt with fear.'

Yevgene's eyes flicked a glance at me through the smoke of his cigarette. For a moment he said nothing, but as I had paused in my story he was prompted to ask, 'And why was that?'

'The well-dressed man slipping out into the darkness was myself.'

I'm thirty-five. For almost ten years I lived in the city and considered it home. It is a beautiful city. The narrow lanes wind through elegant baroque buildings. Streets open out into squares canopied by maples and oak. It is a city of churches, of cafes. It is the city where first I fell in love.

Katya was a dancer. She was as exquisite as blossom I once saw here, caught in a late, severe freeze. It had frozen, then thawed and then in the night frozen once more. The melting ice had trickled down and was dripping from the delicate pink petals when the night frost captured the tiny flowers in droplets of ice. They sparkled as the sun rose the next morning. I stood on the pavement and watched as the spring warmth slowly melted the ice, releasing the delicate blossom. Katya was not freed, however, from her droplet of ice by my attentions.

There is, I realize, a hint of criticism in my tone and that is unjust.

It was not that Katya was so irrevocably cold that she could not respond to my touch, but rather, I feel, a deficiency in myself. I know that despite the fact that I worshiped her, I held back too. A reticence I was raised with did not allow me to take her fully. When our relationship became so tortured that I could not bring myself to see her again, I withdrew into myself a little. There have been no other relationships since then. Occasionally I have used prostitutes.

The figure in the doorway that night did not look startled as he glanced back at me. He was illuminated by the sudden glare of the bare stairwell light bulb. His lips — my lips — twisted into a mischievous grin. And then he was gone. The door closed with a dull thump. I slumped back against the wall, my heart fluttering disturbingly. I must have stood there for some minutes because the timer ran out on the light and I was plunged into darkness. I opened the door and looked out into the street. He was nowhere to be seen.

In my apartment I poured myself a large whiskey. My hand shook a little as I drank. I slumped into an easy chair. My cat jumped onto my lap and I petted it distractedly. It was not that the figure had looked approximately like me, as a brother might; he was the reflection I saw in the mirror. A twin. It was I.

My rational mind searched for an explanation. I stood in front of the gilt framed mirror in my bedroom and ran a hand over my features which, up until that point, I had unthinkingly assumed to be unique. There were, I concluded, only two possible explanations; either I had an identical twin, kept mysteriously secret, who had by some chance also traveled to this country, to this city, to this apartment, or I had suffered some form of delusion.

By the next morning it was the latter that convinced me. Despite this I found myself making a number of errands, popping in and out of the building. No matter how much I chided myself on my foolishness, as soon as I was back in my apartment I found myself longing to go back out. My eyes flicked eagerly around the doors, streets, licking the dark shadows, nooks and crannies like a hungry cat's tongue. He — I — was nowhere to be seen. Of course.

By early evening I had driven myself quite mad and forced myself onto a trolley bus and across the city to a bar with an excellent prospect of the river. There I sat laughing at the absurdity of my behaviour. I drank some of the fine beer they brew in a small town just down the river and watched the sun set over the hills to the West.

Nevertheless I returned home at the exact same time I had the previous evening. My feet dragged down the narrow cobbled street. Each noise attracted my restless gaze. Each figure I surreptitiously scrutinized. I slipped the key into the lock and pushed open the door. For a few moments I stood at the bottom of the stairs in darkness, listening to the silence of the late evening apartment, waiting for the click of a door, the sound of steps. But there was none. I pressed the light switch and made my way up to my apartment.

I had taken off my coat, poured a glass of wine and put on some Verdi when I heard the soft rap at my door. Glass in hand, Callas in full voice, I shuffled to the door and pressed my eye to the spy-hole. It took a moment for my eye to focus on the figure standing, head bowed, before my door. I pulled it open. There he stood before me. There stood I.

He looked up and a sly, sarcastic grin slipped across his lips. Those eyes, blue, almost grey. The hair, thinning slightly. The almost too thick, sensual lips, a quality I have always considered quite crude in myself.

'I have disturbed you,' he said, glancing at the glass suspended in my hand.

Unlike myself he did not seem in the slightest bit perturbed by the fact that he was standing in front of the mirror image of himself. My hand trembled so that the wine threatened to spill from the glass. He reached out and steadied my hand. Short, manicured nails.

'Are you feeling unwell?' The same mocking smile.

'You had better come in,' was all I managed.

He nodded. 'I came only to beg a little coffee.' He squeezed past, close enough for me to smell the cologne he was wearing, surely the same I myself wore?

'I live on the fifth floor,' he said pointing to the floor above my own. 'Just moved in.'

A foreigner here too. His accent, his tone, mine. He padded into the apartment, glancing around, as though weighing up what he saw. He nodded, seemingly approvingly. I closed the door as he slumped onto the sofa. Edging into the small kitchen to pour him a glass of wine, I kept my eye on him. My cat jumped up into his lap and was purring contentedly as I handed him the wine, she did not even open her eyes to acknowledge me. I leant against the doorframe and watched.

If ever you have listened to your voice in a tape recording, or perhaps seen yourself on film, you will, to some small extent, appreciate what I was feeling at this moment. The voice is familiar yet alien, strange. The perspective of our self, unusual. We see our self, hear our self, in those instances, as others do. It is a peculiar, an unsettling feeling. How much more so then, facing this very likeness of myself reclined comfortably on my sofa, sipping my wine, with my cat purring beneath his soft, rather effeminate, fingers.

He raised his glass to me. Bewildered, I raised my own. He sipped at the wine, then nodded as if it was to his approval. I could not help having the rather bizarre feeling he was judging me, to see if I lived up to some standard. I became anxious, ridiculously anxious, all of a sudden, that he should not feel I had let myself, us, down. As if aware of my sudden panic, he smiled benevolently and gently tapped the space on the sofa beside him, inviting me to sit. With legs trembling I crossed to the sofa and sat in uncomfortably close proximity to him.

From the close angle from which I now regarded him, I was able to note that the likeness was more than uncanny: it was exact. The small scar beneath the left eye, which I, in the years of looking at myself in the mirror, had placed on the wrong side of my face. The mole, almost hidden by his collar. The fine, spreading wrinkles, already making tracks from his eyes. I had an almost uncontrollable compulsion to reach over and lift up his cuff to check for the small, primitive tattoo, I had executed upon myself as a teenager.

As I regarded him, he chatted amiably about his move to the city, about his impressions of it, the places he had been to and what he had thought of them.

'And what do you think of the city?' he asked and paused. 'You're not a native?'

I shook my head. 'No,' I said, sensing he knew anyway, that he knew all about me, though we had but this moment met. 'I like the city,' I said. 'It agrees with me. The cafes, the narrow winding lanes, the squares.'

'And then there is the museum.'

'Have you been?'

'Of course.'

'And the Gardens?'

'Beautiful.'

'You must take the trip out of the city, to the forest and the old Summer Palace.'

'I would love to. I have heard it is beautiful at this time of the year. Say, why don't you come along, show me around?'

I nodded. 'Yes. Why not?'

He grinned. That large careless grin I had not seen on my own face, it seemed, in many years. He laid his hand on my knee.

'I'm keeping you up,' he apologized. Standing, he held out his hand. I shook it. 'Let's say this weekend?'

I nodded.

My hand tingled as he left. I stood in the centre of the room staring, dazed, at the door that had closed behind him. I slipped my left hand into my right. It had not felt like that. Our hands had fit like gloves. Such a strange sensation, to hold your own hand. To feel it the way another must. That is how it feels, I found myself thinking. Over and over I found myself thinking, so that is how I look. So that is how I sound. So that is how my hand feels as I lay it, carelessly, upon somebody's knee.

We took the train out of the city early on Saturday morning. The air was crisp and clear with the faint, sharp scent of winter approaching. The city quickly gave way to fields and then the railway lines plunged into the forest. My nervousness about the outing had grown as the days passed following our meeting. I could not sleep. Pacing the apartment, my mind spun madly. I began to convince myself that I had imagined the intensity of the likeness between us.

He rapped on the door at an early hour. He was wearing a beautiful coat and a silk scarf. I could not help admiring him, thinking, immodestly, how good he looked. It made me glow.

He was cheerful company. He reminded me of how I myself had been some years before. He did not seem to have become withdrawn, as I have. Curiously, as we made our way to the station and secured for ourselves a comfortable compartment in the first class carriage, nobody seemed to pay us much attention.

The Summer Palace lies thirty kilometers east of the city. The train pulled into the small station in the village, where we alighted.

We took a horse-drawn carriage of the kind laid on for tourists. As it was late September, and the season almost over, there was not a large crowd. The Great Lake shimmered through the turning leaves as we rode towards the Palace. The road was bronze from leaves already fallen.

The Palace was closed. We strolled, instead, down the long avenue of maples towards the lake. In the carriage we had fallen into a good-tempered argument. I goaded him as we ambled down the avenue kicking at the leaves; it amused and cheered me that he rejected my mocking and cynical attitude. I felt I had discovered a version of myself that had not been worn down over the years. The more we talked, the more I saw that here was not simply a mirror image of myself, but a reflection of a happier me, a version of myself I would very much like to have been.

The morning was warm. A neatly trimmed lawn sloped down to the lake. We sat down by the water's edge and he opened the wicker picnic hamper we had taken it in turns to carry. I noted he had packed a slim volume of poetry along with the local sparkling wine, and I leafed through it while he poured. As the sun glistened from the ruffled surface of the lake we read each other poems, argued, drank.

On the train back to the city I fell to sleep with the feeling of benign contentment enjoyed only by children and the dead. When I stirred, to see the lights of the city glimmering in the deepening dusk, I found my head was resting upon his shoulder. We parted at the door of my apartment. We said goodbye, but lingered, awkwardly. The light clicked off. In the gloom he held out his hand and I shook it. For some moments we stood like that, feeling the strangeness of our skin pressed against itself. Intimate, yet alien. We did not move until a door opened down the passage. He loosened his grip and turned away into the darkness. I closed the door behind me and rested my head against it.

He did not appear the following day. As it was a Sunday I had nothing pressing to take me from the apartment. I kicked around listening for the knock on the door. But he did not come. For some days I saw nothing of him. On the Tuesday I climbed the stairs and debated which of the apartments was his. For some time I stood deliberating what to do. I moved only when I heard the sound of footsteps descending the stairs.

Retreating to my apartment I poured myself a large glass of wine. I knew that it would be good for me to go out, if only to a bar, but I could not drag myself away. I did not even put music on for fear of not hearing him. I had worked my way halfway down the second bottle of wine when finally knuckles rapped on the wooden door.

It was midnight. He had been drinking, too. Silently he stood in the doorway, looking disheveled. Disheveled myself, I motioned for him to come in. We did not speak. He let his coat drop to the floor and slumped onto the sofa. I put on a recording of Verdi arias and poured ourselves each a glass of wine. When I turned, he was grinning. I grinned. A sense of communion deeper than ever I have experienced flushed through me.

I kneeled beside him and lifted the cuff of his shirt. The small, badly executed red rose. I undid my own shirt and showed him the tattoo on my wrist. He beamed. Pulling himself out of his shirt, he turned awkwardly and reached up to a pear shaped birthmark on his left shoulder blade. I laughed. I pulled off my own shirt and turned to show him. He giggled. Thinking fast, I pulled off my sock and displayed the way in which my toes crushed in each against the other. His too. Abruptly, laughing madly, we were pulling at each other's clothes, pointing, poking, until we were naked, identical. Identical. On the soft cushions of the sofa. I embraced myself. Felt the contours of my own body. Felt myself as Katya had felt me. As women have felt me. Strange and yet familiar. Alien and yet intimate. Foreign yet known.

I woke in the morning with a fever and was within hours delirious. How long I lay in that state I don't know. Occasionally I would wake and call out for him, but nobody answered. One day I awoke to find myself in the city's old hospital. Cold winter sunshine flushed my sheets a clinical, unappealing white. Looking through the window I could see that the trees had lost their leaves.

Yevgene Petrovich flicked open his amber inlaid cigarette case. There was only one of the *Davidoff's* left and politely he offered it me. I shook my head. A light sweat had broken out on my forehead and I wiped it away. Feeling inside my jacket pocket I found the quart bottle and pulled it out, taking a good slug. The train was moving into the dirty suburbs of Petersburg.

'It's a strange tale,' Yevgene muttered, lighting his last cigarette. He glanced at me and I did not know how to interpret the look. I took a second deep slug from the bottle and returned it to my inside pocket.

'Yes,' I agreed, 'It's a strange tale.'

I have not seen him. Not once. I have looked, of course. I scoured every corner of that city. I have asked, until I have known that it would be wiser for me to stop, judging by the looks I got. He is gone. And I cannot forget. Hour after hour I sat at the window of my apartment and gazed out. But I saw nothing. He has gone. I have gone.

Reversal

David Belbin

When I first told my employers the idea, they said it was impossible. Otherwise, why had nobody done it before? They underestimated me. The process worked, but there were political difficulties. Implementation would be complicated. Secret committees were swiftly set up. The President herself took an interest. One day, she called me in. It was our first meeting.

"Some things," she said, "are too important to be left up to politicians. The clock is ticking. Committees consider for ever while none of us are getting any younger. I want you to take charge. I'll back you every step of the way. Nobody will interfere as long as nothing goes seriously wrong."

In other words: *you're on your own. Screw up, and you're the scapegoat.* Then she asked me if I'd be able to perform the process on her.

"You're far too young," I said, affected (as most men were, or would be) by her magnetic presence, her matchless face, rich with character that resonated beyond beauty. "Why, you don't look a day over sixty."

She gave me a sideways, aquiline glance that informed me she wasn't susceptible to flattery.

"Not yet," she said. "I'll tell you when I'm ready."

When we had that meeting, the European President was seventy-three, seven years from mandatory retirement age. I was many years younger, but had already gone to seed. Who knew what state I'd be in if I got to her age, and I could expect to live a lot longer than that. In Europe, average life expectancy had reached over a hundred. An unnatural disaster. Evolution had not kept pace with medicine. The human body was designed to wear out by seventy, if you looked after it well. Some things could be fixed if enough money was available. Teeth were easy. Hair could be implanted. Cosmetic surgery worked wonders for the face (but couldn't do anything for the hands). Drugs could ward off senility and make you sexually virile — for a while, at least.

Yet there were always limits. No matter how rich you became, you still ended up with a saggy, wrinkled body, leaking from several orifices. You'd have a fading memory, feel ill much of the time and steadily became disconnected from society. Don't get me started on the problems caused by an ageing, overpopulated planet. Who wanted to end their life living like that?

Reversal's beauty is its simplicity. You're born old and you die young.

***

Finding subjects for the first trials was simple. All we needed were eighty- or ninety-somethings who still had most of their marbles and all of their limbs intact. Fatal illnesses were no problem. Curing them was a by-product of the process. A little memory loss was an advantage if you wanted to get into the program. The results would take years to verify, but this was acceptable, as the second phase would be at least five years in preparation.

Sooner than anticipated, we couldn't keep pace with the numbers coming forward. There was no need to experiment on subjects from care homes. We were inundated with enquiries from the rich and famous. Some offered substantial donations if I allowed them to become part of the program. By the time the five year period was up, the process was still secret, but not very. Coded comments appeared in the media. There was a certain amount of scare-mongering, but it came to little. The process was foolproof.

Meanwhile, in closed sessions, international laws were changed to legitimise the process. Retirement rules were adjusted to encompass the fact that people who had undergone the process aged in reverse. When these closed sessions were over, the politicians involved queued to see me, wanting to join the program themselves.

"What's the rush?" I asked. "Have the process early and you'll be shortening your lives."

According to the new laws, a person could only undergo reversal once. I assumed that people would want the longest life possible, eighty at least. But the politicians — and many others — weren't willing to wait. Most wanted to forget their seventies. Many were willing to forgo their sixties. They wanted to be young again. Some even challenged me.

"You're fifty-six, Professor, yet you don't look a day over forty-five. Are you sure you haven't undertaken the process yourself?"

Cosmetic surgery, I assured them. Soon, though, I had to give in. The laws weren't fully in place, but, for a big enough payment (and the reversee's signature on a document giving me immunity), I would do the deed. I began reversing people as young as fifty. Until recently, after all, a hundred years was considered an awfully long time to be alive.

As news of the process spread, the economy boomed. More housing was needed because so few were dying. We maintained official silence for as long as we could. There was so much we had to prepare society for. Yet, after a few years, even the masses couldn't help but cotton on. Retired sports heroes made startling comebacks. Ageing pop stars recovered their voices. Iconic beauties re-emerged in their prime. Advances in cosmetic surgery couldn't explain such startling changes.

Six years into the Reversal Project, the President came to see me. This was our second meeting and I was as affected by her as I had been at the first. Yet there had been a shift in the balance of power between us. I held the key to the future, and she was only two months from Europe's mandatory retirement age.

"It's time," she said.

I asked her to wait a few months. "Soon, we'll be in a position to offer the process to everybody who wants it."

"I want to be the one to break the news. I intend to announce that, in order to show the process is safe, I will undergo it myself, on my eightieth birthday. Just think, in ten years' time, you and I will be the same age."

This wasn't true, but I didn't contradict her.

"One thing bothers me, Madam President. In your speech, how are you going to explain Phase Three to the world?"

"It's not a problem," the President assured me. "People claim to care more about their children than themselves, but they don't mean it — even less so when they're talking about children who haven't been born yet."

"But, at some point, we're going to have to..."

The President frowned. I didn't complete the sentence.

"You deal with the science," she said. 'Leave public opinion to me."

Two months later, the President made what many listeners were expecting to be her retirement speech.

"Those of us living now are in a unique situation, one which will never be repeated in the history of our species," she told the world. "You may have heard the rumours but ignored them as fantasy, science fiction. Today, I tell you that they are true. Reversal exists. It is a proven technology. Those who undergo the reversal process age in reverse. Year after year they become younger until they are, at last, a babe in arms. Instead of dying after a decrepit, uncomfortable old age, they fade away young and healthy, in the comfort of their families.

"The process is not compulsory and will only be available for the next twenty years. Those undertaking it will be the first and last people to live, not once, but twice. Today is my eightieth birthday, the day when the law says I should retire. But today, instead, I intend to become a pioneer. I will be the first person to publicly undergo the process of reversal, demonstrating its safety to the world.

"In twenty years' time, all people will be born old. They will live for eighty or so years, until they slip, silently into non-being. Youth will no longer be wasted on the young, but will become the privilege of old age, a reward earned, a pleasure to be truly savoured."

She paused, took off her glasses and stared soulfully into the camera. "I leave now to undergo the process of rebirth. When you see me again, I will still be your President, but I will be younger. And the next week I will be younger still. And the week after that, and the week after that until — if I avoid accidents and the few remaining fatal diseases — I will once more be a child, fading happily back into the universe which created me. I thank you for listening, my fellow Europeans. I wish you all a long, fulfilling life."

The President's speech was greeted with great excitement. Polls showed that reversal was hugely popular. The waiting lists were huge. But the equipment was in place. We could reverse all who chose the process within a year. Not that the change was entirely plain sailing. Many people still believed in a god. According to them, reversal made a mockery of his creation. The owners of retirement homes brought a class action against the European government. Parliament made a modest settlement. We bought the buildings at knockdown prices for use as nurseries when phase three came on stream.

The process confused some people. It was a lot to take in. There were, unsurprisingly, a lot of questions about how people would be born in the future. Cartoonists showed teenage girls with enormous bellies carrying a fully grown old person in their womb. We didn't give an explanation, any more than we told people that, post-process, the reversee became infertile. They didn't need to know, but they would work it out. In time.

Reversal ended, once and for all, the world's overpopulation problem. World leaders fell over themselves to join the program. The process we used couldn't be described as ethical, but it worked. Chemical weapons were outlawed, but research on them had never stopped. It was easy to develop a gas that would render every single person on the planet infertile. Once this was released, the old way of having children was finished with. From then on, every single person would be born the new way. Old.

While all these changes were taking place, I grew younger. As many have found before me, using one's self as a subject is often the only principled way to prove that an idea works. I underwent the process when I was fifty. By forty, I was twenty years younger than my wife, Elsa, who said she wanted to wait until her eightieth birthday before undergoing the process. We separated. (As it turned out, Elsa, along with many others, never chose to undergo reversal at all.)

I started seeing a famous actress four years younger than myself. She had been my first celebrity reversee (having insisted on undergoing the process the day she reached fifty). We remained together until, at thirteen, she began her reverse puberty. It was an amicable parting. I was seventeen then, with exploding hormones. It would be nice to think that I had learnt enough to make the most of my second teenage years, but I hadn't. Oh, the girls flocked to me because of my celebrity. Yet, as a teenager who had lived for eighty-three years, I found it hard to relate to my peers. I became lonely and oddly vulnerable — much like the first time round.

The years after they dropped the infertility bomb were one of the most exhilarating times in human history, but also one of the most confusing. Privacy laws hadn't been abolished. Nobody wanted their real age in the public domain and I had my own reasons for keeping things this way. And confusion can be creative, exciting. It was a wild time. The results of reversal took years to become apparent. This was a recipe for trouble. Friendships fractured. Families were wrecked by intergenerational confusion.

Say you're in a bar. The majority of people there are in their first lifetime, growing older. But a few — maybe more than a few — are on their way down. See those two twenty-something women by the pinball machine? The younger looking one is the other's grand-mother. That fifty year old guy at the bar is drinking because his wife had a reversal without telling him. She just left him for a younger man. He still loves her. He might get her back if he goes for an early reversal, like she did. But if he waits a few years, he'll still be cruis-ing bars when she's a kid. See that distinguished looking old woman, being asked to show her ID? She must be sixty-five if she's a day. But the barman's throwing her out, because the woman's part of the third phase. She's only fifteen years old.

Do the members of the third phase, who will only live once, resent us? No. They see the sense in the process. They know that their lives can only get better. By sixty, they will be at university, or in their first job. By forty, they will be at the height of their careers, ready to bring up old children of their own. At twenty-five, they can retire, and enjoy the best years of their lives in perfect health, looked after by loving children who, in turn, are in the prime of their lives. If there is a creator, I have improved on its design.

The hardest concept for people to get their heads around was that of being born old. Let's go to the places we all used to dread ending up in, the old folk's home, or nursery, as we call them now. Look at all those people with lined faces and bent backs. Now, tell me: which are the unreversed old, and which are the young?

You can't tell them apart, can you? But look closer. Some are teach-ing the others: how to walk, how to read. They're telling them stories, singing songs. See that room over there? Toilet training. Where do these new old people come from? They were created from carefully selected DNA and grown in a laboratory. When they are ready to leave, in three or four years' time, they will be allocated par-ents.

Being born old was the final phase of the reversal process. The children's bodies are nourished and matured in expandable sterile units. The new World Government controls the nature of their parent DNA and decides exactly how many children will be born. Projections take into account future labour needs combined with efficient distribution of the world's resources. Since the infertility bomb was dropped, third world poverty has become a memory. Everybody still living on Earth has a quality of life inconceivable a century ago. Reversal has worked.

Were you to see me now, you'd wonder why, when I have just described myself aged seventeen, you have in front of you a very old man. Eighty-one years ago I performed the first public reversal, on the President. Fifty-seven years have passed since I performed my final, private reversal.

I told the world that double reversal was an impossibility. This was a lie. I performed the process just once, when I was sixteen for the second time. The President (she'd long since become the World President) knew what I was up to, but we kept it secret. Sixteen years after that second reversal, my demise was reported. The obituaries were fulsome. I was *the architect of the modern world, the man who thought the unthinkable.* The President herself described me as the greatest man she had ever known. She used the occasion of my funeral to give notice that she intended to retire in four years time, when she would be forty-four (thirty-six in the old sense — she would have lived for a hundred and twenty-four years and been President for sixty of those). She intended, she said, to enjoy her youth to the full. What the President, but nobody else, knew, was that, in four years, for the first time in the century we had known each other, the President and I would be the same age.

You didn't realise this was a love story, did you?

***

Over the last eighty-seven years, society has changed utterly. People no longer think of themselves as living backwards. The words *old* and *young* have lost their meanings. Third-phasers replaced them with new, subtler words that describe the precise condition of every

119

aspect of a person. One of the greatest benefits of the Third Phase has only recently become clear. Third-phasers reach their prime mental and physical condition at the end of their careers, rather than at the beginning. People still do their best work in their thirties and twenties. However, now, instead of lingering on for thirty years afterwards, they retire at the height of their success.

The biggest upheaval was in the Arts. For the breed who came after reversal, the past was a closed book. Most literature lost much of its meaning. Poems, plays, even paintings presented a world the Third-phasers could not relate to. Yet people still thirsted for Art. New work had to be created, and quickly. New forms arose, while others became obsolete. There had never, the President said in her retirement speech, been a more exciting period to be alive. "To be young and at the same time to be very old is a miracle beyond our wildest imaginings," she said.

The President and I embraced our secluded, private life. The first twenty years were one, long honeymoon, our joy heightened by the accumulated wisdom of two lifetimes and the certain knowledge that her remaining time was short, and must be fully savoured. They were a glorious reward for over two centuries of accumulated labour.

Who can blame me, wanting more?

When I was fifty-six and the President sixteen, I suggested to her that she undergo a second reversal, while I undergo a third. In another twenty years, we would again appear to be exactly the same age. The practicalities weren't a problem. We could, if we chose, continue like this forever.

"I don't want that," the President told me. "A hundred and forty-four years is a long time to be alive. I'm looking forward to experiencing childhood again. Have another reversal yourself if you're sure you want to, but promise that you'll wait until I'm gone."

I appreciated her reasoning. In our hideaway, the few people we met took me to be a Third-phaser, the vigorous toy boy of a much older mistress. Yet, I was often weary, too. I longed to reverse, to slowly shrink until I was an unsustainable embryo, small enough to be buried in a matchbox.

I kept my promise and waited, caring for the President until last year, when she faded away. The crowd at her state funeral was awash with small people in their hundred and forties or fifties. Nobody recognised me.

After the President's death, government officials found me in her home. I couldn't tell them who I was — not without confessing that I had undergone an illegal, second reversal. Such a confession would destroy my place in history and put the President's legacy in danger. So I let them think I was a Third-phaser who the President had secretly adopted.

They put me in a junior school, where other people my age had only been alive for seven years. Then they decided I'd lied about my age and moved me to the Infants. Here, they treat me as a slow child, one of the DNA identification process's few failure, because my memory is failing. And it's getting worse. I can't remember how much I'm supposed to know.

Why haven't I reversed myself again? Because, in line with the President's personal directive — which she kept a secret, even from me — all the equipment used for reversal was destroyed, decades ago. The technology needed for reversal has been outlawed. I am too old, too feeble to reinvent it.

She was a wise woman, my mistress, my President. She made sure that, after her death, there would be no double reversals, let alone triple ones; there would be no reversals at all. No chance, consequently, of eternal life. People would live once, with a life span decided strictly according to the planet's ability to sustain it.

There are still people left who have lived twice, one life less than mine. Most of them are toddlers, or they will be, soon. They live in the lap of luxury, where they are revered as wise children, a fragile link to the past. We have much in common, these toddlers and I, but I can't get near them. After my stroke, I tried to tell the truth. But no-one understands the words coming out of my mouth. I live my days out in this cot, wearing diapers, only half awake, feeding from a tube, dreaming, shitting, peeing, remembering, waiting for the day I become the last person on earth to die of old age.

PMQ

Robert Harris

PRIME MINISTER: With your permission, Mr Speaker, I wish to make a statement to the House regarding certain incidents of a personal nature. Some of these incidents have, in the past few days, entered the public domain in a lurid and garbled form, and a number of my ministerial colleagues have urged me to take the first available opportunity to set the record straight. This, with the indulgence of the House, I now propose to do.

Incident at the Greenford Park Service Station
At approximately five o'clock last Friday afternoon I left No. 10 Downing Street as usual to travel to the Prime Minister's official country residence at Chequers for the weekend. The party consisted of two cars. The advance car contained myself, a duty secretary from the Downing Street staff, a driver, and a protection officer from the Metropolitan Police. The backup vehicle contained three additional protection officers.

For several years it has been my practice to take advantage of long car journeys as an opportunity to work. Among the documents which had been prepared for my attention on this occasion was the weekly digest of press coverage compiled for me by my Chief Press Secretary.

I have arranged for a copy of this document, which carries no security restriction, to be placed in the Library of the House. Honourable Members who consult it will see that it conveys frankly, and with detailed quotation, the whole spectrum of press comment about myself as it had appeared in the previous week's newspapers. The comment was, as usual, robust; some might say robust in the extreme. However, I have always taken the view that a free press is an essential element of a free society, and that, if you are in public life, you must, as Kipling has it,

"...bear to hear the truth you've spoken
Twisted by knaves to make a trap for fools..."

The route taken to Chequers is frequently varied for security reasons, and it is not official policy to disclose it. Therefore I shall not do so now. Suffice it to say that the traffic heading west out of London on this particular evening was unusually heavy, even for a wet Friday evening in the pre-Christmas period, and that, after an hour of travelling, we had managed to proceed only as far along the A40 as the Greenford Roundabout, a distance of some seven miles.

It was at this point — that is, at approximately 6pm — that I began to feel unwell. The principal symptom was one of acute nausea, brought on, no doubt, by the effort of trying to read in a car which was repeatedly stopping and starting. I needed fresh air. Unfortunately, for security reasons, the windows of my official car are not designed to open. I put aside the press digest and directed my protection officers to pull in to the next available service station, informing them that I needed to use the lavatory. This request was radioed to the backup car and a few moments later we turned off the A40 onto the forecourt of what I now know to be the Greenford Park Service Station.

I must emphasise that the responsibility for what followed is mine, and mine alone. No blame should be attached to my protection officers, who behaved throughout in their usual exemplary and professional manner. Having checked that the gentleman's lavatory was unoccupied, and having secured the area immediately in front of it, it was on my express orders that they remained outside whilst I went inside, locking the door behind me. Nobody else was present.

Several newspapers have described what followed as a "moment of madness." It would be more accurate, Mr Speaker, to describe it as a series of small but logical steps, whose cumulative effect was to prove fateful. On entering the cubicle I noticed that behind the lavatory basin was a window. This window was slightly open. By standing on the lavatory seat, I discovered that it was possible to open the window fully. I was thus able to bring my face into contact with some much-needed air. Only then did it occur to me that the aperture was, in fact, just large enough for the insertion of my head and shoulders. As the air was having a beneficial effect, this prospect seemed appealing. Unfortunately I then made what was to prove a regrettable miscalculation with regard to my centre of gravity. Questions have been asked about the failure of my protection officers to hear the noise of my exit via the window, but I can assure the House that the roar of the nearby traffic on the wet road was more than sufficient to drown out any sound I may have made.

I left the lavatory in a head-first position and it was this, rather than any subsequent event — and contrary to reports in the media — which produced the slight bruising and abrasions still visible on my face and hands.

It may be that I was rendered temporarily unconscious by my descent. I cannot recall. If I was, it was certainly only for a few moments. Upon rising to my feet, I found myself in a small area, enclosed by walls on three sides. To my left was a gap leading to an automatic car-washing machine. Honourable Members will understand that, given the time of year, it was now quite dark. I had also lost a contact lens. Finding the space in which I was standing claustrophobic, and feeling slightly groggy from the effects of my fall, I ventured out along the side of the car-wash. As the various diagrams printed in the press have shown, I was now invisible from the forecourt, and it was this route which, as chance would have it, led me away from the garage and out onto a neighbouring street.

I have learned subsequently that my protection officers waited two or three minutes before first knocking on the lavatory door and then, on receiving no reply, breaking it down. By then, however, I was several hundred yards to the south. There was, I repeat, nothing they could have done, and no blame attaches to them in this regard.

Telephone Call to No. 10

At this stage of the evening, as I am sure the House will appreciate, I had no particular plan in mind. It may well be that I was slightly concussed. At any event, I was content simply to follow my footsteps where they led me, enjoying the refreshing sensation of the damp night air. Ferrymead Gardens took me to Millet Road which gave on to Beechwood Avenue and later Melrose Close — street names which, more eloquently than I can hope to do, describe the peaceful English suburb in which I found myself. I felt no sensation of danger; rather the reverse.

I am aware that my actions have since been described in the media as "a gross dereliction of duty" (*Daily Telegraph*) and "an unprecedented endangering of national security" (*The Times*). Yet, as the noble lord, Lord Jenkins, has pointed out (in today's *Evening*

125

Standard), there is an historical precedent. On the night of 4 May 1915, Herbert Asquith walked from Mansfield Street, near Oxford Circus, to Downing Street, lost in thought about his feelings for Miss Venetia Stanley, who had just disclosed to him her intention of marrying one of his Cabinet colleagues. If one Prime Minister can walk the London streets unprotected during wartime, why cannot another do the same in peacetime? Does a Prime Minister not enjoy the same civil liberties as any other citizen of the United Kingdom? These are questions which the House may wish to ponder.

Of course, I was aware of the undoubted anxiety which I was by now causing to those who were concerned for my welfare. Accordingly, I took steps to reassure them, The duty log of the No. 10 switchboard records that at 6.27pm a caller claiming to be the Prime Minister attempted to make a reverse charge call to the Downing Street Press Office from a public telephone box in Greenford. The same caller tried again two minutes later. On this second occasion I was finally able to convince the switchboard operator of my identity, and my call was put through. The House will thus see that within approximately twenty minutes of my alleged disappearance, my office was aware that I was safe and well and acting of my own free will. So much for the so-called "night of frantic worry" (*Daily Mail*) to which I am supposed to have subjected them.

My Chief Press Secretary, with characteristic presence of mind, took a careful note of our conversation, and I have arranged for a copy of his record also to be placed in the Library of the House. According to this note, I told him not to worry about me, and reassured him that in due course I would return to Downing Street, of my own volition. He frankly disapproved of this plan. He believed my actions would quickly become public and provoke damaging speculation in the media. He urged me in strong terms to stay where I was, adding that he would arrange for my protection officers to pick me up: they were, he informed me, at that very moment patrolling the neighbourhood looking for me. The duty log shows that I terminated this conversation at 7.01pm.

It was raining quite steadily by now, the streets were quiet, and the realisation was suddenly born upon me that unless I took swift and decisive action to vacate the area, I was likely to face the embarrassing situation of being apprehended by my own security officers.

Irrational as it may seem with hindsight, I was seized with a powerful desire to postpone such an encounter, at least for a little while longer. But how was it to be avoided? A taxi, if one could be procured, was the obvious solution. But now I faced a further, and unanticipated, problem.

The House may be aware that the first thing a Prime Minister loses on taking office is his passport, which is removed from him by his Private Office to ease his official travel arrangements. The second thing to go is his ready money. Why, after all, does a Prime Minister need cash? How would he spend it if he had it? Where would he obtain it if he wanted it? The sudden realisation that I had no money placed me in a quandary.

It was then that I noticed that the telephone call box in which I was sheltering stood adjacent to a small row of commercial premises. Among them was a branch of my own bank. I had retained my personal cheque card from my days as Leader of the Opposition, and it was the work of but a few moments to hurry across the pavement and insert it into the automatic telling machine (ATM). However, my relief quickly evaporated when I realised I had only a vague recollection of my personal identification number (PIN). On my third attempt to enter my PIN, the ATM informed me that it had retained my card.

My reason for giving the House these apparently minor details is to make it easier to comprehend the sequence of events which followed. I was wearing only a light business suit. I was thoroughly wet. I was cold. I was eager to be on my way. The only object on me, I realised, which had any monetary value, was an inscribed wristwatch, given to me during the last G8 summit by the President of the United States.

The sequence of events by which this wristwatch came to be in the possession of a fifteen-year-old schoolgirl, has also excited considerable media speculation, most of it of an utterly fantastical nature. The facts are more prosaic.

"Miss B"

As luck would have it, no taxis were available to hire in that particular part of Greenford at that time of the evening, either for cash or barter. Venturing into the road, I therefore attempted to flag down a

127

passing motorist. Perhaps not surprisingly, the spectacle of a man bearing a striking resemblance to the Prime Minister, bleeding slightly from a grazed forehead, looming out of the darkness on a rainy Friday night with his suit jacket held over his head, caused him to panic. Far from slowing down, he accelerated away, a pattern of behaviour repeated by several other motorists as I made my way up and down the centre of Ferrymead Avenue in search of assistance.

It was at this point that I became aware of another pedestrian on that stretch of road — a pedestrian bending, as it seemed to me, to unlock the door of a parked car. This other person — a female person — who, because of her age, cannot be named for legal reasons — is the person who has since become known in the media as "Miss B."

I cannot, at this stage, remember precisely which of us initiated the conversation that now took place. It may be that Miss B, as I shall also call her, hailed me in a jocular spirit, or I may have approached her. It is not, in any case, a relevant detail. I naturally assumed her to be the owner of the vehicle beside which she was standing, or at any rate a person authorised by the owner of the vehicle to drive that vehicle away, or; at the very least, the holder of a current UK driver's licence. I also accepted at face value her explanation that the vehicle was mechanically defective, and therefore needed to be started by the unorthodox procedure of opening the bonnet and connecting certain cables in the ignition, a technique which, my Right Honourable Friend the Home Secretary informs me, is known as "hot-wiring."

Some will no doubt accuse me of naivety in this matter. That is for the House and the country to judge. The essence of the situation is that I asked a person whom I assumed to be a competent driver to give me a lift, that she at first demurred, that I then offered her as payment the wristwatch to which I made reference earlier, and that she then agreed to drive me wherever I wished to go. The whole case is now in the hands of the Crown Prosecution Service and I am advised that it would be prejudicial for me to comment further on a situation where legal action may be pending.

It was, I should estimate, approximately 7.20pm when, with Miss B at the wheel, we pulled out of Ferrymead Avenue at the start of what was to prove an eventful journey. By this time, unknown to me, British Telecom engineers had pinpointed the precise location of the telephone box from which I had contacted the Downing Street Press Office, my Principal Private Secretary had been alerted, and the Head of Special Branch and the Director General of the Security Service, in consultation with the Commissioner of the Metropolitan Police, had issued orders for the area to be sealed off. The emergency services had responded immediately with their usual superb professionalism. The underground stations of Greenford, South Greenford, Drayton Green and Hanwell had all been closed, and a rudimentary vehicle checkpoint (VCP) was already in operation, blocking access from Oldfield Lane South to the Greenford Roundabout.

It was towards this VCP that Miss B now accelerated.

Journey into London

My precise recollection of what followed is hazy. According to Miss B, as quoted in yesterday's *News of the World*, I shouted "Go, go, go." I believe, in fact, that my actual words were "No, no, no," and that, in the heat of the moment, she misheard me. The truth may never be known. What is not in dispute is that an offence was now committed under the provisions of the 1972 Road Traffic Act, in that our vehicle failed to stop when requested to do so by a police officer. I deeply regret this.

In her account of the night's events, as related in the *News of the World*, Miss B asserts that she had no idea that I was Prime Minister. I believe this to be true. She certainly did not seem to me to be the kind of young person who would follow political events at all closely. When I told her who I was, and that the wristwatch which she was now wearing had been given to me by the President of the United States, she responded with an exclamation of frank disbelief.

I am aware that I have been widely criticised for failing to recognise that she was of school age. It was, however, as I have pointed out, dark; I may well have been suffering the effects of concussion; I had lost a contact lens; and the photographs of Miss B reproduced in the *News of the World* — even with her face masked to protect her identity — show, as I am sure the House would agree, a person of unusually mature appearance.

Her driving skills were also those of a person many years in advance of her true age. The noise of pursuit soon died away and we found ourselves on the A40 heading east, back towards central

London — the very road along which I had been travelling to Chequers a bare ninety minutes before.

Honourable Members may perhaps imagine the thoughts which were running through my mind. I was beginning to see that my actions could indeed be open to widespread misinterpretation, as my Chief Press Officer had warned me they would be. It was now clear that a considerable police operation was under way in the Greenford area. I had obviously inconvenienced many people. Given the numbers involved, there was little chance of what had happened not becoming public at some stage. I needed to think quickly what I should do. Miss B took the view, and expressed it forcibly, that continuing on our present course along the A40 would foreshorten that thinking time considerably, I concurred. Accordingly, we left the A40 at the Hanger Lane interchange and joined the North Circular Road.

Perhaps I might now quote to the House from Miss B's account in the *News of the World*:

> I said to him, 'Are you really the Prime Minister?' He said he was. He seemed like a nice bloke. He'd gone very quiet. He said he was worried he was going to get me into a lot of trouble. He said the papers were going to come after me. I said, 'No way. You're kidding me.' He said, 'You've no idea what they're like.'
>
> He asked if I lived with someone who would look after me? Did I have a husband? I said no way: my dad was inside and my mum had done a runner and I lived with my gran. He said, 'So how old are you then? Eighteen? Nineteen?' I said, 'Fifteen,' and he kind of groaned and went very quiet again. I thought I'd turn on the radio to cheer him up.

Mr Speaker, it has been asked — and fairly asked — why, at this stage of the evening, I did not simply direct Miss B to pull off the road, and await the inevitable arrival of the police. With hindsight, of course, this is what I should have done. I was in a vehicle clearly being driven by someone not qualified to do so. But my situation at the time appeared to me more complicated. Miss B has been kind enough to indicate, via the *News of the World*, that I seemed like "a nice bloke." May I, across the havoc of the past few days, return the compliment, and say that she seemed a nice young woman?

And there was something more. In the drama of the preceding minutes, a bond had sprung up between us — a purely platonic bond, I hasten to add — but a bond nonetheless, which meant that I now felt acutely responsible for the situation in which I had placed her. I knew only too well what was likely to happen to her, a vulnerable schoolgirl, if her part in the night's events became known to the media. Could some means be found of extricating her from this sorry tangle? Our best hope was surely to remove ourselves as far as possible from the scene of police operations, and it was for this reason, as much as any other, that we continued our journey across London, eventually leaving the North Circular Road at the Brent Cross Shopping Centre, and travelling south down North End Road towards the borough of Hampstead.

"Mr A"

I have quoted Miss B as telling the *News of the World* that it was her idea to switch on the car radio. I was frankly curious to know whether any word of the night's dramas had yet reached the media. As it happened, the owner of the vehicle — to whom I have since written a letter of apology — had left the radio tuned to a news station, and immediately I found myself listening to an interview regarding my recent performance as Prime Minister. The House will perhaps understand if I say that I felt a sudden sensation of dread. My political life, if not exactly passing before my eyes, seemed at any rate to be passing rapidly before my ears. However, as the broadcast continued, I realised that the interview, which was part of a regular political programme, had in fact been prerecorded. The tone of the comments being broadcast was one of characteristically lofty abuse and I recognised at once the voice of the speaker: a columnist whom I knew personally, and whose work appears regularly in a number of publications, among them the *Guardian* and the *Observer*. His name will be familiar to members on both sides of the House. For legal reasons, I shall call him Mr A.

Honourable Members who take the trouble to consult the weekly press summary which I have had placed in the Library will see that it contains several quotations from Mr A's recent journalism. By a curious coincidence, I had been re-reading these quotations earlier in the evening, at around the moment when I was stricken with nausea.

In the *Guardian*, for example, he had, written:

> The Prime Minister is, by common consent, a little man: 'a pet-tyfogging political pygmy,' was how one of his Cabinet colleagues described him at a private meeting last week. The gap between his personal qualities and the importance of the office he holds grows daily ever more embarrassingly apparent.

And in the *Observer*:

> It should surprise no one to learn that the Prime Minister is a liar. Lying, after all, is the essence of the politician's craft. What should surprise us — and what alarms his colleagues — is that he is such a bad liar. He is a true phoney: an authentic fraud. As one senior Cabinet Minister recently remarked: 'He's the sort of man who, if he kept a brothel, would bring prostitution into disrepute.'

There is more in a similar vein, but perhaps the House will excuse me if I confine myself to these two, fairly typical illustrations.

As I said at the outset of my statement, I have always believed strongly in the tradition of robust press comment as an essential part of our democratic system. I have nothing against journalists as such. Far from it. I had seen Mr A socially on a number of occasions, both before and after I became Prime Minister. I had been to his house. He had been to mine. He had sent me his books when they were published. I had presented his recent award at the annual *What the Papers Say* lunch when he was made Columnist of the Year. I had always made efforts to be friendly towards him. His position in the political spectrum was roughly the same as mine. He should have been, if not a friend, then at least an ally. Yet in print, for reasons I had never understood, he adopted a stance of unwavering criticism. I return to the account given by Miss B:

> This posh guy on the radio was really slagging him off, so I said something like, 'Sounds like this f***er really hates your guts.' And he said, 'Yes, but he's always very nice to my face.' So I said, 'You mean to tell me you know the guy?' And he said

yes he did, that he used to see him a bit. And I said, 'Well, it's none of my business, but don't you think he's due a sorting, the way he's going on?' And he looked out of the window and he thought about it for a bit, and then he said that funnily enough the f***er lived somewhere around here.

Incident in Hampstead

In deciding to visit Mr A at his home I was aware that I was embarking on a potentially hazardous course. On the other hand, I took the view that I was by this stage

"... in blood
Stepped in so far that, should I wade no more,
Returning were as tedious as go o'er."

By which I do not mean to imply that I consciously intended to do Mr A any actual physical injury, but rather that I had by now concluded that my recent actions would, regardless of what I did, become public knowledge very soon. Once that happened, it did not require much effort on my part to imagine what Mr A himself would have to say about my conduct. The prospect of for once seizing the initiative — of, to use Miss B's phrase, giving him "a sorting," whatever that may mean — held a certain undeniable appeal.

As I have already told the House, our route from Greenford had now carried us as far as Hampstead, the district in which Mr A has for many years lived. I know the area well. As a backbench MP, I had lived around the corner from Mr A in a basement flat. His own, substantial, four-storey house was familiar to me, and I directed Miss B to the appropriate street. For a moment, after we had parked outside, I hesitated. Was this, on reflection, really a sensible course? But then I resolved that I would continue. The media, after all, had frequently turned up uninvited on my doorstep over the years. Why should I not do the same to one of them? I left the car and rang the bell, Mr A himself answered the door.

Mr Speaker, I cannot claim to have the events of the next few minutes arranged with perfect forensic clarity in my mind. I recall that Mr A greeted me with his usual civility, and that he was carrying a bottle of champagne and a half-full glass. He did not seem particularly pleased to see me. He was, he said, expecting dinner guests at any moment, and made a general indication of regret that he was therefore unable to invite me in. Perhaps, he suggested, my office could contact his secretary and we could arrange a suitable date for an appointment the following week.

It was at this point that Miss B left the car and joined me on the doorstep. Her appearance on the scene seemed to affect Mr A's composure. She began quoting back to him several of the points he had been making earlier on the radio, and invited him to step over the threshold and repeat them. He seemed both confused and alarmed by her presence. I explained that she had recently come to work at No. 10 as part of a work experience scheme. This statement, which was part of my continuing efforts to protect her identity, was misleading, and I regret it. He finally agreed to admit us, and asked us to go upstairs and wait for him in his study, while he made arrangements, he said, for one of his domestic staff to greet his guests in his place.

The suggestion in various newspapers that, once in his study, I "ransacked" his desk is absurd. The truth is that the room was relatively small and it was almost impossible for me to avoid glancing at his computer screen and seeing what was written there — namely, his column for that Sunday's issue of the *Observer*. It included the following passage:

Unable, it seems, to tolerate even the mildest criticism, the Prime Minister is said by close colleagues to be exhibiting worrying signs of mental instability. 'All Prime Ministers go mad eventually,' one of his senior Cabinet colleagues told me privately last week. 'The difference is that this one was mad from the start.'

I was still reading when Mr A entered the room.

I now proceeded to make a number of points, of which perhaps four stand out in my memory: first, that it was a pity, given his obvious genius for public administration, that he had never seen fit to offer himself for election; secondly, that it was richly ironic for a journalist, of all people, to accuse all politicians of habitually lying, as I had yet to read any article in any newspaper on any subject of which I had any knowledge that didn't contain at least one factual inaccuracy; thirdly, that I considered it morally contemptible of him to quote anonymous so-called "senior colleagues" who, I was sure, had better things to do than pass the time of day with him; and, fourthly, that if I was mad — and I was beginning to suspect that I might be, for choosing to be a Prime Minister when I could have been a newspaper columnist — then I had surely been driven mad by him, and by people like him.

Mr A responded that he had, indeed, considered a political career during his time at Oxford, but had concluded that real power no longer resided in this House, which was full — I believe I am quoting him correctly — of "little people"; secondly, that he had no views as to the respective merits of journalism and politics, except to observe that nowadays the former offered better rewards, in every sense, and therefore attracted individuals of greater talent; thirdly, that no journalist ever reveals his sources; and finally that he had no particular animus against me personally, but took the impartial view that all politicians were mad and liars, and therefore that whoever was Prime Minister at any given time was, by definition, likely to be the biggest and maddest liar of the lot.

I am not sure precisely how long this conversation lasted. As the House will recall, I no longer had a watch. Nor can I say for certain when I first realised that Mr A was deliberately keeping me occupied. But I should say that roughly twenty minutes had elapsed when Miss B, who had taken up a position by the window, suddenly interrupted our discussion to report that the street below was filling with policemen and photographers. It was then that Mr A disclosed that he had misled us. He had not, in fact, left us alone in order to speak to one of his staff, but rather to alert the picture desk of a national newspaper. The House will appreciate that, until the Crown Prosecution Service has decided whether or not to initiate criminal proceedings, I am not at liberty to describe as fully as I would wish to do exactly what happened next. No party has yet been charged with a criminal offence, and unless and until that happens, Mr A has a right to anonymity. Miss B's published account is, frankly, incoherent. What is not in dispute is that witnesses heard voices raised, and that at some point Mr A and myself both fell, entwined, down the stairs, landing in the hall at exactly the moment when, as luck would have it, the front door opened to admit the first of Mr A's dinner guests, my Right Honourable Friend the Chancellor of the Exchequer.

Conclusion

Mr Speaker, I have tried to set out the facts as clearly and unemotionally as possible. Someone — I think it may have been Abraham Lincoln, or possibly it was Winston Churchill — once wrote that a night in a police cell is good for any man, and I feel that I have personally benefited from this experience. I have been treated as any other citizen would have been under the circumstances, and that is all I have ever sought.

To have been allowed to serve this country has been a great privilege. Over the course of the next few hours, I shall be having further discussions with my ministerial colleagues and others, and later this evening I hope to have an audience of Her Majesty the Queen. After that my own personal position will be clearer.

No doubt much more will be said on these matters in the days and weeks to come. In the meantime, it only remains for me to thank you, Mr Speaker, and through you the House, for the courtesy you have shown in listening to my personal statement.

The Nurture Table

Clare Brown

It was my custom, developed over many years, to observe teachers new to the school without their knowledge; just thirty seconds of watching through the glass at a slight angle and listening to the muffled but usually audible voice, before a brisk knock and push of the door took me into full view of pupils and teacher alike. I was on the look-out for any changes my arrival might elicit: a start, a frown, a tightening of the lips. I have always liked to know to what extent my staff are *at odds with themselves*. A teacher whose tone or posture is transformed at the appearance of the Headmistress is rarely sufficiently convincing, to colleagues or pupils, to succeed in the role.

Ms Craven's reaction to my entrance into the classroom on her first day with us was thoroughly gratifying. Through the window I could see that she was both animated and relaxed and I could hear her speaking confidently. When I eventually breezed in her manner was easy, natural, considerate. All of the qualities which had appealed to her interview panel were very much in evidence and when I left the room, having concluded the brief bit of business I needed with her, I was feeling almost smug at our having made such an excellent choice. She would certainly lead our current crop of Year Twos through their work and play with exactly the right balance of diligence and imagination which a seven-year old requires.

Perhaps it was that smugness, or its sticky remnants, which closed my eyes to what I should have known was a potentially dangerous venture, although I could scarcely have begun to guess how that danger would manifest itself, and with what gravity, when Ms Craven introduced her ambitious idea for the Spring Term Project.

It emerged just before half-term, when I was still occasionally indulging in my surreptitious observations through the glass. I remember that she stood next to the nature table and the tone of her voice indicated that she was reaching a conclusion so I waited before entering and heard her say "....so, Green Class, instead of bringing in all the things you would normally put on the nature table — all

137

the eggshells and twiggy bits which are getting rather whiffy over here...." (she waited for the expected titter, which dutifully came), "...I want you to bring something which is not 'natural', not a leaf or a pebble, but which has a special meaning for each of *you*. Remember, it should be an object which has helped make you what you are — perhaps you have learnt something from it, or it's helped you make a decision. Maybe it made you change, or feel different about yourself. If it's precious please make sure you ask a grown-up if you can take it to school, and don't let's have anything which might rot, like all this yukky stuff..." she wrinkled her nose towards the table, and the children laughed again, forgetting in an instant how Mrs Rhys had carefully arranged and labelled the autumnal treasures they'd collected just before her retirement at Christmas. As I pushed the door open, Ms Craven continued, "...and can you remember what we are going to call this new display, Green Class? Not a Nature Table, but a —"

"Nurture Table!"

"That's right, well remembered everyone. Now, what do we say to the headmistress?"

"Good afternoon Miss Wright," they choroused. I smiled.

"Hello children. I just need a quick word with Ms Craven so perhaps you can look at your reading books for a minute...."

But she interjected: "How about finishing off the worksheet we've been looking at? Remember, put all the actions we can do *naturally* under Nature and all the things we need to *learn* under Nurture." Thirty heads bent to the task and she turned to me with such a sparkle in her clear grey eyes that the note of warning I had wished to impart melted into a weak enthusiasm.

"That does sound complicated, Jennifer! Are you doing it as part of PSE?"

"Yes, I've wanted to try it for a while. It would be a shame if the Personal and Social Education element of the curriculum became completely overrun with all that Citizenship stuff; I thought that we could do something new with the old nature table idea by looking at some of the other forces in the world, things that *shape* us, instead of just looking at Nature as something *outside* and — collectable."

It sounded so plausible, and she seemed so earnest, and I couldn't tune in to the little waves of panic which her words engendered in me;

they were too subtle. I did try, even at that early stage, to voice some concerns. "I wonder if it's wise to ask the children to bring in something which seems to be so very personal and — *totemic*. It depends so much on their home lives..." I scanned the classroom and my eyes rested on a few pupils; the ones who never had a costume for the play or money for the museum trip, the ones whose 'contact in case of emergency' forms were never filled in and returned. There was Joseph, his light brown curls doubtless crawling with lice as usual and Kayley, whose school dinner was obviously her only proper meal in the day. And of course Guy and Gareth, the only pair of identical twins in twenty-five years of teaching whom I couldn't tell apart, who never spoke unless spoken to and even then some of their words were half-formed. "...windfall chestnuts are available for everyone to pick up; what about the children who don't have the sort of — *resources* — you're talking about? For instance, the Hughes boys..."

Ms Craven interrupted swiftly. "I've thought of that, and if one or two of the children seem to be at a loss then I'll make some discreet suggestions about the sorts of things they could bring in. Don't worry, Pamela, please. This is an exercise that will get the children thinking about their place in the world a lot more than getting them to vote for class reps or produce anti-bullying posters."

Of course, this was precisely the problem. There are many things seven year olds needn't think about but there are some which they *shouldn't* think about. And their tiny place in the big wide world, however secure and cosy a place it appears to be, definitely falls into the latter category. But I didn't say so. I allowed myself to be seduced by that light in Ms Craven's eye which seemed to say — trust me, I know what I'm doing, this is a new way and you only know the old way; I will show you the direction in which we can move towards discovery.

I must have wanted her to show me that direction more than I knew, because any other teacher, at any other time, would not have been able to bamboozle me. The governors and PTA were right to chide me for allowing free rein to an untested young woman and her fancy ideas from college. But that was never how she seemed, and now I'm not at all sure that her enthusiasm wasn't zeal, or that her eyes were not shining, but *glinting*. I have shouldered the blame, as it is my duty to do, but I can't slough off the impression of having been duped by Ms Craven. And somehow that makes what happened all the more unbearable for me, since at the heart of it is *anger*. And the anger makes my palms itch; it forces my hands — which are otherwise open in a gesture of shock and pity, and guilt — into fists. I can't forgive her for that.

The first sign that something was amiss in Green Class came around a fortnight after the Nurture Table's introduction. Daisy De'Angelis was sobbing at lunchtime play and the dinner lady who tried in vain to comfort her reported that Ms Craven had told the class there was no such thing as the Tooth Fairy. It was unusual for a primary teacher to make such a sweeping statement and I resolved to tackle her about it at the end of the school day.

As I reached the classroom she was already hurrying out. She was tall and slender and tended to wear close-fitting tops in jewel colours and long, dark skirts, which gave one the impression that she *swept* rather than walked. Her hair was shoulder length, almost black, thick and softly waving. Her complexion was flawless, her eyes were that crystalline grey, and a muted stain of red lipstick was the only decoration she needed. Ms Craven was bound to be an object of fascination; the girls aspiring to her charms and the boys bewildered by their appeal. I remember thinking with some relief, just before offering her the job, that our one male member of staff was nearly sixty and so we wouldn't be confronting one of those difficult, sexually charged situations that seem to spring up around Easter term.

I almost bumped into her in the doorway, but stepped back just in time and said "Jennifer, could we have a word... unless you need to get somewhere quickly?"

"No, no," she replied pleasantly, "I am going to meet up with someone actually, but," and here she smiled at me conspiratorially, "he can wait. What can I do for you?" For the first time in years, I didn't feel up to a staff confrontation but I had to go on.

"I heard that Daisy was upset in the playground today."

"Oh yes, poor love, I'm afraid I shattered an illusion for her, unintentionally."

"We tend not to disabuse the children of harmless beliefs like the Tooth Fairy. They'll come to it when they're ready, usually."

"Well, it was rather unavoidable I'm afraid. Or at least, I fell into it before realising."

"What happened?"

"It was because of the Nurture Table..."

"Ah. How is that project going?"

"Very well, I'm pleased so far. Come and see." She led me to the table, now covered in black velvet, on which several objects were already placed. I noticed a baby shoe and a little vest, a mermaid costume, a couple of photographs, and a Barbie doll in full evening dress.

"So Barbie shows up even here?" I asked, intrigued.

Ms Craven snorted derisively. "Yes, that's Samantha's of course. She wants to be Barbie when she grows up and do you know, I think she'll probably succeed. Bryn brought the vest — it was the first thing he wore, which is clearly significant to him, and whoever brought the shoe did so for much the same reason. I'm rather more interested in Davy's contribution, which is the costume. It's his sister's but he tells me he likes to wear it in his bedroom, along with his mother's shoes!" Her tone suggested that it was all great fun, but I couldn't detect any warmth.

I asked her, "How does the Tooth Fairy fit in?"

Ms Craven rattled a small leatherette jeweller's box and opened it to reveal five milk teeth. "Daisy's mother is saving her teeth to set into a bracelet. At Show and Tell Daisy showed them and told them about this, and Cerys piped up — what about the Tooth Fairy? Daisy said the Tooth Fairy always left her a pound coin but then put the teeth under her mum's pillow for safekeeping. But Cerys insisted that teeth become stars so the fairy couldn't possibly give them away, and the rest of the class joined in on both sides of the argument until of course they referred it to me."

"And you said....?"

"I explained how we often use stories to illustrate things that happen to all of us."

"Was that strictly necessary?"

She paused and for a moment seemed almost humble. "Perhaps I didn't need to be so specific. But there was such a tension in the room; it seemed to demand a rational response... and you know, I don't think Daisy was terribly bothered about the Tooth Fairy. What she kept saying was — my mummy wouldn't lie to me. I think that was what she was really upset about."

"Daisy's mother is a very troubled woman. She's often depressed and can be something of a fantasist."

"Ah. I didn't know the nature of her — illness."

"That is what I meant about this project. It's a can of worms."

She reacted strongly. "Oh, it's not that bad, surely? Daisy could have become upset about any number of things, it just so happens that this project has brought something to light which may easily have come up elsewhere."

She was right, and it was hardly a disciplinary matter. But the expression of humility I thought I'd noticed earlier was gone.

"Maybe so. But perhaps Nurture is going to be a much more problematic subject than Nature." Ms Craven seemed to smirk briefly at this. "Is something funny?" I asked her.

"Oh I'm sorry, I didn't mean to smile. It's just that I'm not quite used to the accent around here, and when you said 'Nature' it sounded rather like 'Nietzsche' and the thought of teaching Nietzsche to seven year olds tickled me."

She may as well have pointed out that I was the headmistress of a small infant school on the Welsh border, woefully near where I had been born forty-eight years earlier, and that she was fresh from teacher training college in London and young enough to be my daughter. I tried to be wry but sounded tart. "I expect you've got that lesson planned for next term, Jennifer. Meanwhile, please be careful with this Nurture business. And try not to spoil the children's innocent beliefs."

"I only told them the truth," she protested.

"The truth can be a blunt instrument, especially when brandished about the heads of children. We must *mediate* it." She said nothing and I sensed resentment. On my way out I glanced at the photographs on the table. One was of a man I didn't recognise but I lifted up the other, a slightly blurred snapshot of a woman in her thirties, smiling into the sunshine under the shade of a straw hat. "Katy's mother!"

"Yes, she said that her mum wears that hat every summer and she's allowed to keep it on top of her wardrobe. I don't think Katy has quite grasped the aims of this project...."

I cut in: "Jeannie Thomas died two years ago last summer. She lost her hair during chemotherapy. She always wore a hat after that." I replaced the photograph and turned to the young woman with a frown, "Did you not sense anything unusual in Katy's manner when she talked about the photo?"

Ms Craven's mouth pursed and her manner was defensive, as she said, "I didn't, no. I've actually never seen a picture of *my* mother so perhaps it seems — alien to me. I was adopted at six weeks old," she continued, in response to the questioning look she must have been trying to elicit from me. "Never got on with my adoptive family, left home at fifteen, never been back in touch. But never traced my birth parents either." She paused and composed her face into a wry smile. "I suppose I've not been terribly impressed by the mothers in my life."

I should have felt sorry for her but, for the life of me, couldn't raise any pity and acted as though I hadn't heard her. I don't know why.

"These are serious matters, Jennifer. Be careful. You've asked the children for something personal as though it's a simple matter, like picking up an acorn. But it's just as likely that something personal involves pain and confusion, even for a seven year old." She didn't answer and I left the room feeling uneasy.

There have been several eventful Parents' Evenings in my professional life, but most of them have proved forgettable, in time. It appals me to know that I will never be able to wipe from my memory the culmination of Ms Craven's Nurture Table project.

I like to be present at a teacher's first Parents' Evening, not interfering, but offering general encouragement and advice if needed. So I hung back in Green Class and listened discreetly whilst viewing the children's artwork. It began calmly enough; a few brief chats during which Ms Craven made an inevitably favourable impression; the mums reassured by her intelligent manner and the dads bewitched by her tight but tasteful v-neck sweater. It was when they began to walk around the room and survey the work of their offspring, when they reached the Nurture Table, that the trouble began, and I could have stopped all of it. The business with the twins was probably unavoidable by then, but if I'd taken the time to check the final display I could have simply gathered up the cloth and deposited its contents in my office, and so much of the other trouble could have been prevented.

It started with the Beesons, Davy's parents. They looked bemused at the presence of their daughter's mermaid costume on the table,

143

and then both read their son's explanatory scrawl on the card in front of it:

This is my favourite pretty outfit. I wear it with my mum's shiny red shoes. The tail feels all silky and nice.

I heard Mrs Beeson whisper ferociously to her husband, "This is your fault, you FREAK — It's perfectly normal, you said, — Just humour me, you said, — I'm still a *man*, you said. Look at this! It's in your *blood*! You've *dirty blood*. Just keep away from me. And from the children. Keep away!" And she ran out sobbing, leaving Mr Beeson looking pale with shock. Beside him, I noticed that Lisa Bridges' mother was trying to remove her daughter's exhibit, while Mr Bridges forced the photograph from her hand.

This is my dad. His hair is the same colour as mine.

"It's him. After all those promises, you kept on seeing that *bastard*. I knew our Lisa didn't look like me, but I couldn't *believe* you'd play a trick like that. You slag. You fucking bitch!"

His wife kept shaking her head, looking more surprised than remorseful. "I can't believe she understood, let alone remembered. She was only three. I just wanted her to see him, to know — just once and then I hid it. She must have kept on hunting until she found it. I can't believe it."

I look after my mum's hat and I think about the summer.

I noticed Huw Thomas hunched in a corner, the photograph of his late wife in one hand and Katy's note clutched in the fist that he pressed to his mouth to stifle his sobbing; and I watched Daisy's gentle, confused mother hanging on to her husband's arm and smiling at her baby's milk teeth while he slipped the card quietly into his jacket pocket...

My mummy told me the tooth fairy gave her my teeth to keep but it was a lie. My mummy goes into our garden with no clothes on.

...unaware that the following week the card would be handed to his wife over the counter of the drycleaners' with a sly wink and she'd be back in hospital, for a month this time.

There were other shocks, further outbursts of anger and disbelief, before I managed to remove the exhibits and see the last parents out. I was about to return to Green Class to confront Ms Craven when I heard a sharp knock on my door and she was suddenly in front of me.

"Something very odd is going on!" she shouted passionately. "It's the Hughes twins, I'm worried about them. Their father didn't come to the Parents' Evening but they just came in and put *these* on the table!" I focused on her shaking hand, which grasped two pieces of what looked like fur. "And I said — no boys, it's not a nature table, remember, we're looking for objects which help us learn about our own lives, our *upbringing*. And they said..." — and here her tone became a parody of the little boys' gruff voices — "'Our vests when we was born — from our mam.'"

"Their mother died when they were born."

"I know, so what do they mean? They don't *have* a mother." She had a little colour in her cheeks, and the sparkle in her eye gave her a febrile look. She was very beautiful. The tiny garments were on my desk now and I could see that each had been roughly stitched into a kind of tabard. They were heavily stained on the inside and faintly malodorous.

"Jennifer, calm down. Those boys are very —" I was about to say very troubled, but I hesitated. Their behaviour was close, they didn't waste their words and kept themselves to themselves. They were behind in their lessons — but not any more than some of their class-mates. I remembered their mother vaguely — she wasn't local and was already pregnant when she married Hughes and arrived in town, so she left only a light impression, of chestnut hair, creamy skin and enormous dark eyes. I'd known him for years, of course. Always was a handsome one, but too quiet, and certainly not interested in pass-ing the time of day with the square girl that was going to university. Not that he passes the time of day with anyone nowadays. Considering the boys had been raised since infancy by a dour wid-ower who worked miles away in a wildlife park over the border in Shropshire and kept no human company, they seemed to be doing pretty well, to my mind. "They are *unusual*. Were they upset when you saw them?"

"Not at all. They seemed quite proud of having brought something to the table."

"And what did you say to them?"

"I thanked them and told them to go home safely. But Pamela, I'm so worried about them. They shouldn't be out on their own at this time in the evening."

"They shouldn't, but this is a small town, they keep an eye out for one another and we can't police the children. What do you want me to do?"

"Well, surely we should tell someone about this...."

"Tell who about what?"

"The social services, or the police, surely...?" her voice tailed off.

"We've no accusations to make. The boys show no sign of having been ill-treated and it would be arrogant for us to sweep in with the long arm of the law and no evidence. It's not our place." Ms Craven looked at me defiantly and left.

I never dreamt that she would act that quickly. Only a newcomer to the town would be so audacious, striding up to the front door of a complete stranger and knocking until it was answered. I heard afterwards how the door had been opened by the boys, how they had said that their dad was at work and nobody could come in, how they had barred her way until she pushed past them, ignoring their tears, and how she just had time to view the shabby hallway hung with photographs — hundreds of photographs, maybe even thousands — of a pale young woman with dark hair, before she heard a growl and turned around, terrified.

The wound on her forearm was a clean scratch and required only an antiseptic dressing. But all the hot sweet tea the police station could provide failed to calm her down and it took a good half hour to establish the facts. In view of her hysterical gabbling about a wild dog and the boys all alone, two policemen had been sent to the house, where the twins' father opened the door and the constables explained that they had to ask him some questions about the boys being home alone, and yes, that did include being left under the protection of the family pet.

This was the point at which I arrived, at the request of the sergeant who accompanied me, to help calm matters down, a task for which I proved dreadfully unsuited. Try as he might to pull himself together, Mr Hughes demonstrated a fast-breathing, sweating nervousness under official scrutiny. I am not one of those highly-strung sensitive types — couldn't have done my job all these years if I was — but even to me the scent of his fear was strong as musk. I sat in an armchair facing the boys huddled at one end of the sofa and their father hunched up on the other while the kindly sergeant questioned

146

him and his men looked around the house. They found room upon room lined with photographs of his late wife, often the same photograph several dozen times on one wall, and a freshly made up double bed beside which lay a ragged and stained sleeping bag, and some food in the fridge and cupboards but nothing which needed cooking, nor any utensils to do so. The man couldn't explain the lack of a bedroom for his sons. The boys had already identified the photographs as 'Our Mother-who-is-in-heaven' but said, on questioning, that they slept 'with our mam' and I sensed that the sergeant shared my nightmarish vision of a decayed corpse flanked by two sleeping children. So, it was almost a relief to follow Mr Hughes down the garden path and into the shed and see the nest of clean blankets and straw, the motley collection of teddy bears, the strewn items of school uniform and, lying at the centre, the wolf.

If it had all stopped there we could have helped. The sergeant's a good man, and the boys trusted me. Their father would have appreciated our discretion; nobody else would have had to know about the night two weeks after his wife's death when, waving aside all offers of help, he had fetched the babies from the hospital, wrapped them in the dead cubs' pelts and laid them beside the grieving she-wolf who had only just survived being smuggled out of the park. And although the tale he told should have been shocking, or even revolting, it just set my mind rolling along a path leading to something — homely. I felt a surge of excitement as I imagined how I would come along after school and at the weekends; I'd clean and paint walls and take the boys shopping to choose furniture; I'd buy them little wooden beds and kit them out with quilts and pillows. I'd get that kitchen sorted; help him get hold of a freezer and fill it with decent food, make sure the family was warm and fed. And we'd say no more about their pet. I'm not ashamed to have had those thoughts, even knowing how foolish they sound now. It could have worked.

But as we left the shed and made our way back up the path to the house, the sergeant lagging behind, preoccupied, and the boys breaking into a relieved run, I heard Hughes gasp and stumble. Turning, I saw his expression change from an anxious frown into a look of surprise, then disbelief, and then finally rapture. "Emily!" he whispered, his gaze beyond me. Following his stare, I immediately recognised the slim silhouette which glided towards us, backlit by the flickering fluorescent strip in the kitchen.

Ms Craven held out her arms to the boys and when they didn't come she made a little run and caught one of them. "It's alright. I'm here now. You're safe now," she murmured and the man was near enough to see how he had been deceived but then, suddenly, so was the wolf, which flew at the woman for a second time. In the dark and confusion I could hardly see what was happening, but I heard three distinct, simultaneous sounds and I don't know which was more heartbreaking: that last, lost cry of "Emily!", the frightened yelp of the boys, or the wolf's desolate howl — of realisation, I'm sure of it — when a clumsy policeman pushed Ms Craven out of the way and the creature's jaws closed, just for a moment, around Guy's face.

"Not again," their father was whimpering when the policemen dragged his sons' arms from around the neck of the tethered and muzzled animal and took her away to be destroyed. Guy's distress was more serious than his injury, though that wound was deep enough, and the doctor administered a general anaesthetic in the ambulance. The sergeant and I left by the front door, and I do wonder if I should have said something to Mr Hughes, perhaps even pushed Gareth towards him so they could comfort one another, but I had to lead Ms Craven, shaking and outraged, from the house, so I never got the chance. Motherless, temporarily brotherless; his father curled in grief beside the empty marriage bed, we left the little boy sitting in the dark living room surrounded by photographs and silence.

***

Summer term. I can't stop looking through class windows, even if my faith in the method has been dented. Not that I really need to check on Green Class: Mrs Rhys has returned for a few weeks before we fill the post permanently. All the children look well enough; the disputes and quarrels begun on Parents' Evening have mostly subsided; no visible scars except for the livid mark the length of Guy's cheek. Children are remarkably adaptable, or adept at appearing so. Gareth hasn't been heard to utter a word since that night, but we're hopeful about his recovery. And now we can always tell them apart.

Mrs Rhys is saying, "Look at this beautiful nest which Edward has brought in. These speckled blue eggshells tell us that two baby blackbirds hatched here in the spring. Now children, if you see a nest with baby birds in it, you shouldn't go near because it may scare the mother away and the chicks won't survive..." I decide not to disturb them. I turn and walk down the corridor as she continues, "...so however much we want to see, we should always hold back, shouldn't we?" I sense an acquiescent silence from the children and imagine their solemn nods as she turns to her display, saying "Right then, let's put this in pride of place in the middle of the nature table."

Mrs Pike: A True Story

Julie Myerson

Once upon a time — and this is more or less a true story — there was a lady called Mrs Pike.

Mrs Pike lived in a lovely new-brick bungalow in Lime Tree Gardens and had a dachshund called Gretchen, an H-reg Alfa Romeo and two lava lamps. Mrs Pike had always been keen on having The Latest Thing. When colour TVs came in, she put her order in straight away, and she always had the very newest model of sports car, never mind about her cataracts.

Why, as far as she knew, she'd also been the first person in Nottingham to get the magnetic soap dish. The magnet soaps were a little dearer than normal soaps but, with the smart little pansy transfers, they made the most ideal guest soaps. Not that Mrs Pike ever had any guests — she wasn't really a people person, never had been, she preferred the TV.

But how proud Mrs Pike was of her possessions! And of her appearance. She wasn't about to reveal her age to anyone, but she still varnished her nails with Elizabeth Arden pearly pink and powdered her face and wore a Persian lamb coat when the weather called for it.

Her kitchen boasted a sunburst wall clock and the latest foil-bubble wallpaper, which — and this was ever so handy — you just wiped down. Only the other day, she'd given it a going-over, amazed at how much grease it had accumulated just from a bit of frying now and then when she fancied it.

If she hadn't been a well-placed widow, Mrs Pike reckoned she could have been an interior decorator for the fabulously wealthy — choosing colour schemes and mixing and matching and so forth. Even the shop-girl at Griffin & Spalding, where she purchased her three-piece suite complete with matching pouffes, had praised her taste. In her lounge, she had a lot of mauve. At Christmas she even had a mauve metallic tree with matching baubles. She'd always been a one for mauve, preferring it to blue, which reminded her too much

151

of the sky. Mrs Pike wasn't keen on nature — never had been, couldn't see the point of all that muck and fuss.

It suited Mrs Pike fine that she was a widow, because she had never been able to abide her husband. He had always been a drinker and it was his own fault entirely that he'd passed away. She was on the point of divorcing him (and fighting him for every penny he had) when she found out he was a goner. Cirrhosis of the liver. This was in the November.

"Put it this way," said the specialist, who had quite a sense of humour as it turned out, "I wouldn't go to the trouble of buying him any Christmas presents."

Mrs Pike had a bit of a chuckle at that. But then, wasn't she having the last laugh? A husband-free Christmas! A husband-free rest of her life! She fancied a winter cruise — if only she could do something with Geoffrey, who was seven and, frankly, a bit of a fly in the ointment.

She told him to please keep out of her way with his long face — otherwise, she'd phone up Mrs White, who would come and take him away in her big black van. Mrs White wasn't real, of course, but Geoffrey didn't know that. Sometimes, she actually picked up the phone and dialled their own number and conducted a nice pretend-scary conversation with Mrs White.

"Is that you, Mrs W? I have a naughty boy here — could you come and take him away please? What's that? Oh, yes, you'd better bring the spanking strap — oh, hold on a moment, Mrs W, I think he's apologising — it's all right, Mrs W, I won't be needing you to come, not for the time being, thanks anyway..."

Even before her husband was safely nailed in his coffin, Mrs Pike set about reclaiming the space he'd taken up in her life, shoving all his mess and rubbish into crates ready for burning. Part of her was itching to start the bonfire and just get on with it, but instinct told her it was better to wait. It was a bit of an anticlimax when he actually went — quietly, one bright Saturday morning, with a half-smile on his face. She couldn't help feeling a wave of irritation at that soppy little smile — until the doctor assured her it was just a medical thing, something the dead do without knowing it.

Lime Tree Gardens was the third such bungalow Mrs Pike had lived in, not by choice, mind you. It was in a quiet cul-de-sac with a newsagent's on the corner. Mrs Lesley, the woman next door, had the hairiest legs — you'd think she'd have them seen to.

The reason Mrs Pike never lived anywhere for long was that she had to move whenever Geoffrey did. Her irritating child had grown into a surprisingly attractive man, and it was to get at his wife Marie that Mrs Pike followed them around the city. Not that it was Geoffrey's fault that they upped sticks all the time. No, it was Marie who had the itchy feet. It was living all those years with an outdoor toilet and then suddenly marrying into money.

"Don't you think Geoffrey deserves a bit of freedom now that he's in his forties?" Marie snapped at her one day.

Mrs Pike went white. "He lived with me until he was 32," she reminded her. "He's always been a good boy."

"Well, he's grown up now," sneered Marie, "and we're his family, me and the kids."

Mrs Pike had stomach trouble on and off for days after Marie's outburst. "Is it such a sin," she wrote in a letter to Marie, "to want to have my own son close at hand? In case anything untoward should happen?"

Geoffrey rang her — sullen-sounding, as though Marie had pushed him into it: "What's all this untoward business, Mother?"

"My hernia," she stuttered, "I never know when it's going to play up."

And she wasn't lying. Sometimes all it took was a slightly stringy piece of chicken, an unexpected bit of bacon. Not that she knowingly ate the fat — she always took off the rind with a pair of scissors and put it out for the tits.

Each new bungalow Mrs Pike lived in, she named herself. She had a flair for it — and she liked to think that something in this world would outlast her. She'd lived in a nice place off Mapperley Plains which she'd called "Saigon" — a topical reference to something she'd heard on the news. The next one she named "The Point", since it was right on the furthermost tip of a triangular new development. Marie had been expecting for the second time when she moved in there. She hated Marie Like That — couldn't look her in the eye with that awful smug lump bulging out of her.

When she was expecting, Marie's game was to take up as much of Geoffrey's time as possible, claiming sickness and the like. At "The

153

Point", this had been especially inconvenient as Mrs Pike had once heard a noise in the night.

"I'm really nervous at nights," she said — and begged Geoffrey to come and sleep over with her, just until she got used to it. So, every night for a week, he came and slept in the spare room. It was marvellous — they'd share a tin of Campbell's soup, just like in the old days, and then watch Bernard Braden on TV. Then — oh my, what a coincidence! — Marie managed to go into labour ten days early and the honeymoon was over, so to speak.

"Couldn't you get a guard dog?" Marie moaned, suggesting a security firm that some friend of hers had used.

"Oooh, I'd be ever so nervous of a great big dog," Mrs Pike protested, knocking that one firmly on the head.

"What about a little dog then?" Geoffrey suggested. "Just an alarm system, as it were?"

And that's how she got landed with Gretchen — not that she'd be without her now, of course. She soon had her lapping sweetened tea out of a saucer and then Gretchen'd insist on having the last two chocs whenever she had a box of Milk Tray. Mrs Pike couldn't abide Montelimar and certainly couldn't tackle the nougat with her dentures.

So Gretchen's teeth went first and then she went all diabetic, which affected her sight. And the blindness made her very tired. She'd nap on and off , and sleep through any noise. "Not much good as a guard dog," Mrs Pike told her son with a degree of satisfaction.

At Christmas, Geoffrey and Marie came over with the children, and Mrs Pike had once again to stomach the sight of that great fat belly all swelled up to bursting — a third one was expected in January.

"I hated giving birth to Geoffrey," Mrs Pike said, when Marie helped herself just like that to more bread sauce. "It was just like going to the toilet, only worse."

"I suppose I'm lucky," Marie boasted. "I just relax and they pop out!" And she leaned over and touched Mrs Pike's sleeve as she spoke.

Quickly, Mrs Pike pulled away her arm. A shudder ran the length of her body. She hadn't been touched by anyone since the war. The feeling made her want to cry and vomit, both at the same time.

When Geoffrey and Marie divorced, she didn't bother to suppress her delight. She poured herself a Dubonnet and lemonade and treated herself to a handful of those pink cocktail biscuits.

On the Thursday after he actually told her, Geoffrey came over for a late soup and cheese supper. Soft white rolls, Lurpak, Dairylea spread.

"You married beneath you," she told him during *Sale Of The Century*. "You want to watch out That Woman doesn't take you to the cleaners."

Geoffrey looked at her and said nothing.

Then he lit a Silk Cut and started answering Nicholas Parsons' questions. He was good at general knowledge, and he got all but one right.

Mrs Pike felt a flutter of pride at the base of her throat. Or was it the cheese so late at night? On the pouffe at her feet, Gretchen snorted in her sleep.

"That animal's poorly," Geoffrey remarked.

"Rubbish," she said. "It's called old age."

But she caught herself smiling at him. The little exchange gave her so much pleasure.

Now she didn't need to worry at night, because Geoffrey moved back in, keeping two suitcases and his valet chair in the spare room.

"Just until I get myself sorted," he said, because the house was up for sale and he said he couldn't face the emptiness without the kiddies.

Mrs Pike hadn't seen the kiddies since the split and neither, from what she could gather, had her son. But she had the photographs on the sideboard — except she'd cut Her out with a pair of nail scissors.

"She's turned them against me," Geoffrey told her. "The doctor's given me something. For depression." For some reason, that word — "depression" — sliced through Mrs Pike's heart. Made her want to catch her breath.

"You're all right," she said brightly, "you're just not the marrying type, that's all. Never have been. I should have spotted it."

"I'm not sleeping," Geoffrey said on another occasion. "I don't know what's going to happen to the business." When he spoke like that, he reminded her of the weedy little boy who'd trail around after her, making her want so badly to kick him.

155

"Let's watch the Eurovision Song Contest," said Mrs Pike. "I listened to our entry and it's not at all bad."

When the police knocked on Mrs Pike's back door, it was very late. So late that she'd taken out her teeth, removed her wig and hearing aid, and had nothing on but a brushed nylon gown under which her flesh always seemed to have a mind of its own.

She'd had mulligatawny soup for supper and it was repeating on her — sometimes an early warning sign of Hernia Trouble.

She pulled on a shower cap, which was all she had to hand, and made her way to the door. She couldn't think why they'd gone round the back when the front porch had a light on. She clipped on the chain and opened it a crack. She knew something was wrong when she heard radios cutting in and out, saw the clouds of several men's breath against the passage brickwork.

"Mrs Pike?" The man spoke too softly, too queryingly. She disliked him immediately. She nodded, unwilling to open her mouth for the lack of teeth. "Sorry to disturb you so late at night. Can we come in?"

"Well —" she managed to croak, and unclipped the chain and stood there, blinking, in the kitchen, her mind all over the place.

"I'm sorry," said the man, who was ever so young — even younger than Geoffrey. "Would you like to sit down. Only we've some very bad news for you, I'm afraid."

"I'd prefer to stand," she said, not wanting to give him any leeway.

"Your son, Geoffrey. He died earlier tonight. He was found at his office. He hanged himself. I'm so sorry."

"Oh my Lord," she said. And smiled.

She could not think. She felt silly. She felt she shouldn't be told such a big thing while wearing a shower cap.

"Mrs Pike? I really think you should sit down."

She felt her lips going wider with the smile and the shock of it. Like a sneeze, she felt a laugh coming. "He hasn't gone and done that, has he?" she said. "The silly monkey. When he had everything to live for."

Mrs Pike was never one to dwell on things. She continued, as she always had, to mooch around her bungalow and pet Gretchen and watch TV with the sound turned well up — never mind about the neighbours.

In fact, the neighbours did their best, she had to admit that. Hairy

Mrs Lesley brought round a piece of apple pie on a plate, even bothered to put on a doily. "Don't worry about returning the plate," she said. "There's no hurry, you take your time."

But Mrs Pike couldn't stand other people's clutter around the place and so she ate the pie, even though the crust was soggy, and then she rinsed the plate in cold water and left it on the Lesleys' doorstep.

Once the funeral was over, she tried to forget all about Marie and the children. One of the kiddies sent her a pair of homemade slippers at Christmas — tatty velvet they were, with silly baubles stitched on all over — and they were much too big, so she sent them back without a note — what was the point?

Then, one evening, as Mrs Pike crossed the hall to get something from her bedroom, she got a terrible shock. There, next to the umbrella stand, was a person — a man, dirty and unkempt, in sports footwear and an anoraky thing.

An intruder.

A burglar.

Mrs Pike tried to scream, but found all her air pockets locked. She gasped. She growled. "Police!" she finally spewed and, her eyes on the figure, staggered backwards. The man, whose face was obscured by the silty dark, groped behind him and let himself out of the front door. The front door, what a cheek!

The police came round. They took their time. It seemed like they'd been there only yesterday. Mrs Pike kept her dignity, sat with her hands in her lap. "Did he take anything?" the young man, a mere child with his spots and his sticky-out Adam's apple, asked her.

"I still have my handbag," Mrs Pike began, then stopped. Suddenly she couldn't remember what else she had. What else she'd ever had. "My mind's a blank," she whispered. In a panic, she took them round, retracing her steps. "I was just finishing my Horlicks," she said, showing them the exact spot where she'd been sitting before she got up. She showed them her cup. "This one's mine, this cup here."

"The dog didn't alert you then?" said the man, as Gretchen roused herself and waddled over.

"The dog's poorly," Mrs Pike said. "And a bit stuck up." She'd meant that last bit as a joke, but no one laughed.

The men went away — nothing resolved.

After that, Mrs Pike kept the lights on, even at night. Electricity burned in that bungalow around the clock — a yellow, throbbing force that sometimes felt like company.

Early in January, Gretchen got a high temperature. The dog's nose was hot and dry. Each breath seemed more snatched and uncertain. She'd not touched a drop of anything for two days when Mrs Pike wrapped her in a mohair blanket and took her to the vet. Who said he was very sorry, but the kindest thing was to let her go."Let her go?" Mrs Pike repeated numbly.

"Put her to sleep — put her down. I'm sorry, Mrs Pike, but I think it's for the best."

The vet asked Mrs Pike if she'd like to have a few moments alone with the dog to say goodbye, but she snapped her handbag open and shut and said she couldn't see the point. She must have looked distressed or something, because the vet put his big hand on her shoulder, moved it slowly up and down.

"I'm sorry," he said, rubbing away at her flesh. "It's always hard, losing a much-loved pet."

It was the second time Mrs Pike had been touched since the war and the sensation upset her. She recognised the feeling, felt it take root in a way that was almost familiar, but couldn't for the life of her place it. Was it good or bad? And if it was good, then why did it feel so much like pain? She moved away, quietly furious.

She drove herself home and when she got in the kitchen she sat and looked at the sunburst clock on the foil wall. Ten past four. Yes, Gretchen would definitely be gone by now. That was that, then.

Mrs Pike put her head in her hands.

And wondered what you did next.

Electra

Eve Makis

Mama was an unusual choice of bride for the son of a wealthy jeweller with forty *donums* of land to his name. The only riches she brought to her union were humility and a good reputation. Grandmother was keen for her son to marry a simple village girl with no pretensions, nurtured to tend house and husband. A girl who would always be grateful to her in-laws for bettering her. 'Choose virtue over beauty, son,' grandmother counselled, 'a beautiful woman is more trouble than she is worth.' Mama was picked, still green, from her mother's simple mud brick cottage and set to ripen 300 kilometres away. Her in-laws built her a palatial house with Corinthian columns and a sweeping marble veranda. When war broke out and the palace was lost, when home became a Red Cross tent, grandmother's crude hypothesis was proven right. The village girl did not sit beating her chest, lamenting her fate. She put her hands to good use. A girl who came from next-to-nothing could get by on very little. She knew how to bake her own bread. How to skin a rabbit and pluck a chicken. How to spend a paltry sum and produce enough food to fill the stomachs of four hungry children who sat with mouths gaping like newly hatched sparrows.

Mama was married in the sleepy Paphos village where she was born and grew up. An olive strewn backwater, set among the gentle foothills of Troodos. Baggy-trousered men, with white moustaches tweaked upwards at the edges, took ringside seats in the village coffee houses to watch the priest lead the bride and her kin across the paved village square, up the flagstone steps that led to the small stone church of Agios Andreas. Later that day they sucked soft, aromatic lamb off the bone and licked their greasy fingers clean. They toasted the newlyweds with swigs of Keo brandy and sweet red wine. They laughed until their stomachs hurt at the satirical chant of the village bard who warned the groom he faced castration by his father-in-law if he mistreated the bride. My parents danced without touching, hands on hips, mother's gaze lowered humbly like a Geisha's. They touched for the very first time in the starchy sheets of their marital bed, which by morning bore the evidence of mama's innocence.

Twenty-five years earlier and déjà vu. My maternal grandmother Elpida — Hope, as she was aptly named — walked across the same village square and mounted the same weathered steps to stand before the altar with a man she barely knew. The wedding festivities lasted three days and nights. Elpida was treated like the Queen of Sheba for seventy-two hours, pampered and fussed over, then promptly forgotten about. Attentions turned to the next transient queen. Elpida's betrothal was negotiated at a formal meeting of parents. A generous dowry was secured by her in-laws and sealed with a handshake. 'I was worth no more than a four-poster bed and half a dozen chickens,' Elpida used to grumble, shaking her head. Everyone in the village was invited. 'May the couple's path be strewn with roses,' they had said, graciously accepting their invitations. 'My path was strewn with your grandfather's whisky bottles,' Elpida complained, scrunching up her cabbage patch face.

On day one of the festivities, women gathered to stuff the wedding mattress, to scatter it with silver coins, to carry the lumbering thing overhead in a celebratory dance. To honour the venerated mattress on which the sixteen-year-old bride would later reject her husband's advances and lie crying, traumatized by the harrowing sight of *papou's* genitalia. The women rolled a baby back and forth across the mattress wishing the couple a fertile union and preferably a boy. To take the family name and propagate it. To become a miniature version of his *papou* and follow in his father's footsteps. 'I prayed for a girl,' Elpida said. 'There is no greater wealth than a daughter to look after you in old age. But I had boy, after boy, after boy before God granted me my wish.'

On the morning of the wedding the groom was lathered and shaved by his father, in the presence of male friends and relatives. 'You are headed for the gallows my friend,' the best man goaded as the violinist played an upbeat tune. *Papou* dry swallowed, unable to react with a razor blade held so close to his throat. Later, when the priest uttered the words 'to love and obey', *Papou* stamped on the bride's large foot, as his best man had instructed, to let his new wife know who was boss. If looks could kill my grandfather would have dropped dead right then and there. The look Elpida gave him was withering. Foot stamping or no foot stamping, the game was lost.

Elpida was large and outspoken and went on to rule the roost. My grandparents were cohabitees, as well-matched as cat and dog, as persian and pit bull. My grandmother raised four boys and a girl. Gossiped over the back yard fence. Cooked and cleaned. Refused her husband his conjugal rights on religious holidays, as any good Christian woman should. No sex for forty days over Easter; no unclean thoughts on those interminable Saints' Days that swallowed up half the year. *Papou* shaved men's stubble for a living and drank the night away in the local *cafene*. He spent little time at home, complaining that his wife was a *faousa*, a nag, the 'plague'. *Papou* died in his forties of cirrhosis, his liver scarred by alcohol and blackened (his mother Andrianou liked to say) by Elpida's incessant nagging. 'That woman drove my poor son to an early grave,' Andrianou sobbed at the funeral. When her husband died Elpida left Paphos, to live with her only daughter in the Karpas peninsula. She refused to lodge with any one of her four sons, saying it was a grave mistake for any mother to share a roof with her daughter-in-law.

'Not everyone can love me, aunty,' I said to Miroulla. We sat opposite one another, sipping Greek coffee, nibbling pastries filled with sugar and crushed almonds.

'Margaret is not everyone,' she replied, 'she is your mother-in-law. What the hell is wrong with that woman? You are a treasure Electra, pure gold. If you were married to my son, if God had blessed me with a child, I would be doing forty somersaults. I would have to lose sixty kilos first, mind you.' Aunty laughed. Her fleshy shoulders shook. Miroulla has no qualms about laughing at her own jokes.

'Adam has never let his mother get between us *thea*.'

Miroulla's mouth shrivelled derisively like a slug doused with salt. 'Do not speak too hastily my love, it is early days in your marriage. Do you think your mother was happy when you took home an English man? The poor woman cried herself to sleep for many weeks before digesting your decision.'

'I gave her no choice, Aunty.'

Miroulla sipped her coffee noisily, a cinnamon-coloured moustache forming on her upper lip. She licked it away and looked at me knowingly. Her eyebrows riding up. Her head leaning to one side above a weight-lifter's neck .

'And your husband? Why is he not so straight-talking with his own mother?'

'Adam has to be more careful.'

'Pah! Why is that? Is Margaret made of cut glass?'

Miroulla leaned back in her chair, resting her hands on an abdominal pouch large enough to house marsupial triplets.

All I could say in my husband's defence was: 'There are reasons *thea*, why Margaret must be treated with care.'

Adam has a formal, respectful, deceitful relationship with his mother. One with crippled lines of communication. In Margaret's presence Adam's comments are guarded, his laughter measured, his emotions controlled. He turns from articulate adult to bumbling boy without testicles. 'I have never been able to talk to my mother,' Adam says, refusing to admit that things have got far worse since he met me. I am a big girl and I insist on the truth. If daughters-in-law were food and could be ordered in a restaurant, Margaret would have chosen a simple salad with a light dressing. What she got was a rather more piquant version with black olives, capers, feta cheese and thick, Virgin olive oil. Margaret finds the Electra Salad unpalatable. This bitter truth hurts Adam more than it hurts me. I have too much love in my life ever to feel unloved.

When she first met Adam my own mother said: 'What do you see in him child? He is so pale. So blonde. So thin. Is he sick?' My reply was *'skase mana'* — shut up mother. I put her in her place before her tongue sprouted wings. I laid down the ground rules early on and warned her against interfering, saying there was only room for two in a marriage. Mama has adhered to my rules, knowing better than to transgress. 'When my daughter opens her big mouth she could swallow us all up,' mama says.

What did I see in him? What did I see in a bunch of long limbs as flimsy as saplings? In the concertina of bones he called a chest? Some women like emaciated men. I never did. I liked them triangular on top, ribs covered with a generous layer of muscle. I liked them dark and healthy looking, preferably astride a Harley. I have sampled my fair share of sun-kissed brawn and generally found it to be vacuous. The excitement aroused by such men explodes into being like a sparkler and quickly fizzles. I come from a seaside town where one can overdose on the body beautiful. Where gym culture, founded by our ancient ancestors, is alive and well, a breeding ground for narcissistic men who fall in love every morning when they look into the mirror. Take a short stroll along the beachside promenade and you will see a fair few beefcakes whose stride is impeded by too much inner thigh. Who sit with their legs wide open airing their gonads. Who pretend to be dark and brooding when in actual fact they have nothing to say. Who will never realise that the brain is a muscle too and needs flexing on occasion.

What did I see in him? Standing us side-by-side would not give you the answer. If blinded by appearances you might say we were ill suited. Adam is tall and slim. *Anamisi*, I call him, my 'one-and-a-half' man. I was denied my fair share of height and too generously allotted curves. Other differences? My husband is health conscious and eats like a sparrow. I could eat my husband and the sparrow and still I would have room for desert. Adam engages his brain before speaking. Me — I say the first silly thing that pops into my head. If I make you laugh I will repeat my joke, again and again until it is no longer funny. Where I am excessive, Adam is restrained, an equation that results in a healthy balance. What did I see in him? My reasons cannot be itemized like groceries on a shopping list. Many are unquantifiable. I have always believed illogical love to be more enduring. Those who choose their partners on the basis of pure logic (good job, tight buttocks, nice car) are more likely to stray when something more logical (better job, tighter buttocks, nicer car) comes their way.

My husband goes to bed with the chickens and wakes up with the crow of the cock. *Ticki, tocko* off to bed he goes, always at the same time, whether he is tired or not. His digital alarm clock shrieks at 6.00am, like a large vehicle reversing, and up he gets in a flash to shower and dress. I have a cousin called Kikis whose bio-rhythms match those of domestic fowl. In his case my earlier comment has more resonance. He lives in a rural village and keeps hens and a balding cock in his back yard. He is an exception to the rule. Early to bed, early to rise is not the norm where I come from. My compatriots are up at dawn, enjoy an afternoon siesta and sleep when tiredness knocks them down like skittles.

Night-time should be savoured slowly, like a rich, custardy *galatoboureko*, not willed away as if it were an inconvenience. When darkness descends I mooch around the house, indulge my sweet tooth, work until I drop or stretch out on the sofa channel-hopping, falling asleep unawares, carrying myself to bed when and if I rouse. If Adam wakes up to answer the call of nature, he frog-marches me to bed, cursing my nocturnal habits, the early bird clucking like a mother hen. I lie down as commanded and run my fingernails gently down his back. Adam's skin pimples, his breathing slows. Out he goes, like a light, my lightweight husband. I get up, determined to stretch out the day until it has no more give.

I sit at my workbench polishing a silver brooch with soft cloth, between thumb and forefinger, rubbing away the dull patina to liberate pure, untarnished metal. Inside a ring of silver are loops and tightly wound swirls of filigree, radiating from a dome of variegated blue and turquoise enamel. The brooch is a birthday present for my mother-in-law, an olive branch, a calculated effort to win her approval. I am compelled to fight a losing battle for the sake of my husband, who will not rest until his mother realises my 'worth'. Our ancient King size creaks in the next room as Adam adjusts his position in the bed. A small television on mute keeps me company, bubbling in a corner of the room like molten lava. It erupts, enticing me to look. I glance, then look away. My mind is on the work at hand, on unfinished projects, on my friend Lydia and her problems with Alvaro, on my sister Martha and her devil of a husband. How fervently I pray that Martha will liberate herself from marital tyranny. My brother-in-law Sotiris is a die-hard gambler with a penchant for East European pole dancers. Every so often Sotiris forgets he has a wife and four children and actualises his fantasies in disreputable pubs that sell women alongside their alcoholic beverages. He imagines, while young women press up against him and stroke his fleshy knee, that he is desirable, a young Marlon Brando. That a woman half his age, with the body of a goddess, can see past the watermelon gut.

Sotiris, I am sorry to say, is not discreet. He has been 'spotted' at late night restaurants, eating lamb's head soup in the company of lycra-clad women. Cousin Kikis, delivering eggs to a customer early one morning, spied my brother-in-law leaving a dingy hotel with a gaudy brunette on his arm. Kikis, egg- and gossip-monger that he is, spread this shocking discovery far and wide. Everyone knows Sotiris is a donkey. They see my sister approaching and duck down behind their palms to whisper: 'Have you heard about her husband, led astray by one of those women. What is this country coming too? No husband is safe from their clutches.' Cyprus is a small place. Infidelity and a taste for prostitutes cannot be kept quiet for long. Everyone knows the truth, apart from my sister, who prefers to believe that her husband is out all night earning the family crust. The only crust Sotiris generates is the one he leaves on musty bed sheets. 'Poor Sotiris,' Martha says when her husband comes home with heavy eyes, exuding breath as rancid as a sweaty shoe, 'that man will work himself to death.'

'Marriage is a game of Russian roulette,' Miroulla says, 'some are lucky enough to draw a blank. Others — BLAM! — they shoot themselves in the head.'

My workroom is a metallurgist's heaven, kitted out with implements for refining, grinding and melting. Once a second bedroom, of little practical use, it is now equipped with soldering iron, burnishing machine and an array of hand-held tools, resembling medieval instruments of torture. Lock me in my workroom for a week with a chunk of metal, preferably gold, and I will re-work it into raindrop earrings or an intricate cross. In this small domestic space where I make my living, I have recreated the workroom above papa's shop. Everyday after school I would climb a circular staircase, with no handrail, defying vertigo to watch papa work, marvelling at his dexterity. With a magnifying glass lodged in his right eye, he would pick up miniscule pieces of metal with pincers, position them on small joints and melt them in place with a soldering iron. He would cut wafer thin lengths of gold into tiny pieces, mix them with acid and melt them in a Greek coffee cup, over a Bunsen flame. When the cooling gold took on the texture of milk skin he would pour it into an old pickle jar fitted with electrodes and filled with a pungent mix of water and cianuro powder. In this noxious smelling solution he suspended his low-grade metals and as if by magic, plated them with 24 carat gold.

'Don't touch that. Don't touch this,' mama warned, 'the workshop is no place for a girl.' Tradition loftily decreed that my brother Minos follow in papa's professional footsteps. TRAD-I-SHON, pronounced as it was with such solemnity in *Fiddler on the Roof*, could go to hell.

Minos gave up his evenings reluctantly, his efforts were half-hearted, his workmanship laughable. His earrings had all the delicacy of door-knobs. Asked to design a simple pendant he would sketch a Medjool date. He lacked patience, imagination and a steady hand. At heart my brother was a white-collar man, who liked to wear a suit and keep his hands clean. He opted for a regimented life, the nine till early afternoon of a bank teller. Against my mother's wishes I became papa's young apprentice. At first I was only allowed to watch and clean, to hurry downstairs whenever the shop doorbell rang to serve customers. I darted down the rickety staircase like a frightened rabbit to secure a sale. 'Kyria Mantovani you look like a princess in that necklace,' I lied, honing the valuable skill of blah-blah required to sell. Mrs Mantovani, her hair gathered up on top of her head, looked like an artichoke gone to seed. 'My daughter, she could sell ice in the north pole,' papa would say, with pride. 'Electra will never go hungry.'

I swept floors. Polished machinery. Gathered up the gold dust and fragments scattered on the workbenches. Sweeping them into a plastic pot using the furry hind leg of a hare — the goldsmith's most valued tool. Papa melted down, purified and re-used these precious scraps. While Martha learned to cook *pastichio* and stuff marrows, I was busy stretching out pencil-sized pieces of solid gold into 20mm strands, reducing the metal in size by feeding it through a series of bronze cylinders, each one fractionally smaller in diameter than the one before. Like papa, I grew three of the nails on my right hand until they were an inch long and used them to hold down lengths of filigree and work them into loops and tight coils. I learned the dying craft of *triferenion* — Cypriot filigree — and produced work beyond the capability of any machine. *Triferenion* is my speciality and my passion.

I have inherited papa's work ethic, his restlessness of soul. Papa sketches designs over breakfast; talks shop over dinner; digests his evening meal and heads back to the workshop, leaving his wife to watch her daily diet of soaps. 'Why don't you stay and keep me company,' mama complains, knowing papa is as difficult to pin down as a fly with chopsticks, as incapable of keeping still as Maritsou, the town's most conspicuous compulsive obsessive. That poor woman spends her days sweeping the streets around her house, filling black bin liners with rubbish, praising God that litter breeds and gives her empty life a purpose. 'The only difference between your papa and Maritsou,' mama says, 'is that she has been certified.' Like papa, I try to squeeze every last constructive minute out of my day, to keep some part of me in motion, be it my feet, my hands or my mouth. Adam is quite happy to get home from work and assume the persona of a slug.

Adam

I feel safe with Electra at close quarters, her warmth oozing through plasterboard. Electra guards my psychological wellbeing, exercises the gamut of my emotional repertoire and saves me from myself. My life would be as bland as tofu without her, yet I cannot assume she will stay with me forever. One in three lose a spouse to divorce, a statistic fed by the five-year itch. Last week I gave my wife a wooden trinket box to celebrate our fifth anniversary. She presented me with a cricket bat to 'get my skinny ass moving.'

My wife is extraordinary. A hand-wrought creature with all its charm and imperfections. Life with Electra is interesting, a challenge, a cultural education. We live in a repression-free zone, where feelings are aired without fear of offending and no subject is taboo. Where one can shout when the need arises and grudges have a short shelf life. Electra has freed me from childhood bonds and circumvented my need for therapy. She has prised me slowly out of my shell, exposing my soft underbelly. For five years I have kept nothing from her. I have been an open book with a partially written prequel. Now, a confession must be made that may consign me to a lifetime of tofu.

I lie in bed listening to early morning sounds, my acoustic senses heightened, following each noise from its genesis to its conclusion. A feline caterwaul punctuates the silence. High heels clacking on concrete grow louder before fading into nothing. The hum of a car engine crescendos, clashes into gear, then splutters its way into the inaudible distance. Far-off laughter echoes, an auditory imprint as lasting as the flicker of a shooting star. I focus on the extraneous, in an effort to stave off the dark thoughts that linger on the periphery of my consciousness, that draw me like a vision in the corner of my eye or the dizzying lure of a cliff edge. Night was once my solace, a sigh of relief at the end of the day. Lately, worrying preoccupations have begun hijacking my peace of mind when I lay my head on a pillow. I used to read until my eyelids dropped, until I sank seamlessly into sleep. Now sleeping is an effort and fiction offers no escape.

I knew a young man once who climbed into bed, went to sleep and never woke up. Climbing into bed at the end of the day is no foolproof guarantee that one will get up in the morning. There were no signs, not an inkling that his heart would stop during the night. An unfinished essay fanned out on his desk, beside it a half-eaten chocolate bar, cigarettes poked from the full-ish packet on his bedside table. His long shoes formed a V-shape, the tip of the chevron pointing towards the dead youth. A vivid description of the room was painted by the friend who found him. It circulated, sending shock waves through the halls of residence that reached me with a dull thud. I was not moved to tears as others were but accepted the aberration with detachment. After all, the chances of dying in one's sleep are statistically negligible. Nineteen years on, the youth who slipped from sleep into death has begun to haunt me. The shock did not rebound off thick skin, as I had thought, but penetrated, and lay in wait.

Once upon a time ominous statistics floated over my head. A cloud of meaningless digits. Blown asunder like the seeds of a dandelion clock. As a child I was told not to blow the clocks lest one of the seeds propelled its way into my ear and took root. An ill wind has blown a more injurious seed in through my auricle. A germ that has sprouted and spread, infecting my psyche with the idea that I am just a number, a sitting duck, waiting for the law of probability to strike me down. Lying in bed, tending the garden, watching television will not save me. I have a one in twenty-something chance of sustaining an injury in the comfort of my own home. Toasters, electric shavers, lawnmowers, sandwich makers have all caused fatalities.

I did not marry Electra for her looks, though her looks were a bonus. She has long wavy hair and eyes like a striated cross-section of nutmeg. Her face would not look amiss amid the Fayum portraits, the ancient faces depicted on mummy cases, discovered in the Greek cemeteries of Roman Egypt. Like the noble faces of her ancestors she can look sweet, wistful, and profoundly melancholic. Electra can also look wild and slightly unhinged, when she has worked through the night and her eyes are streaked with red veins, when she has an idea for a new design and babbles away like a mad professor.

Not everyone can see what I love in her. My mother will never understand. How could she when she barely knows the man who lies beyond the surface of her son? I am no stranger to disapproval; maternal censure has marked every juncture of my life. I left home at seventeen to live on a kibbutz. I studied sociology and dropped out socially after my degree, to travel a portion of the world. I married a woman who does not fit the bill and speaks with the wrong kind of accent. Mother has never openly expressed her bigotry; such a thing would be uncivilised. She thinks her mocking remarks, made behind Electra's back, are entirely acceptable — as is criticism offered up as well meaning advice with the addendum 'I am only trying to help'. Mother should not try to outwit me. Words are my vocation. Nuances my livelihood. I play with words, I shuffled them like cards in a pack, I turn phrases arse about face.

Electra is the only woman who has ever made me laugh from the heart. I laugh with her and at her — but never cruelly. Her sense of humour is typical of the culture from which she hails. It is slapstick, black, Chaplinesque. It exalts the idiosyncratic, the far-fetched and the utterly ridiculous. Electra laughed until her stomach hurt when Mr Bean bowed abruptly and head-butted the Queen. Modelling herself on her comic hero, she has danced the tango with a parsnip and moon-walked for dinner guests. She has perfected the gobble of a turkey and can make a cigarette vanish from her hand and reappear behind her ear.

Electra

I once asked mama why she named me after a woman who despised her mother and conspired in matricide. Perplexed, mama looked at me and asked what in God's name I was talking about. 'I named you after a woman who gave birth to nine children, who laboured in the fields from morning to night, who lived to the ripe old age of 96,' she said. I took the name of my great grandmother. A fertile, hardy, she-devil of a woman, my mirror image according to family forklore, re-written to suit itself. 'The apple fell below the apple tree,' mama says, to emphasize her point. I am the apple. My namesake the tree. A faded black and white picture of great-grandmother Electra shows

169

a small thickset woman with no front teeth and skin as wrinkled as a walnut. 'Look, look, everyone,' mama declares excitedly at family gatherings, holding the picture up beside my face, 'no-one can dispute the likeness.' I can only hope that with the blight of great-grandmother's looks comes the blessing of longevity. The length of the life-line on my right palm would suggest this to be the case. On the side of my palm, at the base of my little finger, two feint lines are scored. They indicate the number of children fate has assigned me.

'I am not ready for children,' Adam says. 'There is still living to be done.' What does he think? That parenthood is a kind of death? Anyone would think he was Peter Pan the way he talks, blessed with the gift of eternal youth.

'Wake up,' I tell him, 'you are no spring chicken. Forty is no longer looming on the horizon my love, but knocking on the front door, waiting to come in and bid *arrivederci* to thirty-nine.' While I wait, playing metaphorical marbles, the tick-tock of biological clock growing louder in my ears, Adam's hair thins and his sperm count wanes. 'Don't panic,' he says, 'men are still fertile into old age. I heard about a man who fathered a child in his nineties.' Bully for him. He may well have sewn his seed and secured his bloodline but did he live long enough to see his child grow up? Could he kick a football round the park without dislocating a hip? I have waited patiently, hopefully, angrily, for Adam's change of heart, popping my daily pill. Risking thrombosis, a stroke and cervical cancer to inhibit conception. Squandering time and my childbearing years. Stewing in resentment.

The flat is as quiet as a hilltop monastery. Adam went to bed hours ago. I lock myself in the bathroom, my heart racing, and open the prophetic box that may set my life on a new course. I pull out the instruction sheet and read it, my stomach bobbing like a buoy below my ribcage. A feeling akin to seasickness holds me in its grip. I have missed a period and must find out why. I did not forget accidentally-on-purpose to take my oral contraceptive. No conscious effort has been made to dupe my husband. If I am pregnant, then our child has beaten the odds and was meant to be. While the world around me sleeps I follow the instructions to the letter. Open packet containing test stick. Hold tip under urine stream for five seconds. Close eyes tightly, cross fingers and wait two minutes.

Adam has littered the road to parenthood with unnecessary obstacles. Our finances must be watertight before we start a family. We must buy a house with a garden in a quiet street. Adam must be promoted and my jewellery business must start making a healthy profit. When will Adam be ready? On the thirty-second of the month, as we say back home. 'It is time my Electra,' Aunt Miroulla says, 'you do not want to wait and end up like me — with only a dog, not a baby to call your own.' To be honest — the thought terrifies me. I need a baby I can swaddle like stuffing in a vine leaf. I am ready. Over-ready. Maternal juices ooze from every pore.

What do I see when I open my eyes? A faint blue cross. Adam's crucifix. The answer to my prayers. The pill, like everything else in life, does not appear to be foolproof. In spite of chemical efforts to suppress ovulation, the test result is positive. I want to shout my news from the rooftops, to poke my head out of the darkened window and stop passers-by with shouts of 'Hey there! I'm pregnant!' What I must do instead is stopper my mouth. How can I share my news with a husband who says he is not ready? What if I tell him and see disappointment in his eyes? I will be tempted to crush his nose with my fist. 'O kindly, benevolent, munificent God,' I will pray each night before I go to bed, 'please save my husband from a bloody nose.'

The Drips and the Drops and the Wedding

Matt Haig

I was going to kill Uncle Alan at the weekend because I had a new plan but I forgot I was going to Sunderland with Mum. So I had to wait until after which was OK because it was only one night.

Sunderland is the worst part of England. It is where Mum comes from and where Nan lives. Mum always tells Nan to move near Newark but she doesnt want to. She wants to stay living in Sunderland and Mum always says Youre scared to go out of your house.

Nan says Its the same all over.

Mum says No mam its not.

Nan says Anyhow I cant leave George.

George is Grandad and he died in 2002 on September the 10th but Nan always talks like he is still alive but she knows hes dead really.

Nan always loves me. I dont know why. I dont do anything. I just sit and eat biscuits. But she always smiles at me like sitting down and eating biscuits is a special trick.

It was Saturday and we got at her door at 11 and she opened the door at 11:05 and she gave me a hairy kiss.

Mum was a shoe done up tight with a double knot and it was because she was scared of telling Nan about Uncle Alan.

And Mum didnt talk about Uncle Alan at first. She talked about all the shops and houses near Nans house which are dead with wood over all the windows and Nan said Its the same all over.

Nan makes the days longer in her house. She checks to make sure with a clock. The clock is on a shelf over the fire. It is a round circle with Roman Numerals and gold round it and it is in a stand which is the shape of a grave. It is white and it has flowers and plants and butterflies painted on it and it goes TICK TOCK TICK TOCK all day but it is the slowest clock in the world and it stays 20 minutes past 12 for half an hour.

Nan does nothing all day just her cross stitch and her cross word and her cross face when she watches the news or the window when girls go by with babies.

Then when it was still 20 minutes past 12 Mum said about getting married to Uncle Alan and Nan laughed like it was a joke. But Nan never laughs so I think she knew it was real.

Mum said Mam Im being serious.

Nan said Oh aye pet of course.

Mum said Mam please. Listen. Were getting married.

Nan coughed over Mums words and said Its all on my chest. It wont come up.

She got a tissue out. She put it to her mouth and put gob and greenies in it. There was spit strings from her mouth to the tissue like wires on cable cars and then the strings snapped and went on the tissue and then she said Sorry pet?

Mum said Alans asked me to marry him and Ive said Yes.

Nan said nothing and then she said Never in the world.

Mum said Now I know what youre thinking.

Nan said Im not thinking anything.

Mum said You think its too soon.

Nan said A month? Why no.

Mum said Two months. Its been two months.

Nan said Well then two months. Why Im surprised you even remember your Brians name after two months.

Mum said Mam please.

Nan said Thats plenty of time for Brian to turn in his grave. And anyhow it makes perfect sense marrying his brother. I mean you wont even have to change your name.

Nan looked at me and then at Mum and her eyes went sharp and she said Youre going to do that to the poor lad?

Mum said Do what?

Nan said I feel heart sorry for the poor bairn.

I was a bairn now. I was a man after the funeral but I was a bairn now.

Mum said Mam dont.

Nan said His Dad dies then you take up with his Uncle I mean what are you trying to do to him?

Mum said Philip go and play in the yard.

I looked out of the glass windows in the patio and the white lines of the blind straight down like prison bars.

The yard is nothing and has nothing in it. Not even one ball. It looked cold and I looked at the sky with big clouds like brains and I said Its cold.

Nan looked at my T shirt and said He needs more than a T shirt in this weather.

Mum said Hes got a jacket.

Nan said Oh that flimsy thing. You might as well put him in a bin liner as make him wear that.

Mum said Its not as cold in Newark.

Nan said Oh aye. Youre practically at the pyramids in Newark. The Trent joins up with the Nile.

Mum said Philip go in the spare bedroom just for a minute while I talk to your Nan.

So I went in the spare bedroom which is on the same floor because all of Nans house is on the same floor. It is a Bungalow because Nan cant climb stairs because of her hip which is made of metal. The metal is called titanium and if you got a really big magnet youd be able to get Nan to fly to it even if you put the magnet next to the wall and she was in the other room youd be able to get her to stick to the wall in the other room. If the magnet was high up it would lift her off the ground and she would be stuck to the wall and not be able to reach anything because the walls are thin like paper. Big white sheets of paper.

Nans metal hip makes her walk with a twisty face because it hurts. She has two metal walking sticks so she walks like she has four long legs like she is a crane fly on the water. She has a bad back as well.

She has ost something osis.

This means her back is like a question mark and she is shrinking. She used to be tall and now she is the same as me and one day we might come and Mum will say Wheres Nan gone?

She will be there on the carpet one centimetre tall saying Help help help Im shrinking and we might lose her again and Mum will say Wheres Nan gone now? And Ill check my shoes and Nan will be on my shoe stuck in my chewing gum going Help me help me Im stuck in the chewing gum.

Mums voice was getting louder and her words came out of the paper wall in whole pieces and they were Do you think its been easy for me? Its been terrible. Youve no idea. Brian left everything in a mess. I had no idea how much money he had borrowed. And how much the Pub was losing. He never bloody told me. And Ive had to deal with all this bank stuff on top of everything else. Philip getting into all sorts of trouble at school. Worrying me to death the way hes been going on. And Alans been so nice and hes been so kind and helped us out with money and

And then her words were getting quieter again and only coming out broken in half pieces ip ot ans ted ing and I couldnt mend them.

I tried to listen but there was another clock by the spare bed tick tock. It was next to the picture of Grandad which didnt look like Grandad because he was young and all grey. It was an old photograph of old times when everything was grey and smart and his eyes looked sad like he knew his future. Like he knew he was going to end up on the sofa all the time getting thinner because he couldnt eat without being sick.

And in between the clock tick tocking Mum was crying. She was always crying all the time now. I didnt know if the crying was about me or money or Dad. It was about me I think.

I looked out the window and there was nothing just the wall of Next Door.

I thought of Dads ghost telling me that Uncle Alan was a murderer.

I felt weird and I said Hello.

I dont know why I just wanted to hear my voice to check I was real but it didnt sound like my voice and the clock was getting louder TICK TOCK TICK TOCK and I got on the bed and lay down and the ceilings swervy circles started spinning round and my skin itched and things you dont think about like breathing in and out I was thinking about like if I stopped thinking about it Id stop breathing and the air was different air like Coke is different to Pepsi it was Cocacola air not Pepsi air and I said Hello again but my voice was still a long way from me.

My heart was doing its funny beating with no stops in it and I thought why am I me why am I not Mum why am I not the ticking clock why am I not a fish why am I not a loaf of bread why am I alive and most people are dead how do I know Im me how do I know Im alive and I thought it must be good to be dead not dead like Dads dead but to be nothing like when you sleep but then I thought it might be a bad sleep with lots of nightmares like the one I had last night when I was trapped in the black box and then my hand started shaking and I was scared why my hand was shaking and I thought I was going to die and I said Mum! Mum! Mum!

Mum came in and opened the door and her eyes were red and she looked at me and said Philip whats the matter?

And far away my voice said I dont know. I feel weird. I dont know my hands shaking.

And she came and felt my head and my heart and sat on the bed next to me and said Its OK its OK Philip youre just in a bit of a panic its OK.

And Nan was a crane fly in the door with her silver front legs and she was saying Dinny chew yourself up lad and Mum said Deep breaths Philip and I said Am I going to die? And she said No which was a lie but I think she meant Not right now and she said Now come on deep breaths and I sucked the Cocacola air in big gulps and still felt empty and the clock was just getting louder

tick

tock
tick

***

I dont like Dr Crawford.

He is the doctor who made me get my willy half chopped off in the Summer Holidays before Dad died because the skin was too tight when it was thinking about girls. I had to go to hospital and I had to have injections and go to sleep with a nurse counting backwards 10 9 8 7 sleep. After the operation I woke up and it was all white like in heaven but there was pain and I looked inside my pyjamas and there were big stitches like thorns. It wasnt good because I had to walk like a hunchback and not let it touch my

177

pyjama bottoms so I had to hold the elastic really far out like I had an invisible fat stomach. When I went to new school it was still a bit sore but the stitches were out. They just fell out when I used to pick them when I went for wees. In the first week of the new school I had to do Games and it was Rugby so Mr Rosen made us shower after Dominic and Jordan called me Helmet because it looks like a helmet on a Roman soldier and Jew Nob and I didnt know why and Dad said Jews have to be circumcised as well and I said Why? and he didnt know why.

Dr Crawford has glasses. I dont know why he has glasses because he looks over them all the time with his chin in his neck. And Dr Crawford is old. He has lines all over his face like he is a map you cant understand and he said to Mum So whats the matter?

Mum said about my heart beating really fast and my sleep walking and my breathing and my shaking sometimes and my other things and Dr Crawford kept looking at me over his glasses and sitting in his chair with his long crossed legs and nodding fast at Mums words like the words were food and he was a bird eating them.

And when Mum had finished talking Dr Crawford said These are all classic signs of Panic Disorder which in this case has probably been triggered by the circumcises of his fathers death.

I dont know if the word was circumcises but that was what it sounded like.

Mum said Oh.

And he turned his long flamingo legs under his desk and started writing on paper and Mum said Will he be all right?

Dr Crawford said Yes. Im sure hell be all right Mrs Noble. Its just a case of controlling his nervous system and controlling the ADREN-ALIN that is causing his heart rate to increase.

Mum said I see. So what are they? I mean the pills. Theyre not erm

Dr Crawford said Theyre called DIAZEPAM.

Mum said Are they. You know. Are they. I mean are they OK for children?

Dr Crawford said In the doses I shall be advising yes it is perfectly suitable for children of eleven.

And Dr Crawford handed Mum the paper and Mum looked at the writing but didnt understand doctor language because only Chemists understand doctor language so she took me over the road to the

Chemist and got me the tablets and she said Youll be better now Philip. Youll be right as rain.

***

Uncle Alan had been in the bath. I could smell his new Salts and I could smell his poo in the toilet. I went in the bath and I just lay there and I wasnt thinking anything I was just listening to the tap go drip drop drip drop drip drop drop.

I kept hearing the voices of Mum and Uncle Alan between the drips and the drops and Uncle Alan was saying I dont scrub up bad if I do say so myself.

Mum said Are my shoes OK? Theyre not too much with the dress? Theyre not too high? Do I look all right?

And Uncle Alan said Like a movie star. Like a magazine.

And then Uncle Alan went past the door and down the stairs whistling what hed been whistling all week.

The whistle was Im getting married in the morning ding dong the bells are going to drip drop drip drop drip drop drip drip drip drop.

And Mum said behind the door Philip love. Philip? Philip?

And I said What?

And she said Weve got to be at the Registry Office half an hour early Philip. How are you getting on?

And I said All right.

And Mum said Ill just go and sort Nan out.

And I stayed in a bit more until the water was cold like the coldest Roman bath which is the Frigidarium which is where Romans went after the Tepidarium warm bath and the Caldarium hot bath and then I got out and dried my body and dried my head under the towel and I liked it under the towel. It was like another world. Like a green towel world that was soft.

Uncle Alan was four hours on the motorway just him and Nan the night before. Nan hates him and Uncle Alan hates Nan but human beings always hate each other and pretend they dont. That is what being a human being is about.

I went out of the bathroom in my green towel like a skirt and I went into my bedroom.

Mum had got my suit out and it was the same suit I had for Dads

179

funeral but with a light white shirt not a dark blue shirt. I looked at the suit on the bed and it looked weird like someone had run over me with a steam roller or turned me flat like paper.

Mum was talking to Nan downstairs but I couldnt hear the words. I put the suit on. I tucked the shirt in after I put the jacket on and that made it hard. My brain was still a bit slow from the tablets but it was speeding up.

I went out of the room and stood on the top of the stairs and Uncle Alan was coming up the stairs in elephant steps and he said All right lad?

I said Yes.

He was wearing his tight suit with his neck pouring out.

He said Shall I sort your tie out son?

I said What?

He said Your ties all wonky.

I said Oh.

He said Shall I do you a knot like mine?

I looked at Uncle Alans knot. It was a small triangle upside down and he said Its a Windsor knot.

I said I dont know.

He said Its a special wedding knot.

I didnt want him to do me a Windsor knot but his big hands were all ready on my tie and he was undoing it and then he lifted my collars up and I thought he might squeeze the life out of me and Mum and Nan wouldnt hear. But he didnt.

I saw Dads Ghost on the stairs behind Uncle Alan and I was on the top stair and Uncle Alan was two steps down so I could see over his shoulder and Dads Ghost said Now is the time Philip.

I said What?

Uncle Alan was putting the tie through the knot and he said I didnt say anything.

Dads Ghost said This is your moment Philip. Push him down the stairs Philip. Push with all your strength son.

I said I I I

Uncle Alan said Are you all right son?

Dads Ghost said Kill him kill him now Philip. Before he marries her.

I said I dont want to.

180

Uncle Alan said Ive nearly finished it now lad.

Dads Ghost said Do it Philip. Do it before its too late.

And I closed my eyes and lifted up my hands and Dads Ghost said Push him Philip. Push him.

And I was going to push him. I was going to do it. But I heard Mum at the bottom of the stairs and she said Whos that handsome man?

I opened my eyes and Uncle Alan finished off the tie and Dads Ghost wasnt there any more and Mum was wearing a light green dress and two light green shoes and her hair was in slides like it was going inside her head and her face had Make Up on and her eyebrows were like wings of birds when you draw them flying in the sky and her pink lips made her teeth pink as well.

She looked at me and the me she was seeing wasnt the real me who nearly killed Uncle Alan because she was smiling like I was a magic boy. Her eyes were shiny with more tears in them and Nan was there behind with her four legs on the carpet that was blue like a pond.

Nan looked up at me and said Ee what a picture.

Uncle Alan went passed me and went into the toilet and shut the door and he started to wee elephant wee.

Mum was two people now. A moving fast person inside a moving slow person. Or a moving slow person inside a moving fast person. I dont know which.

And she said Philip could you start taking Nan to the car?

And then she said Keys keys keys.

I went down the stairs and held onto Nans elbow and her baggy skin with no blood inside it and Nan made a noise like she was hurt just by me touching her elbow.

Sssssssssssss

Mum found the keys and opened the door for me and Nan and went to switch all the lights off and I kept holding Nans arm.

Nan was two people. She was a moving slow person inside a moving very slow person. So I was walking in the smallest Guiness Book of Records steps to the door.

Nan went Ee Aa Ee Aa Ee Aa Ee every time she made a step with her legs or her sticks. When we got to the back door I looked out and guessed it was about 10 normal steps to the car and that is 100 Nan steps.

Ee Aa Ee Aa Ee Aa.

I said Were nearly at the car Nan.

She kept looking at the car and laughing at me like I was mad like the car was 10 miles away not 10 steps away and Grandad used to say that when you get older time gets shorter and walks get longer.

Uncle Alan went past us stroking his suit and making chins and Mum shut the door and clip clopped past like a horse with two legs and Nan said to her Look at me Aa slowing you all down.

Mum said Youre not slowing us down. Were fine for time.

Nan said If you parked a bit Ee closer.

Mum said If you wait there Ill reverse the car.

Nan said I dont want to be any Ee bother pet.

Mum said Its no bother.

Mum got in the car and it went backwards and nearly knocked one of Nans silver sticks over.

Nan laughed and said to me I think theyre trying to finish us off Philip.

I kept holding the skeleton inside her skin and I didn't laugh because Uncle Alan really had killed dad. The car parked in front of us and I opened the door for Nan and I held her sticks and Uncle Alan said Do you need a hand back there?

And Nan said to me Some new legs would do.

Uncle Alan got out of his side of the car and helped Nan get in the car and Nan going Aa Aa Aa Watch Aa Aa and when her legs were in Uncle Alan took the metal sticks out of my hand and put them on the floor of the car in front of her.

I went round the other side and got in and sat next to her and helped her with her seat belt and she was saying I can do it pet but she couldnt.

Uncle Alan said My seats not too far back is it Philip?

I said No.

I thought he is only nice when Mum is there and then he smiled at Mum with eyes like on TV when people are in love and it made me feel sick like it was semolina in my eyes.

Mum drove to the Registry Office which is on the other side of town and the sky was grey and low down and we went past the houses that are yellow like they are ill and no one was talking. Nan was looking out at the kids and going Ssss like she was a lilo when you let the air out and we went by the shops of Newark Players video

182

and J D Sports and KFC and the Chip shop and Caesars Palace. It isnt Julius Caesars Palace it is a Nightclub which is like Drama club but for people who like Night not Drama and it must be owned by someone called Caesar but not Julius. It might be owned by David Caesar or Brian Caesar or Philip Caesar.

We went past the castle wall and the castle park and the castle tramps with no teeth drinking bottles in bags on the bench. One of them saw me looking at him and his eyes stayed on me like they were trying to give me something but I didnt know what. We passed the Chinese and the Purple Door Club where Dad went once and Mum screamed at him I dont know why and Bottoms Up and the woman who shouts about God and Les Miserable walking out of Ladbrokes and we were behind a horse in a box. It was not a posh village Ra Ra horse it was a Traveller horse going left to Tolney Lane where all the big gold caravans and the Travellers and the hard kids live who dont go to normal school and who can beat up anyone even Dane with their fists and big rings and we went on going past Morrisons and past all the houses and then we got there we got to the Registry Office and Newark stopped moving fast.

The Registry Office looks like nothing.

It is just a building with red bricks that you dont notice. This is on purpose so God doesnt notice and so he doesnt put lightning out of his fingers and kill the people who get married again who lied to him in the church.

Mum parked very close to the door so it wasnt far for Nan. There was a two metres tall woman at the door in a suit which was maroon and the woman said when we got out Alan and Carol?

Mum said Yes thats us.

The woman was as tall as Uncle Alan and she said We spoke on the phone. Im Angela. The Registrar.

There was a step and Nan looked at the step and a far away storm went on in her head and Angela the Registrar bent down one metre and smiled at Nan like she was a cat and she said to Nan Hello duckie do you want a wheelchair?

Nan said No pet I dont need a wheelchair.

So me and Uncle Alan helped her up the step and she went Aa Aa Aa and Mum said with crossness inside her voice but pink lips smiling at Angela the Registrar Are you sure you dont want a wheelchair Mum?

And when we got inside there was a hall and four doors and chairs in between the doors and a smelly carpet. Me and Nan sat on two chairs and no one else was there because we were early and Nan was still unflating ssss.

Mum and Uncle Alan went to talk to Angela the Registrar and Angela the Registrar said Right if I could have your passports.

sssssss

Mum went in her light green bag and got out two passports and Angela the Registrar said Smashing. If I could have your birth certificates.

ssssssss

Mum gave her the birth certificates and Angela the Registrar said Smashing. Right. If I could have evidence of your address E G a bill or your driving

ssssssss

Mum gave her a piece of paper and Angela the Registrar looked at it and said Smashing and then she looked at Mum and said And do you have a death certificate for your late husband?

Why are dead people late people? Dad isnt late hes early. Hes in front of everyone whos still alive because you dont start off dead you start off nothing and then you are alive and then you are dead. So it goes

Nothing

Alive

Dead

and if you are dead when you are 41 that is early not late.

Mum gave Angela the Registrar the death certificate. It was just a bit of paper and Angela the Registrar looked at it and said Smashing.

And then people started coming.

There was mums friend Renuka who saw me and made noises because I was in a suit and Carla the Barmaid who was playing with her earrings and looking cross and moving in her suit like it had itching powder in it. She said to her boys Ross and Gary Behave you two.

They were doing dead arms.

Ross said All right Philster?

And Gary said Is that your Nan? like Nan had no ears.

I said Yes.

184

Ross said Is she 100?

I said No.

Gary said Is she older than 100?

Ross said Is she 120?

I said No.

They said What older?

And I said No.

Nan said Ssssss.

Gary said 119?

And then Angela the Registrar went in one of the doors and everyone followed her like she was the Pied Piper going to the river.

***

The room had green stripy wall paper and rows of chairs and a ceiling that was getting lower and lower and a carpet that was thick like grass and sinking my feet.

I was between Nan and Renuka on the second row and they were the only grownups in the room I was taller than and I was feeling weird like my brain was going too fast and I wished Id had my tablet.

Angela the Registrar nodded her high head and made wide eyes at a man at the end of the room and said Derek music and some Derek music came on.

Then she said Derek and the music stopped.

Angela the Registrar looked at Uncle Alan and Mum standing there and Renuka came up in a whisper saying Doesnt your Mum look beautiful Philip?

I looked at Mums bare back over her dress and her bare neck and I said Yes.

She said I bet youre proud.

I said nothing.

And Angela the Registrar pressed her hands together and said Id like to start by welcoming you all to

He was there standing behind. Dads Ghost.

He said You have to stop this Philip.

Angela the Registrar said If any persons present know of any lawful impediment why Alan and Carol may not be joined together in matrimony please speak now.

Dads Ghost said Say something Philip. Tell them about Uncle Alan. Tell them the truth Philip. The truth.

Angela the Registrar looked at Uncle Alan and said If you can say after me.

He said after her I do solemnly declare that I know not of any lawful impediment why I Alan Peter Noble may not be joined in matrimony to Carol Suzanne Noble.

And then Mum said it and put more Nobles in the room.

I do Noble why I Noble know not Noble may not Noble in Noble to Noble Noble Noble.

Dads Ghost was screaming No! No! No!

And the ceiling was getting low low low and the carpet was growing grow grow and I looked behind and saw all the other faces looking at Uncle Alan and Mums backs and then it happened the big blue giant and the little green Mum turned to each other and the words came out of him into Mums eyes.

I call upon these persons here present to witness that I Alan Peter Noble do take thee Carol Suzanne Noble to be my lawful wedded wife and Nan went Ssssss and Renuka touched her eye and went Awwwww and Dads Ghost looked at Mum and said Dont do it dont say it dont say it I still love you please and Mum smiling up into Uncle Alans face I call upon these persons here present Dont do it witness that I Carol Suzanne Noble awwwww do take thee Alan I still Peter love you no to be my lawful wedded husband ssssssssssssssssssssssssssssssssssssssssssssssssss

I am dizzy and I blink and I am in the car park holding Nans elbow and Uncle Alan in front lifting Mum up and taking her in the door like the Romans did and Mum laughing and Uncle Alan laughing and Nan looking at me with her eyes like little milk plates for a cat to drink and her mouth with no lips saying It wont Aa last son it wont last.

186

The First Punch

Jon McGregor

The first punch is a shock. We're taking a short-cut across where the old steelworks used to be, that huge old strip of land between the river and the canal with the motorway flying somewhere way over-head and down here it's almost quiet. Silver birch trees and rowan bushes bursting up through the concrete foundations. Thistles with bright purple flowerheads, stray yellow rapeseed flown in from the fields outside town, those white flowers with the petals like trumpets that wind their way across the ground and up round anything they can get their feelers onto. Butterflies and dragonflies and the evening-song of birds that have lived here for centuries. He says, you wouldn't have thought this was a foundry just five years ago would you. Everywhere there are scattered lumps of machinery, lost cogs and gearwheels, stacks of plate, coils of wire. He says, the way these trees come back you wouldn't believe it. He was one of the last work-ers to be laid off here, and he can still point out where the steel was smelted and poured and formed; the outlines of the old sheds and foundry-halls spread out across the whole site like a giant blueprint, ankle-high walls rearing up to hold a tall window frame, a door hang-ing off its hinges. But mostly there are trees and bushes and birdlife, and it's a good place to walk on a long summer's evening with the sky stretching hazy blue over our heads, a couple of pints swimming through us and one or other of us talking quietly now and again.

So when the first punch comes, it's a shock. Straight into my stom-ach and my body folds around it, the breath knocked out of me and I stagger backwards with my feet scraping and scrabbling on the stony ground. Perhaps it doesn't make sense that I'm surprised, because why else would we be out here, talking about these things, all this talk of I love my wife and if anyone ever tried I know what I'd do, but as I drag the air back into my winded lungs I'm surprised and I don't understand.

I look up at him, laughing, as though it might be a joke or I can somehow turn it into one, and I say what what are you doing what's

187

this? He brings the heel of his open hand crashing into the side of my head like a lump-hammer. I almost fall to the ground, and there's a high-pitched ringing noise in my ears and I can't think and I don't know how to respond. I lift my arms up around my head, turning away, and he pulls my wrists to my side as he slams his forehead into the bridge of my nose.

I'm on the ground, and he is standing over me. Everything is muffled. I'm aware of the sound of running water somewhere. He stoops over me, and punches each side of my head alternately, each punch knocking my head across to meet the next. My arms reach up again to shield myself, but he just punches on through them. He is breathing heavily, watching me, concentrating.

When he stops, there is pain. A hot roar of pain flooding through me. I turn my head to one side and vomit onto the ground. He stands away slightly, getting his breath back.

And this is not right. I should be running away, or defending myself, or calling for help, but I am doing none of these things. I am lying on the dirty ground, watching him, waiting for his next move.

He says what did you think you were doing?

He says how did you even imagine you were going to get away with it?

He calls me a cunt, and he kicks me in the side, his boot fitting neatly between my hip bone and the base of my ribcage.

***

The first time she ever touched me, she touched me on the back of the head, her fingers trailing down through my hair to the nape of my neck, up again, down again, suddenly pulling away as though scorched against a hotplate. She said sorry sorry and for some reason I said sorry too and we didn't say anything else about it. But the way it felt; her long fingers pressing lightly and firmly, the slight scratch of her fingernails. I could feel the lines they had traced across my scalp, tingling.

It had come from nowhere, a lull in the conversation, her hand drifting there with her eyes fixed firmly on mine and I didn't pull away or say anything to stop her, and afterwards I wanted her to do it again and I wanted to leave and I wanted her not to have done it.

We were sitting in the park. We'd finished our lunches and were about to go back to work, back to our different offices in the same building and I can't even think now how it was we'd first come across each other and started talking the way we did. I was thinking about the cases I'd be dealing with that afternoon and suddenly there were her fingers trailing down the back of my neck and she was touching me.

I don't know how we got to that. I've never been clear how anyone ever gets to that.

A few moments later she said excuse me but you just looked a bit sad. I said did I? and she said kind of wistful and I said oh I was just thinking about work and she laughed. That laugh.

She was younger than me, about ten years younger I think but I never really noticed. It never seemed important, meeting for lunch and drinks after work and sometimes being on the same bus. It was only ever about conversation. Our ages, or the rings we both wore, were nothing to do with any of it. We were good at talking to each other was all it was. I could tell her about work, and Eleanor, and fatherhood, and I wouldn't feel like she wanted me to stop. She could tell me about her job, and her husband, and his job, and all the things she liked and didn't like about her life, and I wouldn't feel like there was anything I needed to say. Sometimes our conversation was funny, sometimes it was patient and sad, but always it just came easily and kept on going. And I thought I believed that the sheer startling fact of her physical beauty was no part of the way I enjoyed her company. But the way it felt, that day in the park when she just ran her fingers down through the hair on the back of my head, that was something; and her voice saying because she thought I looked like I was feeling sad, that was something more again.

It had been a long time since anyone had done that.

I wanted to say thankyou but instead I said sorry. She laughed, and she said you look good when you're thinking, pretty. I was embarrassed for a moment. Pretty seemed like a strange word to use of a forty-year old man with lines around his eyes.

But all that happened next was I looked at my watch and stood up to go back to work. She said have a good afternoon, I walked away, and when I turned back to look she wasn't looking at me. She was reading something, running her fingers up and down the back of her

189

head, through her dark tangle of hair. I went back to work, and I tried not to think about it, and the next time I saw her was that afternoon at her house. His house.

***

He comes towards me, and my body tenses, my forearms crossing over my face. He crouches beside me, and pulls my arms away, pinning them to my chest with one hand. I look at him. His eyes are wide and clear, he is sweating a little, there are strands of hair sticking to his forehead. He takes off his jacket, rolls it up, and puts it under my head for a pillow. He doesn't say a word. I look at him, my vision still clouded, my mouth gaping soundlessly. He smiles.

I say, but but what but I didn't do anything.

He smiles again. He says you loved it didn't you?

I look at him, and I don't know what to say. I say, I didn't, what? no, no I didn't.

He winces, turns away, turns back. You fucking liar he says, don't fucking lie to me.

The memory of her. Standing there in that dress. Her bare shoulders and the way she looked at me with those eyes. The movement of the dress when she turned in the doorway, the way it swung around the backs of her legs. That was all it took; her looking at me like that, those eyes, the way the dress swung around the backs of her long bare legs as she turned in the doorway there.

He rushes in towards me and stamps his foot down onto my chest and again all the breath is forced out of me, again there is staggering sickening pain. He does this three times, and the third time, barely realising what I am doing, I roll over and start to crawl away, scraping my hands on the brambles, heading towards the sound of rushing water. I can hear shouted voices somewhere, and laughter. I am crawling for perhaps thirty seconds when I hear quick footsteps behind me and feel a sudden snapping impact to the back of my head. I stop crawling.

He rolls me over, onto my back, and places the pillow beneath my head again, looking down at me with a look on his face as if he wants me to speak. I am shivering. My breathing is ragged and torn. I can hear the shouted voices from somewhere over by the river, I can see

190

the cars rushing across the flyover way up in the sky.

He says don't fucking lie to me David.

He says I don't need people lying to me, I won't have it, I need to be able to trust people, it's not much to ask is it?

I look at him. He takes out a packet of cigarettes, putting the pack to his mouth and biting one out like a splinter from a hand. He puts the packet back and lights the cigarette.

He says she's my wife yeah? I know what she looks like, I know what happens when she's wearing that dress, I know what it does to the way she looks yeah? I bought her that dress so that she'd look like that, he says. I don't know what I'm supposed to say, I watch him and I keep breathing and I listen to the sound of the voices somewhere getting quieter now.

He says and you're telling me you were in the house with her, in the middle of the afternoon, and she's wearing that dress, and you didn't even want to?

He calls me a liar again, he comes closer and he looks at me and he smokes his cigarette.

***

The second time she ever touched me was that afternoon in her house. I can't quite remember why I was there, she'd asked me to pop round and help move a sofa or a table or something but when I got there she didn't mention it. It was a hot day, she had her hair all tied up on top of her head and wisps of it were falling out, she kept tucking them behind her ear, fanning herself with a piece of paper and saying hey I'm hot aren't you? And every time she said it she giggled, nervously or embarrassedly or excitedly I couldn't tell. She had a laugh that made my ears flush red. He was out at work, she told me that, more than once.

She poured us both a cold drink, orange juice with lemonade, and she dropped ice-cubes into the glasses. She dared me to suck a whole ice-cube and I dared her back, and we stood there in her kitchen with our mouths puckered around a block of ice each, grimacing at each other, her eyes watering and sparkling, and when she spat hers out and laughed and leaned towards me that was the second time she touched me. Her two hands flat to my chest, gently, briefly.

191

It had been a long time since anyone had done that.

It was a blue dress she was wearing, pale blue as though it had been washed too often, and it hung from her bare round shoulders on straps as thin as parcel string. It was cut into a sort of v at the back, and when she turned and reached up to a shelf, leaning back slightly, I could see almost down to her waist before I looked away.

We sat in the front room with our cold drinks. She sat beside me, not close enough to touch but turned towards me with her legs folded beneath her and one arm laid out along the back of the sofa. And she talked a lot, quickly, she laughed and the way she laughed made me feel uncomfortable and good at the same time. And when she didn't talk she took a long slow sip of her drink, looking over me at the top of her glass, a long slow look which I wanted to look away from but couldn't.

She asked me how were things with Eleanor, and I said the same, that she wasn't spending so long in bed but that she still wouldn't leave the house and she still looked puffy-eyed when I came in from work. I told her the doctor had been talking about a different medication and that I wasn't sure that was really the answer. This was almost a routine conversation by now. She said it's good you know, what you do for her, I respect that, and I said no, really, I mean she's my wife what else would I do?

She was wearing a long bead necklace, she was twisting it between two fingers and when she let it go it fell against bare skin.

She said I'm glad you're here it's good to have you here and I said well it's good to be here and I was being mock polite but really I meant it. It was good to be there, on her sofa, with a cold drink, her sitting with me, in that dress, tucking wisps of dark hair behind her ear and talking and laughing. She said is it?, suddenly, demandingly, is it good to be here, are you glad you're here? And I said yes, yes it is, yes I am, and I was confused and she was quiet.

I finished my drink. I went to the toilet. I washed my face and my hands, and when I came out of the bathroom at the top of the stairs that was when it happened.

She was standing in the open doorway of the room next to the bathroom, leaning against the doorframe slightly, she'd taken her shoes off and she had one ankle curled round behind the other.

The blue dress hung down to her knees, but with one leg lifted like

192

that it rode up a little, about a third way up her thigh.

I looked at her.

That was all. I just looked at her.

She lifted a hand to adjust the knot of hair at the back of her head, and smiled.

And that could have been enough, that moment, standing there looking at her, and her smile, for me, that hot day with the windows open and the sleepy sounds of summer drifting through the house, a lawnmower somewhere, children shouting.

She said how do I look? and it seemed like she really wanted to know, standing there beautiful and desirable every inch of her, like she wasn't sure, her elegant bare feet and the smooth straight rise of her legs, the way her dress pulled against the curve of her hips and the press of her breasts, her shoulders, her neck, her eyes. Her eyes looked strange for a moment, when I looked, anxious almost. I said you look good and she said do I? really? as if she wasn't sure, as if she thought I might be humouring her somehow, as if there was no-one who told her each day how good she looked. I said, very quietly, yes you do, you look very good. She smiled again, looking away for a moment, looking over her shoulder into the room. I still hadn't moved. When she turned back her eyes looked different and she wasn't smiling. She said, quietly, looking straight at me, do you want me? I did. I wanted her. Hugely and deeply I wanted her. I said, I whispered, yes. She said, her voice quiet and unsteady, oh good, and she turned quickly in the doorway, stepping into the room, out of sight. I didn't even breathe.

That movement, the turn of her hips, the swing and lift of her dress, the backs of her legs.

I don't know how long she waited. I didn't move. I couldn't. She reappeared, and when she spoke this time her eyes spilled clearly over into tears, her voice cracking. She said don't be shy I'm waiting for you. She said don't you want me you said you wanted me. I said I do. She said well come on then, and she opened her mouth slightly, and there were tears down both her cheeks, shining. I wanted her incredibly. I hesitated. I turned and walked down the stairs, out into the afternoon sunshine.

***

My hands are folded together on my chest, I am having trouble breathing and the pain is everywhere now. He looks at me. His cigarette is halfway to the filter. He coughs a little, turning to spit on the ground. He says excuse me, sorry.

He walks towards me and crouches down. He says, listen, you and Eleanor, that's your problem.

He says I don't care if she's not giving you any. I don't give a shit if she makes you sleep in the spare room or if she never even wants to undress in front of you again. I'm not bothered. It's got nothing to do with me. But you're not having mine, alright? He says it very quietly, smiling, as though he's trying not to laugh, and he stands up.

I didn't tell him anything about Eleanor. He shouldn't know all that. I've only ever talked to one person about these things.

He taps the end of his cigarette, and flakes of ash flutter to the ground. He says I'm sorry about all this mate, but it had to be done. He says you got to be able to trust people David, else what's the point?

He says I'm not having you or no-one fucking about with that, alright?

He flicks his cigarette away and looks at me for a few moments, as if he's waiting for me to say something in return. There is nothing I can say.

He turns and walks away from me, heading towards the bridge over the river where the footpath leads to the steps up the side of the hill, through the woods and out into the streets to the house where he lives with his wife.

I watch until he disappears amongst the trees and the bushes. I stand up, slowly and painfully. The sun is low in the sky, everything is bright and clear and peaceful and I feel sick. Dizzy. Confused.

I start to make my way home. It feels like a long way. As soon as I start walking I have to stop for a moment, my breath caught tight in my bruised lungs.

The cars rush across the flyover. Birds crowd together overhead, sweeping across the sky. Dandelions and thistles and blackberry bushes force their way up through the broken concrete.

I walk towards the bridge, towards the steps up the side of the hill and the house where I live with my pale and tearful wife. I will ask

194

her how she is. I will fetch her what she needs from the kitchen. I will take her to the bathroom. She trusts me to do this for her. It's important. You have to be able to trust people.

Home

John Harvey

Resnick was unable to sleep. All those years of living alone, just the weight of the cats, one and occasionally more, pressing lightly down on the covers by his feet or in the V behind his legs, and now, with Lynn away for just forty-eight hours, he was lost without her by his side. The warmth of her body next to his, the small collisions as they turned from their respective dreams into a splay of legs, her arm sliding across his chest. 'Lay still, Charlie. Another five minutes, okay?' Musk of her early morning breath.

He pushed away the sheet and swivelled round, then rose to his feet. Through an inch of open window, he could hear the slight swish of cars along the Woodborough Road. Not so many minutes short of two a.m.

Downstairs, Dizzy, the oldest of the four cats, a warrior no longer, raised his head from the fruit bowl he had long since appropriated as a bed, cocked a chewed and half-torn ear and regarded Resnick with a yellow eye.

Padding past, Resnick set the kettle to boil and slid a tin of coffee beans from the fridge. A flier announcing Lynn's course was pinned to the cork board on the wall — *Unzipping the Agenda: A Guide to Creative Management and Open Thinking.* Lynn and forty or so other officers from the East Midlands and East Anglia at a conference centre and hotel beside the A1 outside Stevenage. Promotion material. High fliers. When she had joined the Force Crime Directorate, then called the Major Crime Unit, it had been as a sergeant; an inspector now and barely thirty, unless somehow she blotted her copy book, the only way was up. Whereas for Resnick, who had turned down promotion and the chance to move onto a bigger stage, little more than a pension awaited once his years were in.

While the coffee dripped slowly through its filter, Resnick opened the back door into the garden and, as he did so, another of the cats, Pepper, slithered past his ankles. Beyond the allotments, the lights of the city burned dully through a haze of rain and mist. Down there, on the streets of St. Ann's and the Meadows, armed officers patrolled with Walther P990s holstered at their hips. Drugs, of course, the cause of most of it, the cause and the core: all the way from after-dinner cocaine served at trendy middle-class dinner parties alongside the squares of Green and Black's dark organic chocolate, to twenty-five pound wraps of brown changing hands in the stairwells of dilapidated blocks of flats.

Bolting the door, he carried his coffee through into the living room, switched on the light and slid a CD into the stereo. *Art Pepper Meets the Rhythm Section*, Los Angeles, January 19th, 1957. Pepper only months out of jail on drugs offences, his second term and still only thirty-two. And worse to come.

Resnick had seen him play in Leicester on the British leg of his European tour; Pepper older, wiser, allegedly straightened out, soon to be dead three years shy of sixty, a small miracle that he survived that long. That evening, in the function room of a nondescript pub, his playing had been melodic and inventive, the tone piping and lean, its intensity controlled. Man earning a living, doing what he can.

Back in fifty-seven, in front of Miles Davis's rhythm section, he had glittered, half-afraid, inspired, alto saxophone dancing over the chords of half-remembered tunes. "Star Eyes", "Imagination", "Jazz Me Blues". The track that Resnick would play again and again: "You'd Be So Nice To Come Home To".

For a moment Pepper's namesake cat appeared in the doorway, sniffed the air and turned away, presenting his fine tail.

Just time for Resnick, eyes closed, to conjure up a picture of Lynn, restlessly sleeping in a strange bed, before the phone began to ring.

It was the sergeant on duty, his voice stretched by tiredness: '...ten, fifteen minutes ago, sir. I thought you'd want to know.'

That stretch of the Ilkeston Road was a mixture of small shops and residential housing, old factories put to new use, student accommodation. Police cars were parked, half on the kerb, either side of a black Ford Mondeo that, seemingly, had swerved wildly and collided, broadside, into a concrete post, amidst a welter of torn metal and splintered glass. Onlookers, some with overcoats pulled over their night clothes and carpet slippers on their feet, stood back behind hastily strung out police tape, craning their necks. An ambulance and fire engine stood opposite, paramedics and fire officers mingling with uniformed police at the perimeter of the scene. Lights flashing, a second ambulance was pulling away as Resnick arrived.

Driving slowly past, he stopped outside a shop, long boarded up, *High Class Butcher* in faded lettering on the brickwork above.

Anil Khan, once a DC in Resnick's squad and now a sergeant, came briskly down to meet him and walked him back.

"One dead at the scene, sir, young female; one on his way to hospital, the driver. Female passenger, front near side, her leg's trapped against the door where it buckled in. Have to be cut out most likely. Oxyacetylene."

Resnick could see the body now, stretched out against the lee of the wall beneath a dark grey blanket that was darker at the head.

'Impact?' Resnick said. 'Thrown forward against the windscreen?'

Khan shook his head. 'Shot.'

It stopped Resnick in his tracks.

'Another car, as best we can tell. Three shots, maybe four. One of them hit her in the neck. Must have nicked an artery. She was dead before we got her out.'

Illuminated by the street light above, Resnick could see the blood, sticky and bright, clinging to the upholstery like a second skin. Bending towards the body, he lifted back the blanket edge and looked down into the dead startled eyes of a girl of no more than sixteen.

Fifteen years and seven months. Alicia Ann Faye. She had lived with her mother, two younger sisters and an older brother in Hyson Green. A bright and popular student, a lovely girl. She had been to an eighteenth birthday party with her brother, Bradford, and his girlfriend, Marlee. Bradford driving.

They had been on their way home when the incident occurred, less than half a mile from where Alicia and Bradford lived. A blue BMW drew up alongside them at the lights before the turn into Ilkeston Road, revving its engine as if intent on racing. Anticipating the green, Bradford, responding to the challenge, accelerated downhill, the BMW in close pursuit; between the first set of lights and the old Radford Mill building, the BMW drew alongside, someone lowered the rear window, pushed a handgun through and fired four times. One shot ricocheted off the roof, another embedded itself in the rear of the front seat; one entered the fleshy part of Bradford's shoulder, causing him to swerve; the fourth and fatal shot struck Alicia low in side of the neck and exited close to her windpipe.

An impulse shooting, is that what this was? Or a case of mistaken identity?

In the October of the previous year a gunman had opened fire from a passing car, seemingly at random, into a group of young people on their way home from Goose Fair, and a fourteen-year-old girl had died. There were stories of gun gangs and blood feuds in the media, of areas of the inner city running out of control, turf wars over drugs. Flowers and sermons, blame and recriminations and in the heart of the city a minute's silence, many people wearing the dead girl's favourite colours; thousands lined the streets for the funeral, heads bowed in respect.

Now this.

Understaffed as they were, low on morale and resources, policing the city, Resnick knew, was becoming harder and harder. In the past eighteen months, violent crime had risen to double the national average; shootings had increased fourfold. In Radford, Jamaican Yardies controlled the trade in heroin and crack cocaine, while on the Bestwood estate, to the north, the mainly white criminal fraternity was forging an uneasy alliance with the Yardies, all the while fighting amongst themselves; at either side of the city centre, multi-racial gangs from St. Ann's and The Meadows, Asian and Afro-Caribbean, fought out a constant battle for trade and respect.

So was Alicia simply another victim in the wrong place at the wrong time? Or something more? The search for the car was on: best chance it would be found on waste land, torched; ballistics were analysing the bullets from the scene; Bradford Faye and his family were being checked through records; friends would be questioned, neighbours. The public relations department had prepared a statement for the media, another for the Assistant Chief Constable. Resnick sat in the CID office in Canning Circus station with Anil Khan and Detective Inspector Maureen Prior from the Force Crime Directorate. His patch, their concern. Their case more than his.

200

Outside, the sky had lightened a little, but still their reflections as they sat were sharp against the window's plate glass.

Maureen Prior was in her early forties, no nonsense, matter-of-fact, wearing loose-fitting grey trousers, a zip-up jacket, hair tied back. 'So what do we think? We think they were targeted or what?'

'The girl?'

'No, not the girl.'

'The brother, then?'

'That's what I'm thinking.' The computer print-out was in her hand. 'He was put under a supervision order a little over two years back, offering to supply a class A drug.'

'That's when he'd be what?' Khan asked. 'Fifteen?"

'Sixteen. Just.'

'Anything since?'

'Not according to this.'

'You think he could still be involved?' Resnick said.

'I think it's possible, don't you?'

'And this was what? Some kind of pay-back?'

'Pay back, warning, who knows? Maybe he was trying to step up into a different league, change his supplier, hold back his share of the cut, anything.'

'We've checked with the Drug Squad that he's a player?' Resnick asked.

Maureen Prior looked over at Khan, who shook his head. 'Haven't been able to raise anyone so far.'

The detective inspector looked at her watch. 'Try again. Keep trying.'

Freeing his mobile from his pocket, Khan walked towards the far side of the room.

'How soon can we talk to Bradford, I wonder?' Resnick said.

'He's most likely still in surgery now. Mid-morning, I'd say. The earliest.'

'You want me to do that?'

'No, it's okay. I've asked them to call me from Queen's the minute he's out of recovery. There's an officer standing by.' She moved from the desk where she'd been sitting, stretching out her arms and breathing in stale air. 'Maybe you could talk to the family?' She smiled. 'They're on your patch, Charlie, after all.'

There were bunches of flowers already tied to the post into which the car had crashed, some anonymous, some bearing hastily written words of sympathy. More flowers rested up against the low wall outside the house.

The victim support officer met Resnick at the door.

'How they holding up?' he asked.

'Good as can be expected, sir.'

Resnick nodded and followed the officer into a narrow hall.

'They're in back.'

Clarice Faye sat on a green high-backed settee, her youngest daughter cuddled up against her, face pressed to her mother's chest. The middle daughter, Jade, twelve or thirteen, sat close but not touching, head turned away. Clarice was slender, light-skinned, lighter than her daughters, shadows scored deep beneath her eyes. Resnick was reminded of a woman at sea, stubbornly holding on against the pitch and swell of the tide.

The room itself was neat and small, knick-knacks and framed photographs of the children, uniform smiles; a crucifix, metal on a wooden base, hung above the fireplace. The curtains, a heavy stripe, were still pulled part-way across.

Resnick introduced himself and expressed his sympathy; accepted the chair that was offered, narrow with wooden arms, almost too narrow for his size.

'Bradford — have you heard from the hospital?'

'I saw my son this morning. He was sleeping. They told me to come home and get some rest.' She shook her head and squeezed her daughter's hand tight. 'As if I could.'

'He'll be all right?'

'He will live.'

The youngest child began to cry.

'He is a good boy, Bradford. Not wild. Not like some. Not any more. Why would anyone … ?' She stopped to sniff away a tear. 'He is going to join the army, you know that? Has been for an interview already, filled in the forms.' She pulled a tissue, screwed and damp, from her sleeve. 'A man now, you know? He makes me proud.'

Resnick's eyes ran round the photographs in the room. 'Alicia's father,' he ventured, 'is he … ?'

'He doesn't live with us any more.'

'But he's been told?'

'You think he cares?'

The older girl sprang to her feet and half-ran across the room.

'Lisa, come back here.'

The door slammed hard against the frame.

Resnick leaned forward, drew his breath. 'Bradford and Alicia, last night, you know where they'd been?'

'The Meadows. A friend of Bradford's, his eighteenth.'

'Did they often go around together like that, Bradford and Alicia?'

'Sometimes, yes.'

'They were close then?'

'Of course.' An insult if it were otherwise, a slight.

'And his girlfriend, she didn't mind?'

'Marlee, no. She and Alicia, they were like mates. Pals.'

'Mum,' the younger girl said, raising her head. 'Licia didn't like her. Marlee. She didn't.'

'That's not so.'

'It is. She told me. She said she smelled.'

'Nonsense, child.' Clarice smiled indulgently and shook her head.

'How about Alicia?' Resnick asked. 'Did she have any boyfriends? Anyone special?'

The hesitation was perhaps a second too long. 'No. She was a serious girl. Serious about her studies. She didn't have time for that sort of thing. Besides, she was too young.'

'She was practically sixteen.'

'Too young for anything serious, that's what I mean.'

'But parties, like yesterday, that was okay?'

'Young people together, having fun. Besides, she had her brother to look after her ...' Tears rushed to her face and she brushed them aside.

The phone rang and the victim support officer answered it in the hall. 'It's Bradford,' he said from the doorway. 'They'll be taking him back up to the ward any time.'

'Quickly,' Clarice said to her daughter, bustling her off the settee. 'Coat and shoes.'

Resnick followed them out into the hall. Door open, Jade was sitting on one of the beds in the room she and Alicia had obviously shared. Aware that Resnick was looking at her, she swung her head sharply towards him, staring hard until he moved away.

Outside, clouds slid past in shades of grey; on the opposite side of the narrow street, a couple slowed as they walked by. Resnick waited while the family climbed into the support officer's car and drove away. ... *a good boy, Bradford. Not wild. Not any more.* The crucifix. The mother's words. Amazing, he thought, how we believe what we want to believe, all evidence aside.

On the Ilkeston Road, he stopped and crossed the street. There were more flowers now, and photographs of Alicia, covered in plastic against the coming rain. A large teddy bear with black ribbon in a bow around its neck. A dozen red roses wrapped in cellophane, the kind on sale in garage forecourts. Resnick stooped and looked at the card. *For Alicia. Our love will live forever. Michael.* Kisses, drawn in red biro in the shape of a heart, surrounded the words.

Resnick was putting the last touches of a salad together when he heard Lynn's key in the lock. A sauce of spicy sausage and tomato was simmering on the stove; a pan of gently bubbling water ready to receive the pasta.

'Hope you're good and hungry.'

'You know ...' Her head appearing round the door. ' ... I'm not sure if I am.'

But she managed a good helping nonetheless, wiping the spare sauce from her plate with bread, washing it down with wine.

'So — how was it?' Resnick asked between mouthfuls.

'All right, I suppose.'

'Not brilliant then.'

'No, some of it was okay. Useful even.'

'Such as?'

'Oh, ways of avoiding tunnel vision. Stuff like that.'

Resnick poured more wine.

'I just wish,' Lynn said, 'they wouldn't get you to play these stupid games.'

'Games?'

'You know, if you were a vegetable, what vegetable would you be? If you were a car, what car?'

Resnick laughed. 'And what were you?'

'Vegetable or car?'

'Either.'

'A first crop potato, fresh out of the ground.'

'A bit mundane.'

'Come on, Charlie, born and brought up in Norfolk, what do you expect?'

'A turnip?'

She waited till he was looking at his plate, then clipped him round the head.

Later, in bed, when he pressed against her back and she turned inside his arms, her face close to his, she said: 'Better watch out, Charlie, I didn't tell you what kind of car.'

'Something moderately stylish, compact, not too fast?'

'A Maserati Coupé 4.2 in Azuro Blue with full cream leather upholstery.'

He was still laughing when she stopped his mouth with hers.

The bullet that had struck Bradford's shoulder was a 9mm, most likely from a plastic Glock. Patched up, replenished with blood, Bradford was sore, sullen, and little else. Aside from lucky. His girl-friend, Marlee, had twenty-seven stitches in a gash in her leg, several butterfly stitches to one side of her head and face and bruises galore. The BMW was found on open ground near railway tracks on the far side of Sneinton, burned out. No prints, no ejected shell cases, nothing of use. It took the best part of a week, but thirty-seven of the fifty or so people who had been at the party in The Meadows were traced, tracked down and questioned. For officers, rare and welcome overtime.

The Drug Squad had no recent information to suggest that Bradford was, again, dealing drugs, but there were several people at the party well known to them indeed. Troy James and Jason Fontaine in particular. Both had long been suspected of playing an active part in the trade in crack cocaine: suspected, arrested, interrogated, charged. James had served eighteen months of a three year sentence before being released; Fontaine had been charged with possession of three kilos of amphetamine with intent to supply, but because of alleged contamination of evidence, the case against him had been dismissed. More recently, the pair of them had been suspected of breaking into a chemist's shop in Wilford and stealing several cases of cold remedies in order to manufacture crystal meth.

James and Fontaine were questioned in the street, questioned in their homes; brought into the police station and questioned again. Bradford spent as much as fourteen hours, broken over a number of sessions, talking to Maureen Prior and Anil Khan.

Did he know Troy James and Jason Fontaine?

No.

He didn't know them?

No, not really.

Not really?

Not, you know, to talk to.

But they were at the party.

If you say so.

Well, they were there. James and Fontaine.

Okay, so they were there. So what?

You and Fontaine, you had a conversation.

What conversation?

There are witnesses, claim to have seen you and Fontaine in conversation.

A few words, maybe. I don't remember.

A few words concerning ... ?

Nothing important. Nothing.

How about an argument ... a bit of pushing and shoving?

At the party?

At the party.

No.

Think. Think again. Take your time. It's easy to get confused.

Oh, that. Yeah. It was nothing, right? Someone's drink got spilled, knocked over. Happens all the time.

That's what it was about? The argument?

Yeah.

A few punches thrown?

Maybe.

By you?

Not by me.

By Fontaine?

Fontaine?

Yes. You and Fontaine, squaring up to one another.

No. No way.

'There's something there, Charlie,' Maureen Prior said. 'Something between Bradford and Jason Fontaine.'

They were sitting in the Polish Diner on Derby Road, blueberry pancakes and coffee, Resnick's treat.

'Something personal?'

'To do with drugs, has to be. Best guess, Fontaine and Ford were using Bradford further down the chain and some way he held out on them, cut the stuff again with glucose, whatever. Either that, or he was trying to branch out on his own, their patch. Hyson Green kid poaching in The Meadows, we all know how that goes down.'

'You'll keep on at him?'

'The girlfriend, too. She's pretty shaken up still. What happened to Alicia. Keeps thinking it could have been her, I shouldn't wonder. Flakey as anything. One of them'll break sooner or later.'

'You seem certain.'

Maureen paused, fork halfway to her mouth. 'It's all we've got, Charlie.'

Resnick nodded and reached for the maple syrup: maybe just a little touch more.

The flowers were wilting, starting to fade. One or two of the brighter bunches had been stolen. Rain had seeped down into plastic and cellophane, rendering the writing for the most part illegible.

Clarice Faye came to the door in a dark housecoat, belted tight across; there were shadows still around her eyes.

'I'm sorry to disturb you,' Resnick said.

A slight shake of the head: no move to invite him in.

'When we were talking before, you said Alicia didn't have any boyfriends, nobody special?'

'That's right.'

'Not Troy James?'

'I don't know that name?'

'How about Jason? Jason Fontaine?'

The truth was there on her face, a small nerve twitching at the corner of her eye.

'She did go out with Jason Fontaine?'

'She saw him once or twice. The end of last year. He came round here in his car, calling for her. I told him, he wasn't suitable, not for her. Not for Alicia. He didn't bother her again.'

'And Alicia … ?'

'Alicia understood.' Clarice stepped back and began to close the door. 'If you'll excuse me now?'

'How about Michael?' Resnick said.

'I don't know no Michael.'

And the door closed quietly in his face.

He waited until Jade was on her way home from school, white shirt hanging out, coat open, skirt rolled high over dark tights, clumpy shoes. Her and three friends, loud across the pavement, one of them smoking a cigarette.

None of the others as much as noticed Resnick, gave him any heed.

'I won't keep you a minute,' Resnick said as Jade stopped, the others walking on, pace slowed, heads turned.

'Yeah, right.'

'You and Alicia, you shared a room.'

'So?'

'Secrets.'

'What secrets?'

'Jason Fontaine, was she seeing him any more?'

Jade tilted back her head, looked him in the eye. 'He was just a flash bastard, weren't he? Didn't care nothin' for her.'

'And Michael?'

'What about him?'

'You tell me.'

'He loved her, didn't he?'

Michael Draper was upstairs in his room: computer, stereo, books and folders from the course he was taking at City College, photographs of Alicia on the wall; Alicia and himself somewhere that might have been the Arboretum, on a bench in front of some trees, an old wall, Michael's skin alongside hers so white it seemed to bleed into the photo's edge.

'She was going to tell them, her mum and that, after her birthday. We were going to get engaged.'

'I'm sorry.'

The boy's eyes empty and raw from tears.

Maureen Prior was out of the office, her mobile switched off. Khan wasn't sure where she was.

'Ask her to call me when she gets a chance,' Resnick said. 'She can get me at home.'

At home he made sure the chicken pieces had finished defrosting in the fridge, chopped parsley, squashed garlic cloves flat, opened a bottle of wine, saw to the cats, flicked through the pages of the *Post*, Alicia's murder now page four. Art Pepper again, turned up loud. Lynn was late, no later than usual, rushed, smiling, weary, a brush of lips against his cheek.

'I need a shower, Charlie, before anything else.'

'I'll get this started.' Knifing butter into the pan.

It had cost Bradford a hundred and fifteen, talked down from one twenty-five. A Brocock ME38 Magnum air pistol converted to fire live ammunition. .22 shells. Standing there at the edge of the car park, shadowed, he smiled: an eye for an eye. Fontaine's motor, his new one, another Beamer, was no more than thirty metres away, close to the light. He rubbed his hands and moved his feet against the cold, the rain that rattled against the hood of his parka misted his eyes. Another fifteen minutes, no more, he'd be back out again, Fontaine, on with his rounds.

Less than fifteen, it was closer to ten.

Fontaine appeared at the side door of the pub, calling out to someone inside before raising a hand and turning away.

Bradford tensed, smelling his own stink, his own fear; waited until Fontaine had reached towards the handle of the car door, back turned.

'Wait,' Bradford said, stepping out of the dark.

Seeing him, seeing the pistol, Fontaine smiled. 'Bradford, my man.'

'Bastard,' Bradford said, moving closer. 'You killed my sister.'

'That slag!' Fontaine laughed. 'Down on her knees in front of any white meat she could find.'

Hands suddenly sticky, slick with sweat despite the cold, Bradford raised the gun and fired. The first shot missed, the second shattered the side window of the car, the third took Fontaine in the face splintering his jaw. Standing over him, Bradford fired twice more into his body as it slumped towards the ground, then ran.

After watching the news headlines, they decided on an early night. Lynn washed the dishes left over from dinner, while Resnick stacked away. He was locking the door when the phone went and Lynn picked it up. Ten twenty-three.

'Charlie,' she said, holding out the receiver. 'It's for you.'

The Contributors

David Belbin has written many novels for young adults, including *Denial, Love Lessons* and *Dead Guilty,* and numerous short stories for both adults and younger readers. He edited *City Of Crime*, an anthology of new fiction by Nottingham writers, published by Five Leaves in 1997. He works part time at Nottingham Trent University where, since 2004, he has been the programme leader of the MA in Creative Writing.
www.davidbelbin.com

Stephen Booth has written six crime novels set in the Derbyshire Peak District, the latest being *The Dead Place*. All feature the uneasy relationship of detectives Ben Cooper and Diane Fry. His books have been translated into many languages, including Japanese and Russian, and have won or been short-listed for several Crime Writers' Association "Daggers". He lives near Retford.
www.stephen-booth.com

Clare Brown's first novel *The Creation Myths* was published in 2005 by Bloomsbury. She is co-editor (with Don Paterson) of *Don't Ask Me What I Mean: Poets in Their Own* Words (Picador 2003). Clare spent seven years working in theatre and another seven as Director of the Poetry Book Society, before moving to Nottingham and becoming a full-time writer. Her second novel will also be published by Bloomsbury in 2007.
www.bloomsbury.com/authors

Elizabeth Chadwick's latest work, *Shadows and Strongholds*, is a novel about the lords of Ludlow in the twelfth century. Her novel *The Greatest Knight*, based on the life of William Marshal, is published in November 2005. She is the winner of a Betty Trask Award and four of her previous novels have been shortlisted for the Romantic Novel of the Year.
www.elizabethchadwick.com

Stephan Collishaw's first novel, *The Last Girl*, was set in pre-war and modern Lithuania, his second, *Amber*, in Afghanistan during the Soviet occupation. Stephan was selected as one of the British Council's 20 best young British novelists in January 2004. He lives in Nottingham.
www.stephancollishaw.com

Tom Cox was born in Nottingham in 1975, and born again in 1988 when watching golf on television. His life as a teenage golf rebel became the book *Nice Jumper*. His second, *Educating Peter*, chronicled a road trip with a melancholy Slipknot fan. Tom was The *Guardian*'s rock critic, writes features for a variety of national newspapers and is currently working on his first novel.
www.tom-cox.com

Matt Haig's first novel, *The Last Family in England*, was published in 2005 by Vintage, to great acclaim from newspapers and Labradors everywhere. 'Drips and Drops' is extracted from his new novel *The Dead Fathers Club* which will be published by Jonathan Cape in 2006.
www.matthaig.com

Robert Harris was born in Nottingham in 1957. He is the author of *Enigma*, *Fatherland*, *Archangel* and *Pompeii* as well as several books of non-fiction. He was formerly a journalist, his career including a spell on *Newsnight* and as Political Editor of the *Observer*.

John Harvey recently returned to Nottingham, the setting for ten Resnick crime novels and numerous short stories, one of which, 'Cheryl', first appeared in *City of Crime*. *Flesh & Blood*, the first of his novels featuring Frank Elder, won the Crime Writers' Association Silver Dagger for Fiction, and, in the U.S., the Barry Award for the Best British Crime Novel of 2004. His most recent book is *Ash & Bone*. For many years he ran Slow Dancer Press.
www.mellotone.co.uk

Clare Littleford has written two psychological crime novels, *Beholden* and *Death Duty*, both set in Nottingham. She was one of the "24-8" group of East Midlands writers in 2003, which led to her touring as part of the Hazard Warning group of crime writers. www.clarelittleford.net

Jon McGregor's *If Nobody Speaks of Remarkable Things* was the only book by a first novelist on the Booker Prize long-list in 2002, before winning a Somerset Maugham award the next year. Jon was awarded an Arts Council/British Antarctic Survey Fellowship to visit Antarctica. His second novel *So Many Ways to Begin*, will be published by Bloomsbury in September 2006. He was born in Bermuda and now lives in Nottingham.

Eve Makis was born in Nottingham to Greek Cypriot parents, who had emigrated to England in the 1960s. Her first novel, *Eat Drink and Be Married*, was published in 2005 and was inspired by her parents' life here and the wider Greek Cypriot community. Eve formerly worked as a reporter in Britain and a print and broadcast journalist in Cyprus.

Nicola Monaghan taught for several years before a career in finance took her to London, New York, Paris and Chicago. In 2002 she returned to her native Nottingham to do an MA in creative writing at Nottingham Trent University. She graduated with distinction in 2004, and now works in Arts Marketing at the Broadway Cinema and Media Centre. Her first novel, *The Killing Jar*, is inspired by lives she witnessed on the council estates where she grew up, and will be published by Chatto in 2006. www.nicolamonaghan.co.uk

Julie Myerson grew up in and around Nottingham, which provided the setting for her first novel *Sleepwalking*. Her most recent novel is *Something Might Happen*, which explores the effect of a murder on the inhabitants of a small seaside town in Suffolk. Her latest book is short memoir of childhood, *Not a Games Person*. One of her other short stories appeared in *City of Crime*.

Kat Pomfret's first novel, *Paradise Jazz*, was published in 2005 by Snowbooks. The *Daily Telegraph* described the book as having "A great ear for sassy dialogue and jazz club rhythms". The book is set in the Deep South of America, and in England.
www.snowbooks.com

James Urquhart worked for some years as a bookseller and as a secretary for a Labour MP, but is now tending his family and writing full time, primarily reviewing for the broadsheet press.

GOOD BUSINESS

by

Sheena Carmichael
&
John Drummond

Good Business

A Guide to Corporate Responsibility
and Business Ethics

Sheena Carmichael and John Drummond

Business Books

Copyright © Sheena Carmichael and John Drummond 1989

First published in Great Britain by
Business Books Limited
An imprint of Century Hutchinson Limited
62-65 Chandos Place, London, WC2N 4NW

Century Hutchinson Australia (Pty) Limited
89-91 Albion Street, Surrey Hills,
New South Wales 2010, Australia

Century Hutchinson New Zealand Limited
PO Box 40-086, 32-34 View Road, Glenfield,
Auckland 10, New Zealand

Century Hutchinson South Africa (Pty) Limited
PO Box 337, Bergvlei 2012, South Africa

British Library Cataloguing in Publication Data
Carmichael, Sheena
    Good business: a guide to corporate
    responsibility and business ethics
    1. Business enterprise. Ethical aspects
    I. Title II. Drummond, John
    174'.4

    ISBN 0-09-174028-2
    ISBN 0-09-173949-7 Pbk

Phototypeset by Saxon Ltd, Derby
Printed and bound in Great Britain by
Mackays of Chatham PLC, Chatham, Kent